TO
PIECES

# TO PIECES

*A Novel*

## KATI ROCKY

**TEMPUS PRESS**

Berkeley, California

ISBN 9780692122341 (print)
ISBN 9780692122488 (ePub)

"Those who danced were thought quite insane,
by those who couldn't hear the music."

—FRIEDRICH NIETZSCHE

$\mathcal{A}$T THE BEGINNING of junior year, the words my classmates would have used to describe me were: normal, average, everyday, medium at everything, B person, Plain Jane. At the end of junior year, the words they would have used to describe me were: weirdo, schizo, psycho, "F" for freak person. How does a solid B tumble to a solid F in the space of one semester? It happens when she is hiding a giant secret about who she really is. It happened slowly and all at once, when my cover was blown and the real me seeped out and changed everything. For good.

# ONE

*I*T ALL STARTED on my seventeenth birthday. That's the day I started dying from the inside out. Or maybe something inside was coming to life—something I wanted to stay dead. My older sister Maya, my mother and I were celebrating my birthday in the morning before school. Maya had made the trek home from college the day before and spent the night so that she could wake up with me on my birthday and present me with a gift and a breakfast of chocolate cake before she headed back to school. She knew how much I missed her and, probably, she was a little worried that if she didn't come, my mother might forget the occasion.

They sang the last verse of "Happy Birthday" and I blew out the candles, sensing something inside burn out along with them—a spark plug, or a light bulb that had been fading in and out, on the fritz, and then was finally extinguished. In truth, it had been coming for a while. I had been sinking down a hole since Maya had left for college several months before.

We dove into the birthday cake, which tastes as good at seven a.m. as it does at seven p.m. "Open my present first," Maya said, handing me a box covered in silver wrapping paper. I recognized the label on the outside of the box inside. It was an expensive lingerie store not far from our house. I opened the box and inside was a beautiful, light blue, silk nightgown.

"I love it," I said, rubbing the soft silk against my chin. The nightgown must have cost a fortune—over half Maya's monthly allowance for food and whatever else she needed at college. I felt guilty. She shouldn't have spent so much on me.

My mother slid a tiny box across the table. I lifted the lid and waiting inside was… a gold necklace with a sequined unicorn charm hanging from it. "I know how much you like unicorns," she said, smiling proudly. Yes,

I did like unicorns – when I was in the third grade. She might as well have gotten me a Barbie cash register. I mustered up a smile and thanked my mother. The gift confirmed what I already knew and had known for years – my mother hadn't a clue about who I was. Once we'd finished our slices of cake, Maya hopped up from the table and told me to collect my things. She wanted to drop me off at school before she drove back to college.

Maya pulled her car into my high school parking lot and double-parked outside the entrance to the school Atrium—next to the five choicest student parking spots on campus. "I don't go through the Atrium, remember?" I told her. "I'm Bench."

Maya's mistake was understandable. She was used to parking and entering next to the Atrium entrance because when she was in high school, she was an "A" group person – "A" for Atrium. The A group was at the top of the food chain—the coolest, most popular. A group kids weren't creepy, they were just… special. Or, as one of the A girl's license plates read, "2speshl."

"Oops, I forgot," she said. "Do you mind? I've got to get on the highway before it turns into a parking lot, otherwise I'll be late for my classes."

"Peace out, girl scout," Maya said as I climbed out of the car.

"Keep it real, happy meal," I returned. We waved to each other as she drove away. I watched her car until I couldn't see it anymore. Every time she left for school, I got that abandoned, helpless feeling you got when your mom dropped you off on the first day of preschool. Maya was my idol (perfect in every way), my anchor, and my pseudo-mother. If I was a kite, she was my string. If I was a tightrope walker, she was my net. Without her around, I felt wobbly and disconnected.

I wandered through the Atrium, which was the most attractive part of West Hills Prep School. There were redwood picnic tables shaded by umbrellas, a hammock, roses, and lots of quiet. I had never felt comfortable in the Atrium. Even when Maya and I were both at the school, I would have her drop me off at the Bench entrance before she swung around and parked in the A lot.

I smiled at Ariana and Alexis, twin sisters, as I passed them. Ariana and Alexis were genetically engineered to perfection—perfect teeth, perfect hair and bodies with curves in all the right places. They were sitting with their boyfriends. Stella Mercury, the one creepy A, was swinging in a hammock next to them. Stella glanced up as I walked by and gave me a lackluster smile that said, "I know you want to be me, but it's not happening."

What Stella didn't know was that I had no interest in being her—or any of the As. Technically, I might have been able to get in the As, since I was a legacy and I could look cute when my kinky blonde hair was cooperating, but being an A meant basking in the spotlight, a spotlight that I did not want trained on me. I strongly suspected that under scrutiny I wouldn't hold up, and when I finally tripped, my fall would be news—because As were watched and talked about.

I was a solid B, and that's where I aimed to remain—comfortably and inconspicuously under the radar. Some people shoot for the stars. I shot for the place equidistant between me and the stars—the midpoint. My thinking was that if you don't stick your neck out, it won't be cut off. Blending in was my goal, and so far I'd done a pretty darn good job at it. I was contentedly Plain Jane. Jane Doe.

I made my way out of the Atrium and continued on toward the CEA— Covered Eating Area, home of greasy food and C people—the working class. Only nerds and losers frequented the CEA. (Nerds and losers who would probably turn out to be winners in adulthood, since there is no correlation between high school popularity and success in later life. How many boyfriends you collected or goals you made by age eighteen was no indicator of building a successful career at anything.) CEA people did things such as: dress for the weather, wear sensible shoes, eat greasy cafeteria food, and quote *Star Wars*.

Zeke, the C with the most cooties, noticed me and lumbered across the lawn with his arms outstretched. Zeke was overweight, had b.o. and no social i.q., and was likely a genius. "Jane! Happy birthday!" Zeke shouted. He reached me and gave me a smelly hug. "Hey, did you know that if it's really quiet and you listen hard you can actually hear your eyeballs move?"

"No, I didn't know that," I answered. "I'll remember to listen close next time I'm . . . in the Gobi Desert." I smiled and continued walking.

Charles Dickens, wearing an ascot and a triple-breasted tweed vest, marched across my path. He was not the real Dickens, of course. He was Charles Duncan. In eighth grade, after we read *Great Expectations*, Charles assumed the role of a nineteenth century British dandy. He went so far as to speak with an English accent and talk about where we lived as "one of the former colonies." I actually thought it was kinda cool that Dickens unapologetically did his own thing, even knowing that lots of kids made fun of him. "Happy day of your birth, Jane, how many years has it been?" he asked.

"Seventeen," I answered.

"Ah, youth is wasted on the young," he said, a strange remark from a sixteen-year-old.

No, I wasn't so fascinating that everyone had memorized my birthday. Our school website posted birthdays in an effort to "make every student know that we value them."

My phone chimed. A text from Nell, one of my two best friends: "Happy birthday! Would you rather sleep with Charles Dickens or have every hair on your body plucked out individually?" I looked up and saw her waving at me from the main entrance to the school before she disappeared inside.

"Pull out the tweezers," I texted back. Sorry, Dickens, but as bold as you are, I don't want to see you naked.

I continued past the CEA, heading across the lawn for the big cluster of Benches, home of the B people. My people. We were the largest group of the school—the middle class. We were all the usual variations: jocks, preppies, skaters, surfers, theater people, brainiacs, stoners, student government. Mostly, we were regular, average teens muddling through high school in an unremarkable way.

The three groups coexisted fairly peacefully—we all knew our place and stayed there. The social structure of the school made some strange kind of sense to me when Maya was there—because she was involved in the hierarchy, it couldn't be wrong. But, now, with each passing day, the whole scene seemed more pathetic… and wrong.

Tiffany, my other best friend, tackled me as I reached the Benches. "Happy birthday!" she squealed, planting a kiss (in bright pink lipstick) on my cheek. "I've got a big surprise for you. We're going to cel-e-brate tonight!" she chirped. "Nell is leaving after third period to go to the doctor. She has a swollen gland." Nell always had something. "But I told Nell that I didn't care if the lump was cancer—she had to be at your house at seven. The trio is together every birthday—no matter what. Subject change. You'll never believe what happened this morning."

I nodded, knowing this was going to be about Tal, the Israeli exchange student who had moved here in the fall. Tiffany had had a crush on him since the first day of school and, so far, had gotten absolutely nowhere with him. Nobody had gotten anywhere with him. Tal was cute, with dark brown hair and light brown skin, a knockout smile, and the bluest eyes. And he had an accent that was so seductive that he probably could read a computer manual and it would sound sexy. "This morning, on my way here, I stopped at the Verona," she said. "I ordered my usual, a gingerbread latte, and who do you think was behind me in line?"

"I can't imagine," I said.

"Tal. And he ordered a gingerbread latte, too," she gushed.

"Am I missing something?" I asked.

"Obviously, he ordered what I ordered to show me that we have the same tastes," she deduced. "I could tell he was about to say 'Hi,' but his phone rang."

"That's great, Tiff," I said. A week ago, she was convinced Tal was going to ask her out because he had dropped a Hebrew English dictionary on her foot in the halls and said, "Sooo sorry." Apparently, the way he drew out the soooo was significant.

The bell rang and everybody began fleeing for class. "See you at lunch!" Tiffany shouted after me.

I wandered to my locker, grabbed my history book and headed for class. Before I'd reached the classroom, I got another text from Nell: "Would you rather have nine fingers or eleven toes?" Nell knew I had history with Nine—aka Astrid Inch. Her unkind nickname was due to her having nine fingers, the result of a car accident that cost her a pinky. Astrid skate-boarded everywhere, had a shaved head, pierced lips, and hated society— or so she said. When she graduated, she wanted to become a tattoo artist or a revolutionary guerilla and fight against "the man." She nodded at me as I took my seat next to her and then went back to doing what she was usually doing—staring at something on the horizon. I secretly admired her. She didn't give a rip what anyone thought of her. She wasn't sneaking through life like I was.

Class began and Mr. Vega (or Vegas as we called him because he was so not Las Vegas—he had the personality of Muzak) started in on the specifics of yet another war. It was always a war—with the occasional famine or flood or the description of a forgotten, ancient society thrown in for variety. And all the wars were the same—lots of bloodshed and then somebody wins. Hadn't anything important happened over the course of history that didn't involve feuding and mass execution?

I hobbled through the rest of the uninspiring school day like I always did—waiting for Spanish. School had been reduced to six hours of waiting for Spanish. Finally, it was time for sixth period. Before heading to class, I stopped at the girls' bathroom, where I checked my teeth for food particles, applied lipstick with a topcoat of berry-colored lip-gloss, and scanned my overall appearance for glaring flaws. I stayed in there while I finished a breath mint, practicing different smiles I might give him. Him was one Ben Sanders.

Ben had transferred midyear to West Hills Prep from another private school because our school had a better crew team and the best boys' coach in the league. It was crush at first sight for me on his debut day at school, when he shot me a shy grin and took the seat kitty-corner to me in Spanish class. My toes curled and my stomach did flip-flops. "Break me off a piece 'a that," Tiffany texted me as he pulled a laptop from his backpack.

Almost every Spanish class, Ben did or said something that made me more into him – like when, during one particularly lackluster lesson, he painted all his nails blue with a sharpie, or when Senora Flores was trying to teach us some new verbs and she pulled out a lighter wand (to use as a pointer) and waved it over Tiffany's head and asked, "What am I doing, Ben?" Instead of answering "waving" (in Spanish) he answered, "Trying to light Tiffany's hair on fire."

Another Ben plus was that we were both rowers (I was on crew, too), and even though he was a star he didn't brag about his skills or hang out exclusively with his teammates. I liked how he rotated around the various school locales and hung out with the different groups, not confining himself. He even had lunch with Zeke and Dickens occasionally. Unlike the other students, he seemed blissfully ignorant of the caste system.

Ben had shaggy blonde hair that hung over glow-in-the-dark green eyes, a dimple in his left cheek and a tall body that was lean from years of rowing. Then there was his smile, which reeled me in from moment one. It wasn't a beaming grin. There was a touch of sadness or trouble at the corners, like he was content but not convinced that life was a joy ride. This made me feel akin to him—like we were cast from the same iron.

I finished my mint and wandered into Spanish, trying to appear casual and carefree—like I noticed Ben but wasn't dying for him. He shot me one of his awesome smiles and I took my seat near him. I reflexively gave him just a regular, stupid grin, not one of the cool ones I'd practiced in the bathroom. "Hi," I said, trying to think of something else to say – anything

– but my vocal cords always froze when I saw him. As per usual, I felt like a family of deer in floodlights. I fumbled as I clumsily pulled my Spanish book from my backpack, almost dropping it. I was making way too much noise. Why couldn't I gather my book without so much rustling and thumping? I cleared my throat, out of nerves, and immediately worried that I sounded sickly. I raised my arm to tighten my ponytail and detected b.o. Great. He'd probably smelled my stink. I started wishing I hadn't sat so close to him because simply being alive around him was embarrassing.

Just then Stella bounded into class, plopped into her seat next to Ben, and leaned into him, her T-shirt showing just enough cleavage to be provocative.

"Are you busy this Friday, Ben? I have tickets to Southland Music Festival," she said.

I crossed my fingers. Please say no. Please say no.

"Sorry, but yah—I am busy," he answered. "Thanks anyway." I breathed a deep sigh of relief that I hoped he hadn't heard. I didn't want Stella stealing Ben away before I'd gotten a chance to go out with him – or even had what could be considered a conversation with him.

Stella had been drooling over Ben for months without even a nibble from him, but she continued her quest for his heart—or at least his hormones. Ben wasn't biting. "Too bad," Stella said, giving a pouty smile. "Next time." Stella leaned into Ben further, studying some writing on his binder. "Is that a poem?" she asked.

"A few stanzas of my favorite Dylan Thomas poem," Ben answered.

"I absolutely adore Dylan Thomas," Stella purred. She picked up his binder and studied the verses:

> *The force that through the green fuse drives the flower*
> *Drives my green age; that blasts the roots of trees*
> *Is my destroyer.*
> *And I am dumb to tell the crooked rose*
> *My youth is bent by the same wintry fever.*

She handed the binder back to Ben. "Mmmm," she groaned. "Those are some words to savor."

"Yah. It's really evocative," I said, quoting what my language arts teacher said about almost every poem we read. I was grasping for something else to say. Something interesting. But my brain wasn't firing fast enough.

"I'm so glad you like the verses," Stella said, before I could spit out another comment. "Does this mean you've come around and started enjoying poetry?"

"You don't like poetry?" Ben asked.

"Not really," I stammered. "Just . . . certain kinds of poetry. It's complicated . . ." I could feel blood rushing my cheeks. I was sure I was blushing. I wished the floor would open and my desk and I could be sucked underneath the classroom. Now I looked stupid in addition to extremely socially awkward.

"Huh?" Ben said.

"The greats—she hates—or has hated for years," Stella insisted. "All the poems that are taught in school. Can you imagine the fun she's been missing out on? Shakespeare, for example?"

Just then, before I could utter even a word of defense, Señora Flores decided to show up—not before this excruciating conversation began or somewhere in the middle before it had taken this unfortunate turn, but right at the point where I was left looking like a nonintellectual, unsophisticated dip who had dismissed one of the most revered, ancient forms of expression. I wanted to punch Stella in the face and turn back the clock and not even have sat near Ben. I felt my chances with him circling the drain.


It was seven-thirty by the time Tiffany and Nell arrived at my house—later than planned because Tiffany's tutoring session ran long. I could tell that my mom was itching to be doing something else when they suggested that we, once again, light the candles on the cake so they could sing to me. The cake now read "Happy Bir."

"Yum," Tiffany said as she licked the frosting off her fork. "Why couldn't frosting be a food group?"

Nell and Tiffany giggled and chatted while I sat quietly eating cake. I wished we were celebrating one of their birthdays and not mine. Birthdays are supposed to be occasions where you're happy and lighthearted and enjoy having friends and family fawn over you. I was none of those things. I was trying to feign a festive attitude, but I wasn't excited that I'd conquered another year and was starting in on a new one and I was tired of faking it. The only thing I was glad about was that the day was coming to a close.

I opened Nell's present first: a large flashlight, complete with a compartment containing a Swiss army knife.

"Nothing says 'I love you' like a flashlight,'" Tiffany groaned.

"It's not just a flashlight. It's a survival device for when the Big One comes," Nell said. Nell liked to always be prepared for the worst—probably because she was always focused on the worst. Lately, I'd been relating to Nell more and more.

"My gift is homemade," Tiffany said, sliding an envelope to me. "I don't have any money because my mom cut off my allowance until I pull my grades up."

Inside the envelope was a card with an address written on it. "It's a surprise you're going to like," she said, winking. "But, we've gotta drive to get it. Let's go." We all stood up from the table and headed for the front door.

"Have fun girls," my Mom shouted to us as we reached Nell's car. "I'll be home late tonight, Pumpkin. I'm going to Cookie Diamond's house and we have tons to do. We're working on the seating chart for the Furry Friends fundraising dinner." Furry Friends was the dog rescue charity she headed. She climbed into her car and shut the door. "XOX," she shouted out the window before she drove off. "XOX" was my mother's virtual hug and kiss. And "Pumpkin" was the nickname she'd had for me since I was a baby. I was "Pumpkin" and Maya was "Sweet Pea." The names suggested that at one time, when we were very young, my mother had felt some warmth for us. Who knew why it all dried up before I'd even graduated kindergarten.

Upon Tiffany's instruction, Nell first drove us to the dead-end at the top of the hill behind my house and we drank a bottle of champagne that Tiffany had filched from her mom's stash—toasting to my becoming Mrs. Ben's Girlfriend, a year of good hair days, my boat winning the Spring Classic Regatta, and my GPA taking wings and soaring—all highly unlikely. The champagne was warm and the bubbles stung my throat and the alcohol wasn't giving me a buzz. It was making me tired. I gave most of my champagne to Tiffany, and she seemed glad to have it.

Once the champagne bottle had been drained, we piled back into Nell's car and Tiffany plugged the address on my birthday card into her phone and got directions. "Now for the good part," she said. Tiffany was trying to create a mood of drama and suspense as we rode along, making me guess repeatedly where we might be going. The charade was boring me.

I just wanted to sit and be left alone. As we drove along, it was becoming increasingly clear that my two very best friends had no idea what was going on inside me. We were sitting together in a small car, yet I was light years away from them.

After driving down from the hills and about five miles across town, we arrived on a tree-lined street full of large, traditional-looking homes with manicured yards. Finally, we arrived at a white Tudor home. "Park the car," Tiffany instructed. Nell pulled over to the curb and turned off the engine. "Cut the lights and take a look. Specifically look at the second story window on the far right."

"Please tell me this isn't what I think it is," Nell said.

"That, dude, is Ben Sanders' bedroom," Tiffany announced.

"Are you nuts?!" I asked, panicking. "He could see us. He'll think I'm a stalker." Nell started the car and peeled away from the house.

"Jane is right," Nell said. "Hanging out in front of the house of the guy you have a crush on is a sure way to public humiliation."

"You're both so uptight," Tiffany said. "I was just trying to be helpful. Now you can put a house with the face. Do you know how much research I had to do to get this address?"

"God, I hope he didn't see us," I said. "Especially not after that embarrassing poetry conversation in Spanish." I loved Tiffany, but this was about the worst birthday present I could have asked for. The day had officially gone to hell.

"Don't worry. It's dark inside the car. He couldn't have seen us even if he was looking out his bedroom window," Tiffany assured me. "And the poetry conversation wasn't even all that embarrassing. You made it into a much bigger deal than it really was." All I could do was hope that Tiffany was right.

"I've gotta get home. I've got crew practice early tomorrow morning." Crew had been my sport for three years now. I liked crew fine, and I was pretty good at it, but the original draw for me was its offer of anonymity. Crew wasn't like volleyball or gymnastics or track, where you could shine above the rest or screw up conspicuously. It was a true team sport where everybody was equal. If the team had a glorious victory or a miserable loss, all nine of us got the credit, not one of us stood out. Crew was a safe sport to hide in.

Nell drove us out of Ben's neighborhood and headed back to my house. We were stopped in traffic, waiting for the light to turn, when

Tiffany pointed to the black minivan in the lane next to us. "Isn't that your mom?" The light turned and the car pulled up ahead before I had a chance to look at the driver. I studied the car. It looked just like my mom's car – it even had the same dent on the driver's door—but I couldn't make out the license plate. The car turned on its blinker to make a right into the parking lot of a large, shingled building.

"Get up closer," I told Nell. A second before we reached the car, it turned right and disappeared into the parking lot. I only caught the first three letters of the license plate VEV. Those were the first three letters of my mom's license plate.

"That was definitely my mom's car," I said.

"What's your mom doing in there?" Tiffany asked.

"I don't know," I answered. "She's supposed to be working on the fundraiser at Cookie Diamond's house – which is miles from here. Why would she lie to me about where she was going?"

"Maybe there's someone in that building that they're delivering a dog to," Nell said.

"No," I answered. "They have a shelter where you pick up the dogs."

"Maybe she has a boyfriend who lives in there and she doesn't want you to know about him," Tiffany said.

"My mom doesn't date," I said. My father, whom I'd never really known, had died young and unexpectedly years ago and my mother hadn't had a man in her life since then. When friends would try to set her up she would always say that my dad was her "one and only." Could she have found a new "one and only?"

"I'm sure there's a perfectly good reason why she's in there," Nell said.

Something about the situation seemed off. It was almost ten o'clock at night and my mom was arriving at a random building several miles from our house. Of course there was a reason, like Nell said, but just what that reason could be I had no idea.

When I got home, I was sleepy, but I kept myself up waiting for my mom's return. I purposely sat reading in the living room, because it was where the front door was. I didn't want to march into my mom's room to ask her where she'd been. I wanted it to feel more natural and not like an interrogation that might scare her off from telling the truth. I'd casually bump into her in the living room when she got home and pepper her with a few questions about her night. It was after eleven when she got back. She seemed surprised to see me. I asked her how it went at Cookie Diamond's. She told me they got a lot accomplished and that she was tired. I could tell she wanted to get away from me, but I pressed on. "Did you guys leave her house and go anywhere?" I asked.

"No, no," my mother answered. "We were way too busy to go off and have fun." Then she marched purposefully out of the room. "Get some sleep, Pumpkin."

My mother had told a big, fat lie. I was stunned. She had been a lot of things over the years, but a liar was never one of them. What the heck was she hiding from me and why? I intended to find out.

Twenty minutes later, tucked safely in my bed, I ran over the events of the day: Maya going back to school, her visits home getting spaced out further and further; my mother giving me a present for a nine-year-old and racing from my birthday dinner; her lying to me about where she'd been and how little I really knew the woman; looking like an idiot in front of Ben and why it had to be so hard and complicated to get anywhere with a guy you liked; the whole lame social structure of school and how the Cs just accepted their peasant status and the As greedily and guilt free gobbled up the good stuff; how we all allowed others to label and define us; my perpetual struggle for mediocrity; my lack of balls to be who I really was. And who was I really? I'd been so feverishly trying to blend in that I didn't even know who I was. What was I so afraid of? That the me inside was totally unacceptable?

None of it was making sense. Something grey and ugly was closing in on me. I felt myself opening the door to a cruel, uninvited guest who wanted only to tell me how much I sucked and how pitiful my little life was.

The next morning, I was late to crew practice because I stayed in bed too long debating whether or not I should go. As soon as I climbed into the boat, I wished I hadn't gone. "Catch, drive, finish, recover," Claire, our coxswain yelled to us. I moved my oar lackadaisically, only wanting to do the recover part of the stroke. Claire noticed how little energy I was putting into my stroke and asked me if I was feeling "under the weather." I answered in the affirmative so that I had an excuse to quit practice early.

I arrived at school and checked in with Nell and Tiffany at the Benches. They were blabbing on about something that I had no interest in. I nodded, pretending I was listening, and glanced around at the others. Everybody looked happy and full of enthusiasm. That must have been how I looked up until lately. I couldn't remember what I used to smile about – what I knew then that I didn't know now. It seemed like I was watching the scene through a plastic bubble – like I had stepped out of the world going on around me and was now only an observer, not a participant. Like I was an alien who had been parachuted down from a saucer into a world I'd never visited before.

I'd thought that maybe I could lose myself in the 1940's during history class, but unfortunately the 1940's were all about World War II. Between learning about the tragedy of the Holocaust and all the soldiers who died in combat, I left the class having an even bleaker view of mankind. Math class, Nell noticed my low mood and mistook it for me worrying that Ben had seen us at his house the previous night. I let her think that was my problem. It was much easier than describing my real problem, which she wouldn't be able to do anything about anyway.

There was a little spring in my step when Spanish time finally arrived. Knowing I was going to see Ben bumped up my mood a notch. But, Stella arrived at the classroom seconds before me, plopped down next to Ben and started hogging all of his attention, talking about the celebrities she'd met at a movie premiere the night before. She got him so wrapped up in conversation that I couldn't even squeeze in a "hi" to him. I started worrying that maybe he did like her after all. Tiffany caught me staring at them. "She's got her claws in him, but she'll never get her hooks in him," she whispered. "You look like you're coming down with something," she added, studying my face, and told me to get some rest. Rest is exactly what I wanted. I wanted to fall asleep and wake up when it was time to graduate.

My homework took three times as long as it should have that night because I couldn't focus. Dinner with my mother was awkward. I choked down what I could, I didn't have much of an appetite, while she rattled on about the Furry Friends fundraiser. She didn't seem to notice that I said approximately three words the whole meal. The thirty minutes I spent with her made me lonesome for an actual mother, someone who could wrap me in their arms and tell me it would all be okay. The likelihood of that happening was less than the likelihood of my getting killed by a rhinoceros stampede on my front lawn.

Each morning I heaved myself out of bed with a little less oomph and went through the motions as best I could. Things weren't getting better. They were getting worse. And on and on it went.

And then:

One morning, a few weeks into my black hole, I was at my locker, desperately twisting the lock in circles, so psychically fried that I couldn't crack the combination. The bell had rung and I was going to be late to history to learn about another bloody battle. After I pounded my fist against the locker a few times, the girl who had the locker next to mine arrived and told me that when she couldn't remember her combination she would make her mind as blank as possible. After a few minutes of going blank, she'd let her mind return to the combination—and the correct numbers would pop up.

I shut my eyes and attempted to go blank when I felt a hand on my shoulder. I pirouetted around and there stood Ben, smiling shyly at me. He started uhm-ing and aw-ing and staring at his tennis shoes. "So, did you finish all your Spanish homework? I blew mine off because I had to go to the doctor yesterday for my knee it's been aching a lot so I thought maybe I had torn something but it's just a little strained so I can keep rowing through the spring and summer regattas. Now I just have to do these boring stretches," he said. He was talking fast and without punctuation, words running into words, his eyes darting dizzily back and forth and over and up and down. He waved an umbrella. "Thought it might rain the news said so last night but then the paper this morning said only a forty percent chance but forty percent is enough to . . ." He took a breath and then looked up at me, swallowing his words, "What are you doing . . . uh . . . over the weekend? Because I was thinking that if you're up for it maybe we could sort of hang out or do something—or not if you're busy."

I should have been over the moon and Mars with excitement. It had happened. My dream had come true. Ben Sanders had asked me out. But I was so wasted and crumpled that all I could do was start walking to class with him alongside me, trying to think of a way to say 'no' that wouldn't hurt his feelings and would leave room for us to go out later if I recovered. There was no supply of witty banter in me and only enough words at my disposal to order off a menu. I didn't have a half hour's worth of smiles to give, and there was a gigantic possibility that I'd burst into tears at some point during our time together and he'd know what a truly psycho mess I was and go away forever.

"That sounds good," I stammered. "But, my . . . our house is being . . . fumigated so I . . . well . . . we have termites and that isn't good. . ." Termites? Could I have thought of a lamer excuse?

"Hey. I get it. Don't worry," he said, cutting me off and talking even faster than before. "It's cool. I'm kinda busy too. We'll do it some other time when we're . . . both... you know, don't have so much to do." As I watched him rush away from me, I remembered the combination to my locker.

And then:

Maya got overloaded with school demands and didn't come home for spring break as planned. I had been waiting and waiting for her. Waiting to spill out all the anguish and confusion and have her help me sort it out. Now that wasn't happening, the only thing I thought might drag me out of the muck. Further down I slid.

And then:

Our boat, just as mediocre as I was, came in second to last in the Spring Classic Regatta. Just to make the loss a little more humiliating, Ben witnessed the entire race and was standing on the dock as I climbed out of the boat—a disheveled, defeated mess—and he looked right past me, like I was completely invisible, which I wished I was.

Night became the darkest and most dreaded part of the day. Without the distractions of classes, homework, and texts—that's when the pain pulsated the hardest and the wicked voice inside screamed the loudest: "Your life is meaningless. You're a loser. It's all a hopeless waste."

One night, when I was sick of staring at the ceiling for six hours and facing the eight a.m. school bell and the long school day on zero night's sleep, I decided to take matters into the hands of the drug industry. I pulled myself out of bed and crept down the hallway to my mother's bathroom and quietly found my way to her medicine cabinet. Lined up on the middle shelf was a row of pills. I knew one of the bottles contained sleeping pills because my mom used them when she traveled. Two of the five bottles contained painkillers, which I knew because I'd used them when I'd had my wisdom teeth pulled. Another bottle was antibiotics.

There was a bottle of bright orange pills that would keep a person up all night with their neon glare. I settled on some tiny pills in a comforting baby blue color that looked, well, restful.

I returned to bed, took one and waited twenty minutes. Nothing. I swallowed another pill and waited fifteen minutes. Sleep still wasn't on, and I was beginning to wonder what these blue pills were actually for—but I kept going with them. After four pills I was finally out cold.

When I woke up at the sound of the alarm, my head felt like it was stuffed with down and my feet felt like they were being drawn down below the floorboards via some extra strength gravity. I was more pole-axed than ever.

Up until then, I'd kept it together. I'd dragged myself through the school days wearing a blank face and then escaped home to curl up and cry. But, during trigonometry, the numbers became too much. I was drowning in cosines and Pythagorean identities and arcs. I felt a panic attack charging for me. I shuddered as it passed through, having a hard time catching my breath. Then I choked up and tried to hide my face as salty, raindrop-sized tears welled up and then trickled down my chin and onto my worksheet, turning the paper to pulp. Luckily Nell, who was sitting next to me, noticed. She yanked me from my seat and helped shield my face as she towed me into the bathroom. She hugged me while I shook hard, sobbing.

"What is it? What's going on?" Nell asked.

"It's like I'm being tortured all day."

"Tortured by what?" she asked as I hugged her tighter.

"This horrible voice inside," I answered.

Nell pulled away and stared at me—wide-eyed, stricken. "Whoa. Whoa," she said. "You're hearing voices?"

"No, it's not like that," I tried to explain. "I'm not delusional. I know the voice is mine. It's a part of me I don't want but can't shut up. It's like I'm whipping myself and I can't stop."

"This isn't cool," Nell said. She hauled me out of the bathroom and down the hallway. "There's something not right with you, Jane, and I'm not falling for your 'I'm just tired' excuse anymore." We reached the administration office and she disappeared inside for a few minutes, warning me not to leave or else.

"I told the guidance counselor you had a fever and I needed to take you home," Nell said as she walked me to the parking lot. She opened her car and shoved me into the passenger seat. "Look, I know what a drag this scene here is and what a shambles our world is in and how hard it is being a teenager—but even I don't have an imaginary person yelling at me all day."

"You're not getting the voice thing. I just don't feel well. It's not that big a deal," I said.

"Whatever," she said. "You haven't been eating and you're so skinny you could sleep in a pencil sharpener. You don't return my texts, you don't return my e-mails. And you never want to hang out. You barely even talk to Tiffany and me. I called your sister. She's meeting us at your house as soon as she can get there."

"Maya? Why did you call Maya? She's really busy with schoolwork," I said.

"You need help. Maya is finding you someone to talk to. Maya loves you so much," Nell said. "She's worried. We're all worried."

Maya was coming. Selfishly, I was glad she was coming home. I'd been resisting calling her because I knew she was studying for finals and didn't want to bother her, but I needed her. If anyone could help me it was Maya. The urge to cry some more let up as I thought about how good it would feel to hug her.

# TWO

*T*HE NEXT MORNING, I piled into my mother's minivan with two of our five dogs. With only one child left at home (and that one being a teenager who had her license), one might wonder why she drove a minivan. But the van had never been about her kids. The van was about our dogs, which my mom was constantly carting to the vet or the pet spa or a dog park or on hikes or to places with good views for the dogs to enjoy (not sure dogs realize a view is a view) or just out and about. That morning we had Storm, a Chihuahua Yorkshire mix who was named after the rainy day on which she'd been rescued, and Monica, a Rottweiler pit bull mix named after Santa Monica, where she was found hunting rodents in the storage room of a diner with a health inspection rating of C. (We also had two cats, a parakeet, and two rabbits.)

After a twenty-minute drive, during which my mother talked mostly about the kitchen remodel she was planning, and after telling me more than twice that she thought Maya was overreacting and that I didn't need to be seeing a psychotherapist and that I should have taken more time with my appearance so that I could "make a good impression," we pulled up in front of a tall, drab medical building flanked by two mirrored office buildings that were reflecting so much light that it felt unsafe to open my eyes completely. I waited for my mom to cut the engine and park, but she continued checking her makeup in the mirror. "Go on, Pumpkin, you don't want to be late," she instructed.

I stepped out of the car slowly. "I'm going to run a few errands while you see Dr. Goode," she said. "I'll be back in an hour. Feel better. XOX."

I kicked myself for thinking my mom would provide some support in the fashion of walking me to the doctor's office and maybe telling me I had nothing to be nervous about. I knew by now to expect nothing from her but the emotional bare necessities, but it gave me a hollow, discarded feeling nonetheless as I watched her drive off.

Dr. Goode (a doughy looking fiftyish man with an amorphous, lumpy body) seated me in a big, comfy leather chair and settled into the barca lounger positioned across from me – taking forever to adjust the chair just so. I knew nothing about what this visit was going to be like and the anticipation was making me jittery. I wanted to get it going so that it could be over

Finally, Dr. Goode looked at me and asked, "How are we feeling today?" I didn't answer because I didn't know how "we" were feeling. I only knew how I felt. He pulled out a folder and leafed through the pages inside while I took inventory of his office. The room was large and rectangular and painted a cheery yellow and there were bowls of choco-late and boxes of tissue on every available surface. A dozen shelves were filled with books with titles like *Breaking the Spell of Obsessive Compulsive Disorder, The Faces of Schizophrenia, Repair Despair, Riding Out the Ups and Downs.* Clearly, the room had seen plenty of heartache and was ready to absorb mine.

Dr. Goode read aloud from one of the pages in the folder. "Let's see. According to your mother, no behavioral or learning problems during childhood, reached all your developmental milestones on time, no history of mental illness in your family... Your mother tells me you might be grieving your father's death." He looked up. "Do you want to talk about that?"

"Grieving my father's death? Seriously?" I replied. My mother was working on a PhD in self-delusion. "My father died when I was four and the only vivid memory I have of him is of me falling off a pony at Griffith Park and cutting my cheek and of him swooping me up and running in circles around the parking lot because I told him the wind made the cut stop stinging."

I paused, trying to download another memory. People always tiptoed around the subject of my dad, fearing that mentioning my deceased father would make me sad. But, I knew my father so briefly and remembered so little about him that the subject of him packed no emotional punch.

"I can also picture my sister and I leaving a fair with him, each holding one of his hands and holding a caramel apple in the other hand," I said. "I remember my apple fell to the ground and I started crying. He picked out the tiny pebbles and specks of dirt stuck to the caramel so that I could still eat it."

My father had died from a freak aneurysm at thirty-eight and left us behind with some money that had been passed down a few generations from a grandfather who invented and manufactured an improved torpedo propeller that corkscrewed through the water at the speed of sound and blew ships to smithereens during World War II. Great Grandpa then invested his windfall in oil and real estate and businesses that were still earning money—not millions, but enough that we had a comfortable life and my mom didn't have to work. Plainly, we were carving out a nice living off the dead backs of foreign enemies whose bones were decomposing on the ocean floor—their flesh eaten long ago by sharks.

"So, you don't really remember your father. Correct?"

"Correct."

Dr. Goode jotted down some notes. "Your mother also informed me that you recently turned seventeen and that it's a milestone that has been challenging for you. Tell me about that."

"I turned seventeen, not forty." My mother had totally brainwashed this sap.

"Seventeen is close to eighteen, which brings up college and living on your own," he said. He'd left out getting to vote and being old enough to drink in Europe, Mexico, and Canada, two other things that were weighing heavily on me.

"Apparently, you aren't eating," he said. "Why is that?"

"I try," I said. "But everything tastes like, I don't know . . . lighter fluid."

He stopped writing and looked up, concerned. "You've swallowed lighter fluid? Did you do it on purpose? Were you trying to hurt yourself? I need to know."

"No, no, not like that. It's just that food tastes . . . yucky. And it's hard to swallow. I'm pretty much never hungry."

"No appetite," he said. "Hmm . . . The significant differences between what your mother told me and what you're telling me make me wonder if your mother is in denial or you two aren't communicating well. Do you have anything to say about that?"

"My mother lives in a houseboat on Da Nile and possesses zero listening skills," I answered. "She might as well say, 'You lost me at hello' when you start a conversation with her. We're not close at all and never have been."

"So, your mother is absent, possibly narcissistic?"

I nodded my head "yes." "My older sister claims she was more caring when we were little. She froze us both out starting when I was pretty young."

"Interesting . . . High school is tough for a lot of kids," he said. "There's peer pressure and feeling like you don't fit in . . . do you have many friends?"

"Some," I said.

"So you have some friends you enjoy?"

"Why are you repeating what I just said?"

"Is it bothering you?"

"Yes."

"Why do you think you don't like repeating yourself?"

"It seems like a waste of time—mine and yours." This whole *visit* was feeling like a waste of time. I didn't see how answering a bunch of boring questions and hearing the fibs my mom told about me was going to make me feel better. The visit wasn't excruciating, like I feared it would be, it was just dull. All I wanted was to be walking out the door.

"Understood," he said. At a much quicker clip, Dr. Goode asked if I dated, were my grades good, did I play any sports, did I find my school workload manageable, did I use recreational drugs, was I content with my size and looks, did I get along with my sister, and on and on and on. After I answered in the affirmative to every question (except the drug one), he tapped his pencil on his notebook, baffled.

"It sounds as if your life's circumstances are acceptable to you," he said.

"Normally, I can deal," I said. "But, I've never found life easy. Lots of the time I feel like I was planted here without an instruction manual—like everybody's flying north and I'm flying south. I've always believed that I am different than everyone else."

"Different how?" he asked.

"I don't know. Like I'm weird inside and that if everybody knew the real me nobody would like me," I said.

"Interesting," he said. "Let's talk about what you like. What do you enjoy?"

The ickiness inside me was so overpowering and so far reaching that it was hard to remember ever liking much of anything. I squeezed my eyes shut and pictured myself smiling and slowly, slowly began recalling the good stuff: "Thanksgiving. Warm nights when you don't need a sweater. The sound of my blade skimming across glassy water on a quiet morning. Puppies. Skiing in fresh powder." I stopped. Suddenly, I was filled with nostalgia for all the things I could no longer enjoy.

"Is there more?"

"Yah, uhm . . . When you get really into a book and can't stop reading. The sound of rain. A guy named Ben . . ."

"So, you have a boyfriend named Ben?"

"No. And let's not get into that. Not a pleasant topic," I said, wishing I hadn't brought up Ben. Just the mention of his name was enough to sink my mood down further.

"Would it be accurate to say that there is enough about life that you enjoy that you want to remain here?" he asked.

I shrugged. "In the past, but not so much now."

"Why don't you want to be here? What is upsetting to you?" he asked.

"I'm upset because I have panic attacks that leave me light-headed and there's black pit of horribleness in my stomach and there's nothing that I want to do besides sleep, and I can't sleep. I'm tired of being tired all day at school and struggling so hard to learn things I'm not even interested in and can't imagine I'll ever use in real life. And I'm sick of watching all the kids at my school marching behind their self-imposed border lines, like a colony of ants, and how unfair it all is, but how everybody just goes with it—myself included. I hate that I've totally screwed up and sent away the only guy I've ever liked. I hate that I've devoted so much time and effort to crew and my boat doesn't win races. And I can't get rid of a voice inside that hates me and tells me that everything I do is a waste of time."

Unlike Nell, Dr. Goode understood the voice deal and didn't think I was cracking up. Phew. "We all have a negative interior voice," he explained. "When we don't feel well or are in difficult circumstances that voice can get very critical and self-limiting. Then it's a vicious cycle."

"My voice gives me doom," I said.

"I call that enemy voice the Beast," he said. "The trick is to talk back to the Beast; to tame the Beast and bring it back into check. Do you think you could do that? Try to get into a dialogue with the Beast and tell it to leave you alone and that what it is saying isn't true?"

"I guess I could try," I said.

"Does this exercise sound like it might be helpful?" he asked.

"Possibly."

"What else do you think would help you to feel better?"

"Aren't you supposed to tell me that?"

"How do you think I can make you feel better?"

I couldn't do the circular conversation anymore. I checked my watch and saw there were only ten minutes left, so I decided to zip it and run out the clock. At the stroke of noon, I was sprung, but not without copies of *How to Survive the Loss of a Parent* and *Positive Thinking in a Negative World*, an appointment for the next week (which I knew I wouldn't keep), and the promise to start a journal of my feelings about turning seventeen. As I moved through the doorway, so relieved to be exiting, Dr. Goode stopped me and handed over a card. "I'm going to recommend you call this number and make an appointment with Dr. Rice," he said. "He's an excellent psychiatrist. Deals with a lot of teens."

My stomach churned. The newly christened Beast was celebrating, giddy and laughing uproariously: "Even a trained psychologist, a professional, can't help you." I had the urge to puke, but where? The garbage can? A tissue?

"From what I'm hearing, you're suffering from depression and medication may be in order," he said. I must have looked as flipped out as I felt because he reached out and squeezed my hand reassuringly. "Don't worry," he said. "Dr. Rice and I have dealt with many young people in your shoes and you can and will get better. If it's okay with you, I'm going to brief him on our visit."

So there it was. He'd pulled out the big guns. I'd graduated from shrink to turbo shrink. My problems were even worse than I'd thought.

I walked out of the office and reached the curb, where my mother was waiting inside the car, talking on her phone. As I climbed into the car, she whispered, "Feeling better? How was it?"

"This is how it was," I answered as I handed her Dr. Rice's card. She glanced at the card and then pulled away from the curb and picked up her cell phone conversation where she had left off.

"And how does it feel when your mother acts dismissively like this to you?" I could picture Dr. Goode asking me.

My answer: "Familiar."

Dr. Rice, or Minute Rice as I named him, because during our entire appointment he looked at me only for as long as it would take to cook a pot of instant rice, didn't rise from his seat, peek up from his computer, or shake my hand when I stepped into his sprawling office. He was a squat, nerdy-looking man who was drowning in an enormous brown leather chair and moon-shaped glasses that swallowed his tiny head. I glanced around as I walked through the office and to the couch, surprised that the place was so generic looking – not a straight jacket or a stretcher or at least some sign of a person who dealt with psychos. While I knew kids who went to therapists, I didn't know anyone who went to a psychiatrist. Or at least nobody I knew had admitted to having a brain that required medical attention. All I'd ever wanted was to be normal and being here confirmed that I wasn't. I resisted the urge to tell Minute Rice that I was all better and just ditch the whole thing and live with whatever was wrong with me.

"Take a seat Janelle," Minute Rice said—an inauspicious way to kick off our relationship.

"Jane," I corrected him as I sat. I despised being called Janelle—not because it was an ugly name but because it was my full name and the only people who ever used my full name were my gynecologist, my dentist, my allergist, airport security officers and ticket agents, and my mother and teachers when they were angry with me. Every long line I'd ever waited in, every painful shot or cavity filling I'd endured, every time I'd had a finger wagged at me—every one of these situations had either begun or ended with the name Janelle.

Displaying about as much warmth and effort to connect with me as a clerk at the market scanning my groceries, he started in: "I spoke to Dr. Goode about your symptoms and what is going on with you. I know he asked you a lot of questions, but I have more." More questions? Dr. Goode had asked me so many questions. How could there possibly be more things to know?

His first round of questions was mostly medical. Did I have seizures? Was I on any medications? Was I being treated for any serious illnesses? "How long have you been clinically depressed?" he asked. So it was clinical depression, not just depression? Putting the word "clinical" in front of "depression" made my condition sound more serious. I could feel the panic attack train chugging towards me.

"About two months," I answered, taking deep breaths as I fended off the attack.

"That's a while. You should have been in here sooner." His fingers started clicking away on the keyboard. "We're going to skim over some emotional history now. Please try to be as honest and thorough with me as you can. I can't diagnose or help you if I don't know the facts. Okay?"

"Okay," I replied. Normally, I would have thought it would be difficult to give somebody I'd just met my "emotional history," but Minute Rice was such a blank slate that I didn't think it would be that hard. It would be like telling your secrets to a hole in the ground.

"Did you ever feel the way you do now when you were younger?" he asked.

"No. But I did get sad a lot," I said. "I've always spent at least a few days of every month feeling blah."

"Were your moods reliable, or did they seem to change at will?"

"My moods have always done their own thing. Years back, I asked my sister how to predict what mood you're going to wake up in when you go to sleep at night. She told me that when you go to bed happy you wake up happy and vice versa. But, it's never worked that way for me."

"Have you had times of great happiness and exuberance—times where you had too much energy and couldn't sleep?"

Just what he was getting at here I didn't know, but I continued, "At least a night a week I have trouble putting myself to sleep. Sometimes I stay up until two, three in the morning, watching TV, listening to music, cleaning my room, reading. But, the weird part is that I'm not so tired the morning after a late night. The insomnia I've had lately is different, though. I stay up all night depressed and I'm exhausted in the morning."

"Possibly bipolar disorder," he said. Bipolar disorder? I'd heard the term plenty of times. But, usually it was used to describe the kids at school who were significantly off. Often, it went along with terms like wack job or nut bag or schizo – a few more labels I didn't want.

"Sometimes, when I'm on one of my late-night jags, I write and write—song lyrics, even though I'm not a musician, short stories, lists of things I want to do. I'll write for hours."

"Hypergraphia," he said.

"Hyper-whatia?" I asked.

"When scads of ideas are racing through your head and you feel compelled to get them all down. It's a symptom of hypomania. What about hypersexuality? Have you ever felt so acutely sexual that you made an impulsive choice? Maybe had intercourse with someone you didn't know well?" I wanted to know what, exactly, hypomania meant if I was being diagnosed with it, but Minute Rice was moving through his questions so fast that there was barely time to breathe.

"I've only slept with one guy and it was so much the opposite of good that I've never done it again. And it wasn't hypersexuality that drove me into his arms. I was drunk, the first and only time I've been drunk or will be drunk, and I was curious to see what the fuss was about."

It was in Hawaii with a tan and slick windsurfing instructor named Reese. After the third day of lessons and flirting, we took a choppy, moonlit ride on his catamaran and shared a bottle of champagne, and wound up naked. What came next was anything but sexy—it was painful and icky and I couldn't wait for it to end and for him to get off me.

Once the session was over, I was glad that I had become a member of a worldly, mature group of sophisticated people who'd been devirginized. But the whole ordeal grossed me out enough to file it under B for Big Mistake (along with breaking both ankles when I was seven by jumping from a second story balcony holding an umbrella to see if I could fly like Mary Poppins; trying to drive a tractor parked in a vacant lot and crashing it into—and toppling—a chain link fence; and faking a heart attack in fifth grade to get out of a social studies quiz and having to pick up trash around campus for the month as punishment for lying.)

In fact, I was so grossed out that I didn't want to wake up next to Mr. Windsurfer and get talked into a round two. After he fell asleep, I took my chances and dove off the catamaran and swam to shore.

Maya was awake and sitting up in bed when I arrived back at our hotel room. "Where have you been?" she asked, leaping out of bed and grabbing me. "I searched everywhere. You don't know how much covering I had to do with Mom."

"I lost it," I said, pulling off my wet clothes.

"Lost what, your purse? Where are your shoes?"

"No. I lost IT it."

"I hope you used a condom," she said, crawling back into bed. "And please tell me it wasn't that old guy on the beach."

"Negative on the condom and he's only twenty-seven."

"Yippee. At least you can charge him with statutory rape if he gave you herpes or got you pregnant."

"I don't get the big deal," I said. "I hated it."

"It gets better. You'll see," she yawned, pulling up the covers. "And it helps if you actually know and like the guy." She dropped her head onto the pillow and shut her eyes. "I'm not even going to ask why you're soaking wet."

"Any times of intense sexual desires even though you might not have acted on them?" Minute Rice asked.

"Not really. None of the guys in my school do much for me and I don't feel a desire unless there's a person I like."

"You're lucky. Hypersexuality is a part of bipolar disorder and it can get one into a lot of trouble—pregnancy, sexually transmitted diseases," he said. "Any other feelings or behaviors that made you or make you feel . . . different . . . uncomfortable . . . or upset?"

I poked around my brain for answers. Dumping the contents of my brain into a stranger's lap was a new experience. I'd never told anyone these things – not even Maya. I folded my arms around myself, wishing I had a coat so that I could at least cover up my body, since I couldn't cover up my brain.

It took a few minutes, but I was able to uncork some troubling memories. "In fourth grade, I got obsessed with the number seven," I answered. "I'd always had an affinity for the number seven. Six is such an opportunist and a kiss up, always trying to get a leg up on seven, and eight is haughty—so satisfied with himself that he's divisible by four and two. And even though five is an odd number, it's ubiquitous—twenty-five cents, fifty dollars, and five times twenty makes a hundred, the grand poo-bah of numbers. So, I befriended seven and started doing everything in seven. I'd take seven bites of cereal before I swallowed. I'd open and close a door seven times before I shut it for good. I'd switch the lights on and off seven times. It got so distracting that I couldn't concentrate on my schoolwork or conversations, but I couldn't stop. It went on for months."

"Obsessive-compulsive disorder," he reported

"There's a name for living under the spell of the number seven?" I asked in disbelief.

"Feeling compelled to do things and being unable to stop. Common."

This was amazing. Everything I'd thought was my personality was a diagnosis. I was legitimately ordinary—albeit ordinary for a person with a potpourri of mental disorders. It was a little comforting to know that I wasn't completely alone in my weirdness. I'd always felt so singled out.

Minute Rice stopped typing but still didn't look up from his computer. "Okay. Enough for now," he said. "My preliminary diagnosis is that you have early-onset bipolar combined with OCD, obsessive-compulsive disorder, and that you are currently in a bipolar depression."

Bipolar. There it was again. "Bipolar?" I asked.

"I'll give you the DSM definition," Minute Rice said as he pulled out a giant grey book and leafed through it. *"The Diagnostic and Statistical Manual of Mental Disorders"* is published by the American Psychiatric Association. It gives the official definitions of mental disorders. They're arranged by numerical codes . . . Let's see . . . Here we are. 296.7." Now I was not only a diagnosis—I was a code number.

Dr. Rice handed me the tome. I read: "Bipolar Disorder DSM 296.7: condition that causes extreme shifts in mood, energy, functioning . . . Mania (euphoria) alternates with depression . . . Symptoms include: acutely elevated mood followed by acutely low mood . . . Affects 2 to 4 percent of population . . . Biological and genetic in nature . . . No known cure."

"I'm not certain you're bipolar, but I have a strong hunch," Minute Rice said. "However, if you are bipolar, I don't know if you are bipolar one, bipolar two, or bipolar spectrum. Bipolar spectrum is the mildest and bipolar one is the most serious because the highs are much higher and the lows are much lower than spectrum or bipolar two."

"So do you have something that could lift my mood? Lift it fast?" I asked. My heart quickened with anticipation. Maybe this troll of a man, with all the knowledge he had in his little head, would be able to get me feeling better soon.

"I most likely can find something that will help you, but just what medication that is I'm not sure," he answered. "And as for how long it will take, that is a question mark, too. Some medications work quickly for some people. Other people don't get relief for weeks—that is, if the medication even works for them." Ugh. I had wanted a fast fix. Minute Rice was looking less like a savior and more of a bearer of bad news. He continued, "If it is bipolar two or bipolar spectrum, as I suspect, it is very treatable. Bipolar one is treatable, though it can be more challenging, and the disorder is usually more debilitating."

Debilitating. The Beast inside was amused: "Debilitating. You're disabled. Unable."

Minute Rice plucked a sheet of paper from his desk and handed it to me. "Don't worry," he said. "If you're bipolar you're in good company."

I read the list of names on the paper: Peter Tchaikovsky, Ernest Hemingway, Sylvia Plath, Zelda Fitzgerald, Vincent Van Gogh, Jimi Hendrix, Jim Morrison, Dylan Thomas, Kurt Cobain, Buzz Aldrin. Every single person on the list had either killed, drunk, or drugged himself to death, with the exception of Buzz Aldrin, who had, instead, landed on the moon. This was good company? These people had tragic lives. I didn't want to be part of this elite group of miserables, no matter how brilliant and cool they were.

Minute Rice pulled out a prescription pad and started writing. "I'm giving you a prescription for an antidepressant I've had good results with. Ten milligrams once a day for now, in the morning. We'll talk in two weeks and bump up the dose. I like to start small. Along the route, we'll be able to tell if the antidepressant is working." He continued writing. "I'm also giving you a prescription for a sleeping pill and a mild sedative to use for your anxiety."

Minute Rice rose and handed me the prescriptions and then moved to the exit door, opened it, and motioned for me to leave. Like Dr. Goode, he had two separate doors—an entrance door and an exit door. All these doors so that nobody will see you coming out of a psychiatric office? Was I supposed to feel even more ashamed and embarrassed than I already felt about seeing a psychiatrist?

"See you in two weeks, Janelle," Minute Rice said as I stepped out of his office. A double whammy: Janelle start and finish.

"Oh," he called after me as I stepped into the hallway. "You might get a headache or dry mouth. Those are normal side effects. But check in with me if you have rapid heart rate, vomiting, or suicidal ideating."

"Suicida—what?"

"If you start planning to kill yourself," he answered as he shut his office door.   I left the office building more puzzled than I'd ever been by a physics lecture or the number infinity or when I first learned about the birds and the bees. I had a prescription for a medicine that might work or might not work or might make me arrange to kill myself for a disorder I might or might not have, and there was no telling how long the medicine might take to work, if it even worked. I didn't know whether I should feel hopeful or doomed.

The next morning, after a sleeping-pill-induced night's sleep, I woke up, padded into the kitchen, poured a glass of orange juice, and opened the bottle of antidepressants. I shook one of the light green oval pills from the bottle and into my hand. I held the pill and stared at it for a beat. It was tiny, barely an eighth of an inch across. I couldn't imagine how something this minuscule was going to circulate itself through the five feet seven inches of real estate between the top of my head and the soles of my feet and get it all into working order. I raised my glass to the pill and clinked the two together in a toast. "Here's to a happy working relationship," I said and then washed down the pill with the juice. I may have doubted the powers of the tiny pill, but I was putting my brain in its hands – praying it could dull the pain. I had to at least try and believe things would get better.

For the next four days, I woke up every morning and performed a body check. Stomach: churning. Throat: still felt like upchucking. Heart: grinding. Legs and arms: tired and weak. Brain: being strangled by a wet blanket. Overall: still riding a bad one.

By day five, with no change in mood, I was starting to believe the relentless voice of the Beast when it said, "The meds won't work. Nothing will ever work—never ever. You'll feel this way forever." I tried to talk back to the Beast and tell it that what it was saying wasn't true, like Dr. Goode had suggested I do. But, it's hard to fight a negative voice when you believe every word it says.

On day seven, I was forced to go swimming with my p.e. class. Mrs. Blodgett, the teacher, told me that that she would no longer let me hang out in the locker room, like I'd been getting away with for the past few weeks. She said that whatever illness I'd claimed to have was clearly gone, and that I looked "plenty healthy to participate in athletics."

I didn't bother doing a body scan during swim class because I was too numb from being in the freezing pool and from standing in the brisk wind outside the freezing pool to feel anything but cold. We were doing a freestyle relay and I was on the blocks, waiting for the swimmer in my lane to tag the wall so that I could dive in and kick my lifeless legs and stroke my lifeless arms for two laps.

Mrs. Blodgett was lumbering along the concrete path next to the pool with a whistle in her mouth. Mrs. Blodgett was easily two hundred pounds, not a great advertisement for the health benefits of physical education, and she was so sour that she was able to pull off whistling and scowling simultaneously.

Suddenly, just before I was about to dive off the blocks, Mrs. Blodgett tripped on a crack in the concrete and the whistle dropped from her mouth. She reached down to retrieve the whistle, lost her balance, and tumbled into the swimming pool with a cannonball splash. Immediately she began thrashing around frantically, trying to swim to the edge of the pool. Either she didn't know how to swim or her plus-sized clothes were pulling her under.

Luckily Latham, a star rugby player with bodybuilder arms, was swimming in the lane she had fallen into. He kicked toward her and guided her to the edge of the pool. Like a little kid just starting swimming lessons, Mrs. Blodgett walked her hands along the edge of the pool until she reached the steps. She trudged out of the pool and onto the cement, where she stood, befuddled and with her white blouse clinging to her chest. Then she blew her whistle, spewing water onto her face, and bellowed, "Class dismissed."

It wasn't nice and it wasn't fair, but the whole scene was so humorous that once all ten of us girls were safely inside the locker room, we let loose with the laughter we'd been stifling for the past ten minutes—big, doubled over, slumber party laughter. The laughing was tickling my insides, brushing away the soot. It was like the sun had broken through the night sky. I had forgotten how delightful laughter was. I had forgotten even what it felt like to find something funny.

We giggled through our showers, giggled as we toweled off, giggled as we dried our hair, and left the locker room still giggling.

By the time I reached Spanish, I had downsized my laughter to a grin. I plopped down in the seat next to Tiffany and pulled out my binder.

"Oh, my God! Oh, my God!" Tiffany squealed. "You're smiling!" She leaned into me and gave me a peck on the cheek. "You're smiling! I've been waiting weeks to see you smile!"

Was I really smiling? I was smiling. I was smiling for real! I quickly moved through a body scan as class started. Stomach: was my stomach growling? Could I actually be hungry? Throat: didn't feel so tight, could swallow. Heart: beating just right, not too fast or too slow. Legs and arms: I raised my arms and uncrossed my legs and it didn't feel like much of an effort. Brain: no Beast inside telling me that I sucked. I looked over at Ben and Stella, chatting quietly, and, though it still made me sad, I didn't feel as busted up and broken as I usually did when I saw them.

I arrived home from school and burst through the front door. All five dogs greeted me in the foyer and I crouched down and kissed each sweet critter on the mouth, even Friday, an ancient bulldog with decaying teeth, named after the day she was rescued, and Monica, who never had a shortage of gelatinous drool. Then I proceeded into the kitchen and shocked my stomach (which hadn't been asked to digest much besides pills for a while now) with a quarter of a jar of peanut butter on crackers, two pears, a few squares of dark chocolate, and a bowl of tortilla soup.

My whole body was smiling. I skipped upstairs to the bathroom, reached into the medicine cabinet and pulled out the bottle of antidepressants. I placed the bottle on the counter and kneeled on the floor, bowing to the bottle. "Thank you, green pills, thank you, thank you, thank you," I repeated. "Thank you scientist who invented you, thank you factory that cooked and packaged you, thank you Dr. Goode for sending me to Minute Rice so that he could prescribe you. Thank you."

At six-thirty, after finishing my homework, I logged in an hour on my rowing machine, which I hadn't touched in forever—let alone go to practice. I showered afterward and then made my way down to the kitchen, where my mother was feeding the five dogs three different kinds of dog food. "Wanna have Chinese food for dinner?" I asked.

"For dinner. You mean you're hungry?" she asked.

"Starving," I answered.

"I'll bet. You've been living on orange juice and air," she said. "Where do you want me to order from?"

"I thought we'd go out," I said. I picked up a couple dog dishes and filled them with water.

"I'd love to, Pumpkin, and I'm thrilled you're hungry, but I've got more work to do at Cookie's house. This Furry Friends fundraiser is a monumental chore," she said. "I'm already late." My mom stood and pulled a Chinese take-out menu off the counter and handed it to me. "This place just opened. It's supposed to be good," she said. "And they deliver. Save some for me. I'll try to be home before you're done eating."

I stared at my mom, wondering if she was really going to Cookie's or if she was going off to the building I had spotted her at last time she was supposedly working on the fundraiser. "Are you going anywhere else besides Cookie's?" I asked.

"Just Cookie's," my mom answered, searching around the countertop for her keys. I was about to tell her that I'd seen her at a random building and ask her what she was doing there and why she lied, but I stopped myself. She'd probably just lie again. I would find out on my own what she was up to. My mother finally spotted her keys and tossed them into her purse. "XOX," she said as she disappeared out the door.

I didn't want to waste time waiting for Chinese food to be delivered, so I made a meal out of some of my mom's leftovers from an Indian restaurant she'd been to the night before. After I'd eaten, I got into my car and drove away from the house. First, I drove to Cookie Diamond's house and searched for my mother's car. It wasn't in the driveway, it wasn't in the street. She was not at Cookie's house.

I remembered the street the building I'd seen her at was on and I remembered what it looked like, but I didn't know the exact address or even the intersection. I cruised the boulevard several times before I spotted the large, shingled building I had seen before. If my mom was in the parking lot, I didn't want her to spot my car when she left, so I parked around the corner and walked to the front of the building, keeping an eye out for her. I stopped at the front door to the building and read the sign, "Brookside Assisted Living Center." There went the secret boyfriend theory. My mother certainly wouldn't be dating a man who needed assistance with being alive. She was not a nurturer of people. I tugged on the front door, toying with the idea of entering, but it was locked. There was a doorbell, but I wasn't going to ring it. People were probably already asleep. I wondered if my mom had a key to the place.

I stood staring at the building for a few minutes and then made my way into the underground parking lot. Sure enough, there was my mom's minivan – big as God. She had some explaining to do, but I would have to pick the right moment for my questioning.

# THREE

*D*URING THE NEXT few days, as my mood and confidence went from better to better to best, I greeted each morning with a little more pizazz. Each day my smile grew wider, my energy grew greater, I talked a little more and a little faster, I had more new ideas on a collection of subjects, and my gratitude for just plain old being alive grew greater. I required less and less sleep every night. I would stay up late listening to music and posting online – about how good life was and how we all needed to get along and destroy the high school social pyramid that was crushing us and how I loved everybody, no matter their status.

School was tough for me. It was on slow motion while I was on fast forward. It was challenging to sit still. I would cross and uncross my legs dozens of times per class and invent excuses to go to the bathroom. I also had a hard time keeping from blurting out answers. I had to practically duct tape my mouth shut. The teachers weren't happy with my behavior and I was sent to the guidance counselor's office on more than one occasion.

By the end of the week, I had soared to even higher heights and ushered in a brand-new kind of good mood that was nothing short of a mystical experience, a mood that could be described as ecstatic.

Thursday morning, I rose at five a.m., after having awakened at four-thirty jubilant and buzzing with restless energy. Blood was coursing through my veins and my heart was beating like a bongo. I was high on life in a way I'd never been before.

I roused the dogs and led them into the backyard and out the gate for a run. Crew practice (which I'd started going to again) didn't start for a couple hours – and I needed to move immediately. I couldn't wait. Muscles wanted to flex. Legs and arms wanted to pump. The dogs and I chased each other around the neighborhood, up and down the streets and alleys in circles. Speeder, a greyhound who was rescued by the side of the freeway (hence the name), kept up with my breakneck speed and even got ahead of me a few times, but I was in the lead for two-thirds of the run. After half an hour, Friday dropped out, then Storm, followed by Monica, who quit after forty-five minutes. An hour and fifteen minutes later, the dogs followed me through the backyard gate and into the kitchen, where they collapsed, pooped.

"Pancakes for all," I announced as I retrieved the ingredients from the cupboards. Soon I was frying soy bacon (due to our affinity for animals, we were a meatless household) and flipping pancakes over a griddle. Only half of the pancakes were making it back onto the griddle after being catapulted a foot above the stove. The other pancakes were landing on the floor, where the dogs were scarfing them down. The dogs seemed so happy to be eating the pancakes that I didn't have the heart to stop them. I wanted them to be as happy as I was.

"I smell something good," my mother trilled from the family room. She entered the kitchen and screeched, "No!" desperately pulling the pancakes out of the dogs' mouths. "Out doggies! Outside!" she hollered as she shooed the dogs through the back door.

"Ready for breakfast?" I asked as she returned to scraping up pancakes from the floor.

"Jane, what are you doing?" she asked. "You know Friday's teeth are decaying. She can't eat this stuff. Neither can Storm. She's allergic to wheat. And I'm trying to get Monica to lose weight."

"I'm celebrating because I'm feeling amazing," I said. I turned off the fire under the griddle and drenched a tower of pancakes in maple syrup.

"I'm glad you're feeling better. I knew there wasn't anything wrong with you," she said. "But try to think of the dogs before you do something like this."

"I did," I said. "They were starved because I took them on a long run."

"Thank you, but remember we have the dog walker," she said. "He knows where the dogs should walk and how far and fast each one can go. Please leave all the exercising to him or to me."

"Yes, ma'am," I answered, saluting her. I pulled out a fork and drove into the stack of pancakes with venom, congratulating myself on being an excellent chef.

I arrived at crew practice early and sat on the beach in the marina, watching the sun rise. Nature had flicked on its light bulb for me. I watched a bird describe an arc and listened as it sang a lullaby—for me. The tide washed in and out for me. The sand was soft for me.

By the time crew practice started, I'd already done a half hour of push-ups and sit-ups and more than a dozen handstands. My teammates arrived and stared in disbelief as I tried to lift our boat off the rack and carry it to the water by myself. Normally, all nine of us carried the boat to the water, but I felt like I had the strength of eighteen longshoremen. Unfortunately, I could barely budge the boat and the others had to help me.

Once we'd lowered the shell into the water, I hopped into Devon, our stroke's seat, the most important seat in the boat. "Mind if we change it up today?" I asked Devon. "I have a few pointers for you."

"Yes, I mind," she said. "And I don't need pointers."

"I'm just trying to help us win. I thought I could demonstrate a few things that might help you hone your skills," I said.

"Out of Devon's seat, Jane," Claire, our coxswain, shouted into the cox box.

"Fine," I said, making my way to the seven seat, soon to be somebody else's seat. Seat seven was the least important spot in the boat—the spot where (as usual) I'd been hiding. But I was better than seat seven. Coach Beverly had even recognized that I was capable of a more important seat. But every time she suggested I try a new place in the boat, I had declined. For the past year, she'd been eyeing me suspiciously, like she was onto the fact that I was a diehard underachiever and couldn't figure out why. I was done being an underachiever and she would soon see what I was truly capable of.

"Coach Beverly wants us to do an endurance run followed by some starts," Claire said. "I want laser focus on technique today."

We paddled out into the marina, past the sailboats and yachts. "Good, guys, keep it up," Claire droned on. "That's a nice pace. Oarsome."

"C'mon, everybody, synchronize!" I shouted. "It sounds like we're thrashing around in a bathtub. I want to hear one oar, not eight. Think of us as one being with sixteen arms. Like a millipede."

"Leave the talking to me, Jane," Claire said.

"No offense, but we've all heard everything you have to say a million times," I said. "All the 'oarsome' and 'way to go' and 'dig in harder' mean nothing anymore. We're desensitized. I'm going to give you some new material." I'd been thinking everything I was saying for months, but I'd been too nice to say something so harsh. However, it needed to be said if we were going to get better – and "nice" was just my cowardice.

"You're being rude, Jane," Claire said. "I'm the coxswain. I know what to say, not you."

"It's time for a sprint! Up two beats!" I shouted. I dropped my blade into the water and pushed my legs as hard as I could.

"We're not sprinting yet," Claire said. But I kept the boat going at the fastest clip possible, for as long as the others could keep up.

After about four minutes, I saw Coach Beverly maneuvering her boat closer to ours, checking her stopwatch. "There's Coach Beverly. Let's show her our stuff! Fuel those legs!"

I could feel the girls pulling harder with me, driving through the water. The shell was swinging forward, our blades in unison. We were kicking ass like never before.

"Excellent work, girls," Coach Beverly yelled into her bullhorn. "You're looking really strong! That was one of your best sprint times!"

"We are strong!" I said. "Keep going. Refuse to be fourth and fifth placers. Our new place is numero uno! We have the talent! Let's win South Coast Regatta! Let's get those college recruiters begging us to row for them!"

"Zip it, Jane!" Claire yelled. "No more giving orders or I'm going to tell Coach Beverly."

"Me, too," Devon said. "I'm the stroke, not you."

"Jeez," I said. "I'm just trying to inspire us to be better. We're never going to win regattas until we truly believe we're winners." I couldn't understand why Devon was so dead set on mediocrity.

"We become winners by following Coach Beverly's training plans and respecting the rules of the boat," Claire said.

Which has been getting us nowhere, I thought. I didn't want to get in trouble with Coach Beverly, so I shut up and behaved for the rest of the ride, letting Claire spew her clichés and Devon set an unskilled, too-slow pace. When we'd disembarked and put the shell back into the boathouse Audrey pulled me aside. "I'm going to talk to Coach Beverly about getting you in the stroke seat for the South Coast Regatta. You're better than Devon. I told you that last year, but you wouldn't listen."

"Well, I'm listening now," I answered, happy that somebody was onboard with my plans to make our boat the best it could be. "Let's do it."

I arrived at school and noticed a space open in the A lot. "Who deserves this spot more than me?" I thought as I slid into the spot and proudly exited the wagon that was my mom's before it got old and then was Maya's before she saved up and went halfsies with my mom on a convertible MINI Cooper and then recently became mine.

I marched through the Atrium with my head held high. "Good morning, As," I said, waving to a few of them. "What a beautiful day to enjoy the umbrellas and the roses. Maybe someday you'd like to let some of the other students enjoy them."

I marched past the CEA with pride. "Good morning, Cs," I said, waving.

Dickens tipped the top hat he was wearing at me. "Top of the morning, Jane."

Zeke approached us. "I just noticed the other day that the Mona Lisa has no eyebrows. Do you know why that is?"

"Mona Lisa was the Renaissance," Charles answered. "A couple centuries before my time, so I wouldn't know."

"I'll get to the bottom of it by the end of the day," I promised. My phone chimed, and I looked down at a text from Nell: "Would you rather repeat junior year or have a metal pin in your jaw that constantly picks up talk radio stations?"

"I would rather skip senior year and invent a metal pin that, when inserted into the brain, adds one hundred points to the I.Q so that everyone can be as smart as me," I texted back.

"Buenos dias, Bs," I said as I reached the Benches. "It may be very sunny out later today and, seeing as how there is no shelter here, maybe some of you would like to dine in the Atrium under the umbrellas? The As don't own the Atrium any more than the Bs own the Benches. Just a thought." The bell rang and I headed for history.

At the start of history, I asked Vegas why we had done nothing but study wars all year and why we couldn't study some more positive events that had taken place in the past; and why our textbook, and every history textbook I'd ever read, was chock-a-block with disaster and bloodshed. "It's like world history is combat and strife and nothing else," I said, feeling like I was far more qualified to teach than he would ever be.

"I don't choose your curriculum," he answered. "The principal does, and much of it is based on what colleges require you to have learned to earn acceptance. And wars are important. They have shaped and influenced our culture and the state of the world today."

I pressed on. "Maybe if we started learning about the good things that have happened over the years and not just the fighting, it would make us less aggressive and we could relate to each other in a more peaceful way. We could learn more about how different holidays started and the gold rush and what people did with their newfound wealth or the first inmate to be rehabilitated and leave prison and be a good citizen."

"That's an interesting thought, Jane," Vegas said. "And now, if you don't mind, I am going to continue with World War II."

I held my hand over my mouth to keep from talking anymore. But the perpetual interior chatter and slew of thoughts made me want to shoot up my hand and ask, "Is this noise inside my head bothering you?"

When class ended, Nine turned to me and, for the first time ever, I saw her crack a smile.

When it was time for lunch, I headed straight for the CEA, where I ordered a grilled cheese sandwich. I'd never ordered food from the CEA before, always worried that it would make me look like a loser. But, now that I was certain I wasn't a loser I would eat food from wherever I wanted.

It was cloudy out, so I decided to hang out at the Benches, where I could warm up. I found Tiffany and Nell and sat next to them, unwrapping my sandwich and taking a bite.

"Did you get that from the cafeteria?" Tiffany asked, pointing at the sandwich like it was something I'd fished out of the sewer.

"Yep," I said. "And it's delicious."

"You actually went inside the CEA and ordered something?" Nell said. "What were you thinking?"

"I was thinking that I was hungry," I said. I waved the sandwich. "Want a bite?"

"It does look kinda good," Tiffany said. She glanced around to make sure no one was looking and took a bite. "Wow. Mmmm."

"See what we've been missing out on," I said. "From now on I'm getting lunch in the CEA when I'm hungry for it."

"I don't recommend that," Nell said. "Unless you want to become a C."

"I will not become a C because I am not a letter. I am a person," I answered as I walked off from the Benches and headed back to the CEA for a drink. Before I left the CEA, I rounded up Charles Dickens, Zeke and three other Cs and told them they were coming with me to eat in the Atrium. At first, the C gang was giggling excitedly, like we were going off to rob a bank. But when it was show time and we were supposed to enter the Atrium, everybody got scared and took off except for Dickens and Zeke. It was so frustrating to try and elevate kids and have them chicken out and remain in their lowly comfort zone.

"How come you guys are having lunch *here* today?" Stella asked while we settled down at a table in the Atrium. She looked bugged, which was my goal. She had bugged me for years. It was her turn.

"It's sunny out and we don't feel like getting burned when there are plenty of umbrellas in here," I replied.

"What about the CEA?" Stella asked as Zeke and Dickens seated themselves at a table and got comfortable. "There's no sun in the CEA and plenty of seating—and lots more burritos if you want seconds."

Zeke, probably from nerves, started laughing. "What's so funny?" Stella hissed. Zeke, who had never understood social cues, kept right on laughing. Stella, blushed from rage, picked up the small stack of pencils Zeke had set out on the table and snapped each of them in half and handed them back to him. Zeke examined the pencils for a few seconds and then smiled up at Stella. "Thank you," he said. "I will use these in my scientific experiments." Then everybody cracked up, even Ariana and Alexis.

Stella shook her head in disgust and then started for the exit. "I'm going off campus for lunch. It's gotten too… crowded in here." Game over. I won.

"That was brilliant," I told Zeke, after Stella was gone. "But, how do you take it? How do handle the . . . disrespect?"

"Being at the bottom of the heap is surprisingly freeing, because there's nowhere lower for me to fall," he said. "It's like . . . I don't have to worry about doing a good job because I've already been fired."

I got to Spanish class and took Stella's seat next to Ben. I didn't know why I hadn't taken the seat before. She didn't own it, and it was where I wanted to sit. Next to the guy I liked. The only place to sit if I wanted to start building something with him. My insides started fluttering just at the feeling of being near him. I'd forgotten how charged up his aura got me. Ben screwed up his face, looking puzzled as I pulled out my Spanish book. I gave him a big, warm smile. Just then, Stella arrived. She stomped over to me and stopped, glaring at me. "Excuse me, Jane. You seem to be confused. That is my seat."

I glanced around the chair. "I don't see a name tag on this chair."

Stella sighed and threw her backpack on a nearby seat. "I hope this mood of yours is temporary," she said. "Because everything you're doing is annoying."

Seconds later, Señora Flores arrived and started in on a dull lesson—the conditional tense. A few minutes into the lesson, I raised my hand. "What is it, Jane?" she asked.

"Why don't we all pretend we're Che Guevara today, or even Shakira, and answer your questions with something they would say," I suggested. "It would make the conditional tense a lot less humdrum."

"Maybe another day," Señora Flores answered.

My hand, which I seemed unable to control, shot up for every question Señora Flores asked, and even though I kept saying, "Oh! Pick me! Pick me! I know the answer!" she didn't call on me once.

Three-quarters of the way through class, I hatched another idea. "I figured out what the Spanish language is missing and what would make it better," I blurted out. "Let's talk about it after class," Señora Flores answered. "I'll be rapido," I replied. "The lingua es missing contracciones como he's, there's, we're, I'm—and the possessive contracciones tambien —Jane's, Ben's, Tiffany's. Si Espanol had contracciones it wouldn't take so mucho time to get across what you're saying and conversaciones would be more eficiente and … "

"That's enough," Señora Flores said. "I don't want any more interruptions." I could tell I'd pushed her too far, so I sat on my hand to keep it from shooting up and clenched my jaw tightly to keep myself from talking for the remaining ten minutes of class. It was torturous.

At school dismissal, Nell and Tiffany ambled to the parking lot with me. "You're acting bizarre, Jane," Nell said. "You're so ramped up and you're walking around the school like you own the place. And you're hanging out with people you never even used to talk to. You're getting dangerously close to becoming a C. Would you rather return to being the Jane we know and love or spend the rest of high school stuck in the CEA eating cheese sandwiches with Zeke?"

"Did you know that the CEA grilled cheese has both gruyere and cheddar in it?" I asked. "And FYI, Zeke is a cool guy and I'm over your 'would you rathers.'"

"Fine. What's with all the goofy theories and questions you're spouting out?" Nell asked.

"Goofy?" I asked. "Maybe you find them goofy because they're too smart for you to understand." I was beginning to wonder if Nell was as bright as I'd thought she was all these years. At the very least, her view of the world was narrow, more narrow even than mine had previously been.

"They're not smart. They're ridiculous," she said, looking more and more frustrated with me. "And as for all your chipper posts and texts about how grand life is—you need to get into reality. There's starvation and disease and poverty in the world. This planet is a polluted mess and the polar ice caps are melting and we're going to run out of water one day. Remember?"

"You know what your problem is," I told her angrily. "You're too negative. Life is incredible and amazing and you don't get it. The glass isn't even half empty for you. It's smashed to bits on the floor."

"Get off her case, Nell," Tiffany said." Can't you see that Jane is just excited about how much better she is doing? Personally, I find her zest refreshing." She turned to me. "But I will say that you're pushing it by hanging out with the Cs."

"You're wrong on your last thought, Tiffany, but I forgive you," I said. "I've got plans for us. We're going shopping – on me. Without Nell. Let's hit the road." I swaggered off toward my car with Tiffany following me. `

After driving about fifty miles an hour on five miles of surface streets, we arrived at a high-end department store, where I valet parked the car and instructed Tiffany to hop out, but she just sat there.

"We can't go shopping here," Tiffany said. "They don't even sell a barrette for under fifty dollars."

"Enough with the sensibility," I said. "Now come on in and pick out what you want, or I'll just buy you a bunch of stuff that you might not like."

I talked Tiffany into getting herself a pair of gold sandals and got myself a pair of over-the-knee brown suede boots, which I couldn't be bothered to try on. Trying on things was for cautious people who wouldn't take risks.

Next came the handbag department, where I bought Tiffany (over her protests) a beaded clutch purse. Jewelry department: long gold chains for both of us. Makeup department: eight tubes of lipstick in eight different colors for us. Then came a skirt for Tiffany and three orange T-shirts for me. "One can never have too much orange," I explained. To further prove my point, I bought an orange motorcycle jacket. The shopping spree price tag—$3,285.53. I didn't even blink as I signed the receipt. Who knew how fun it was to shop without worrying about prices? More importantly, who deserved these things more than me and my best friend?

Tiffany and I had driven merely a mile from the store when an irre-sistible plan hit me between the eyes. "Want to buy a bottle of tequila and some margarita mix and head somewhere picturesque and have our own little happy hour?" I asked Tiffany.

"But, how are we going to buy tequila?" Tiffany asked as I pulled into a liquor store parking lot.

"It's about attitude," I said as I swung open the car door. "Act like you own the joint. Like nobody can stop you from doing what you want to do—like you're the prime minister of a superpower."

Once inside, I chose an expensive bottle of tequila, grabbed some sweet-and-sour mix and a package of plastic cups and marched confidently toward the cashier, a pimply-faced guy who looked barely twenty-one.

"I.d.?" he asked.

"Uhm . . . Right . . . The problem is . . . that . . . my wallet, with my license in it, was stolen yesterday… from the… library," I said. "From the library. Can you believe that? The library? Wouldn't you think a place where people read books was safe?"

"I didn't bring my i.d. because she's driving," Tiffany said.

"One of you needs i.d. or I can't sell the tequila to you," he said.

"Listen," I said, leaning over the counter. I could tell from the flustered look on the guy's face that he was ripe for manipulating. "It's my twen-ty-second birthday and we just want to have a few drinks and party at the beach. Celebrate that I've made it this many years without dying."

"Why don't you hook up with us after work?" Tiffany asked, flashing a flirty smile and tugging on her sweater so that an inch of cleavage was peeking out of the V-neck. "We're going to be at El Matador. You know where that beach is?"

"I get off at six. Will you still be there?" he asked.

"We'll wait for you," I said.

"Okay," he said, ringing up the merchandise. "That sounds all right."

With absolutely no intention of going to the beach, Tiffany and I drove to the top of my street, to our special drinking spot we'd visited on my birthday. We found a small clearing with a view and started mixing up margaritas. Last time we'd been here I'd wanted a sink hole to appear and swallow me up. This time I wanted to call out to the hills and tell them what a glorious day I was having.

"To us being BFFs for this life and every life after," I said, raising my glass to Tiffany's. I continued toasting, on and on: "To this mountain, which was thousands of years in the making, specifically created for us so that we could sit on it today." "To us kicking ass at school and graduating with honors." "To us dismantling the West Hills cliques and breathing life into the classes."

After a couple drinks, it started to drizzle. "What's a little mist going to do?" I asked Tiffany when she expressed more than a passing interest in splitting. "It's not like it's nuclear rain. It's just water the atmosphere whipped up fresh for us." As the rain poured down harder, I opened my mouth and let the drops land on my tongue. The rain made my tongue tingle and tasted good mixed with the tequila.

Soon we were soaked. And Tiffany was pissed. I wouldn't let her have the car keys, so she had no choice but to sit crouched under a tree that was providing little in the way of shelter. "I gotta get home," she whined. "I have lots of homework." But, I didn't want to leave.

"Come on," I pleaded. "Just one more drink." But Tiffany was set on bailing. The fact that she was the reasonable one in this scenario was an upset. Tiffany was one of the biggest partiers in our school, infamous for being the last one to leave a gathering, for hooking up with guys she barely knew, and for draining every cocktail glass she touched. Her grades weren't good, she regularly cut class, and she didn't play any sports, preferring to hang out at the coffee shop and gab after school or scour the Internet for bargains on clothes and accessories.

I drove Tiffany home, refusing to use the windshield wipers because I liked the warped way the road looked through the raindrops. I thought about the one-eighty my life had taken in the past couple weeks. It had all happened so fast—from zero to sixty. I'd gone from miserable to content to euphoric—and nothing would ever darken my spirits again. I had slain my evil Beast and burned him in a fiery pyre. He was dead and buried and would never darken my doorstep again.

After I'd dropped off Tiffany and was about to merge onto the freeway and head home, I got an excellent idea for how to spend the rest of my afternoon. I did a U-turn and headed east, in the opposite direction.

I reached Brookside Assisted Living Center in ten short minutes. I turned into the parking lot and slid into a space and cut the engine. I walked up to the front door of the center and hesitated. I didn't have a plan for what I was going to do or say. I just wanted inside. I wanted to poke around and see if there was any evidence of what my mother was doing there. I decided to wing it. I pushed open the front door, which was unlocked this time.

I stepped into the building and was met by a receptionist at the front desk. She looked up at me quizzically. "Good afternoon. Who are you here to see?" she asked.

"Oh, I... I'm...," I started. "Uh..." I was tripping over my tongue while the receptionist glared at me, not smiling. I now wished I'd figured out a lie to tell about why I was there before I'd just barged in the place. "I was just walking by and I thought that... I would have a look inside because... because..."

"Because?" she asked, looking suspicious.

Then it hit me. "Because I wanted to know what your center was like," I said, speaking more confidently now that I had a plan. "I have a grandmother who could use some assistance... with living."

"Is she ill?" the woman asked.

"Yes... She has... uhm... heart problems," I said.

"Well, we specialize in caring for people who are ill," she said. "That's why our prices are higher. I let people know that from the start, because you don't need to pay for this level of care unless you have health problems." She pulled out a stack of literature from a shelf behind her desk and handed it to me. "This should have all the information you need, including pricing."

"Could I take a look around and get a feel for the place?" I asked.

"You'll have to schedule a visit with our director," she said. "Her name and number are on one of the sheets I gave you. You should bring your grandmother when you come. She needs to be somewhere she feels comfortable." Terrific. Where was I going to find a pretend grandmother?

Just then I heard the front door open. The receptionist looked up and smiled. "Hello, Ruby. I was worried you weren't coming," she said as a middle-aged woman walked in, towing a small terrier on a leash behind her. "Three of our patients already asked when you were going to get here."

"Sorry. I got held up in traffic," the woman said as she took off down the hallway. "I'll make it up to them. Today will be an extra-long visit."

I watched the woman disappear around the corner and then turned back to the receptionist. "She's a pet therapy volunteer," the receptionist told me. "She brings her dogs for visits. The patients love it."

Dogs. Now I knew just what to do. "I have dogs and they're all really well-behaved and sweet," I said. "I'd love to bring them here for visits."

The receptionist grabbed a sheet of paper from inside her desk and handed it to me along with a pen. "We're always looking for pet therapy volunteers," she said. "Our patients can't get enough of them. Fill out this form and I'll give it to our director. She'll be doing a background check. If she okays you, we'll call you and schedule a visit. It may take a while before you hear from her. She's on vacation right now and she'll be swamped when she returns."

I was shaking I was so excited. I was going to be able to visit the entire facility and meet everyone in it. I was en route to solving the mystery of why my mother was coming to this place. I filled out the form, handed it back to the receptionist, let her know how enthusiastic I was about volunteering and then took off.

That night, my mother and I had dinner together, the third dinner we'd had together in two weeks. I found myself staring at her while she ate, wondering just what was going on in that lying brain of hers. Usually she bored me, our conversations were always so surfacy, but in her deceit she had become fascinating to me.

"I know nothing is wrong with you and that you're just having fun, but maybe you can tame down at school," my mother said. "The administration tells me that they're having difficulty getting you to follow the rules and you're behaving erratically. They're confused because you're usually a good student." Apparently, my teachers had complained about me and some of my "friends" had chimed in. Principal Hodge told my mom that my "comportment was so out of bounds" that he was threatening suspension if I didn't start minding my manners.

"I'm trying to reform the place," I explained. "It's boring and a lot of the students are treated unfairly."

"School is supposed to be boring so that you want to do your work and graduate on time. And it isn't fair because life isn't fair," she said. "I explained to Principal Hodge that you've had some health problems—some problems with your glands that have thrown you out of whack. But, he's still threatening suspension if you don't shape up."

Gland problems? It sounded so medieval—like my humors were out of balance or I had the vapors—something to be cured by leeches or smelling salts.

"I didn't think you'd want him knowing you were having emotional problems."

"You mean *you* didn't want him knowing." The knowledge that my mother was ashamed of my mental disorder should have hurt, but it had the opposite effect. That she had taken the time to think about me enough to come up with her preposterous lies about my "glands" meant that she had actually given me some thought. That was a new one.

"Also, I got an alert from the credit card company this afternoon about your bill at the department store. It was astronomical. I don't mind you buying yourself a few presents, but your tab was exorbitant. I want to see what you bought because a lot of it's going back. Any more bills like that and I'm taking the credit card away."

"Since you were the one who first brought up the money topic, how much will you give me if I toss the salad up a couple feet and it all lands back in the bowl?"

"Nothing. It's not a good idea."

"Here it goes," I said as I picked up the salad bowl and launched the lettuce up a foot. Impressively, almost every leafy green made it back into the bowl.

"That's enough, Janelle," my mom said.

I picked up my plastic glass, which was filled with water. "How much if this makes it into the sink?"

"Stop it, Janelle."

I wound up my arm and pitched the glass, which splashed water all over the floor before it landed in the center of the sink.

"Yes!" I shouted triumphantly, pumping my fist in the air.

Speeder and Monica rushed into the kitchen and began barking at me. "Look," my mom said. "You're upsetting the dogs." She rose from the table to pet the dogs. "Shh . . . It's alright. Janelle is just a bit worked up." Then she turned back to me. "Since you've already ruined dinner, I'm going to say something you probably don't want to hear. I don't think the medicine you're taking is agreeing with you. I knew you didn't need MDs or prescription drugs, but Maya made a big deal out of your slump and now look what's happened."

"My slump? Is that what you call clinical depression?" I asked.

"I don't know what those psychiatric terms mean," she continued. "You're staying up until very late and leaving the house at the crack of dawn, and I've never seen you so . . . defiant and sped up. Dr. Rice's assistant told me you missed your appointment and haven't returned his calls to reschedule. You skipped your appointment with Dr. Goode, too."

"I don't need those two anymore," I answered. "I'm all better."

"I agree that you probably don't and didn't need them, but since you've already started with Dr. Rice and the medicine, you need to visit him and get him to take you off that crap so that you can return to being yourself."

"You mean go back to being depressed?" I asked. "No way. Anyhow, the directions say you're not supposed to quit the medicine when you feel better. You have to keep taking it."

"Do me a favor and call the doctor."

"Fine," I said. I stared at my mother as she tucked back into her lasagna. My curiosity was so great that I couldn't contain it any longer. "Have you ever heard of a place called Brookside Assisted Living Center?"

My mom took a nervous sip of water and coughed. "It's not ringing a bell," she answered, not making eye contact.

"I thought I saw you there," I said. "Are you sure?"

"Positive," she said. "And why are you spying on me?"

"I'm not spying on you," I said. "I just thought I saw you drive in there."

"Well, it wasn't me," she said, fibbing with great ease. "There are a lot of people with black minivans. If I had been there I would tell you. I'm an open book. You know that."

Open book? If she was an open book then there was literally nothing to her — because I knew nothing about her other than what I saw her doing around the house. She had shared nada of her interior life with me. And now she was hiding secrets from me. I felt the divide between us growing even greater. Where there should have been a bridge or a path, there was a barbed wire fence shooting up taller and with more spiky points.

"Go call that doctor, please," my mother said. I stomped out of the kitchen and up to my room.

My mother and I had eaten late, so it was already nine-thirty when I finally uncovered Minute Rice's card and picked up the phone. His office was, of course, closed, but there was an emergency cell number on the voice mail. I dialed it, and Minute Rice answered. He sounded testy. "What's the emergency?" he snapped.

"It's not an emergency, but my mom wanted me to call you, since I haven't been in to see you yet," I said.

"If it isn't an emergency you should have left a message on the machine or e-mailed me," he said. "It's late. I'm playing bridge."

"Sorry," I said.

"Since you have me on the phone already, why don't you tell me what's going on. How are you doing with the medication?" he asked.

"Incredible. I've never been better. I'm so grateful to you. You're my most favorite person ever. And you'll be glad to know the medicine didn't take long to work." I was talking at runaway-train speed.

"I'm not glad that the medicine worked so fast. It's not supposed to," he said. "It could be evidence of a switch."

"A switch?"

"A switch, meaning an extreme and rapid change in mood—either up or down," he said. "A bipolar switch is occasionally triggered by an antidepressant. Are you sleeping?"

"I don't need sleep," I said. "The medication charges my batteries for me."

"Are you keyed up? Impulsive? Aggressive?"

"I have hundreds of ideas and I'm super excited about everything I'm doing."

"It sounds like hypomania," he said.

"Hypomania? No. I think I'm just hypohappy," I said. "But, let me check. Can you hold on a minute?"

"No, I can't. I . . . ." he objected as I set down the phone.

I picked up my laptop and quickly googled hypomania. I grabbed the phone. "'Hypomania DSM 296.40,'" I read into the phone. "'Mental state characterized by persistent and pervasive elevated mood . . .' "

"I know the definition of hypomania, Janelle," Minute Rice cut in. "Will you please . . ."

I continued reading: "'Symptoms include: mild euphoria, racing thoughts . . . lots of ideas . . . self-confidence, irritability, hypersexuality . . . increased activity and energy . . . decreased need for sleep...'"

"Enough, Janelle," Minute Rice said. His voice was getting louder.

"'May impair a person's judgment . . . reckless behavior . . .'" I finished reading and shut the laptop. "Nope. Not me. I'm more like . . . SUPER BITCHIN' DSM CODE 1000."

Minute Rice sighed. "Stop the medicine and make an appointment for Monday morning. You sound most definitely hypomanic. Try to relax and get some rest. Use the sedative and sleeping pills to slow down your mind. Good night."

I hung up the phone having zero plans to follow his suggestions. I wasn't going to visit him for a talking to or stop taking my happy pills. In fact, I was devising a plan to siphon my happy pills into the reservoirs and turn everybody's frown upside down. Why did Minute Rice want to pull me down from this glorious, creative place I was presently living in? Slowly it dawned on me. There was a conspiracy and Minute Rice was part of it, along with my mom, Nell, and the school administration. It was a conspiracy of people who wanted to dull my mind and squelch my ideas.

Great minds and geniuses are often ostracized and hated—even executed—for the extraordinary change they symbolize. Change frightens regular people. I was a chosen one, a genius, a revolutionary—like Martin Luther King, Jr., Jesus, Abraham Lincoln, Joan of Arc. All these years I'd been bumbling around feeling different and now I knew why. I was different. I was operating on a higher level. I was one of the anointed, and I had been placed here by divine powers. It was all making sense. I was here to do great things. I would start with reforming my school and create a domino effect that would spread reform to schools all over the county. Then the country itself.

I headed to the den downstairs, which had once been my father's office, for guidance. My mother wasn't much of a reader, but my dad had been a voracious one, and she had left all his books in place and untouched.

Actually, she had left almost everything of his in the den untouched. It was creepy—like she was waiting for him to return. The photos of her and my dad with their arms around each other, staring at one another with goo-goo eyes, weren't so surprising, since I'd heard how in love they were. What amazed me were the photos of Maya and me with my mom. There were pictures of her holding us, kissing us, reading to us. It was so hard to imagine her kissing or holding anything that wasn't covered in fur—unless, maybe, she had a pet fish. Was it possible that she had really cared about Maya and me at one time? Or maybe she was just one of those people who enjoyed babies or was good at posing for the camera.

I moved slowly through the room, looking for books about leaders and revolutionaries. Thomas Jefferson seemed like a good place to start. He'd done a masterful job of turning this land into a country. I leafed through his biography and found that he had some words for me: "Every generation needs a new revolution." Agreed, Mr. Jefferson, and I'm on it.

I flipped through a book about African leaders. It turned out that Nelson Mandela, the anti-apartheid activist and former president of South Africa, and I had similar visions: "I have cherished the idea of a democratic free society in which all persons live together in harmony and with equal opportunity." Substitute "high school" for "society" and he and I were on exactly the same page.

I browsed the bookcase for more wisdom and found a volume on the brilliant artist and inventor Leonardo da Vinci—maybe not a political revolutionary but certainly the most diversely talented person to have ever lived. The book detailed many of da Vinci's innovative scientific theories. But, it wasn't so much Mr. da Vinci's genius concepts that inspired me. It was what da Vinci did with the concepts that intrigued me. To keep others from ripping off and tampering with his groundbreaking discoveries, he recorded them backwards, in mirror writing. "Thank you for the tip, Leo," I said as I shut the book. "I will do the same if I feel like recording any of my ideas."

I moved around the den, glancing at more books until I came upon my mom's filing cabinet. Her locked filing cabinet. The filing cabinet had always been there, but it had never been of any interest to me. However, now that I had a detective case on my hands, anything my mom had locked up was of interest to me.

I searched around the room for the key to the cabinet and found it in a desk drawer. The filing cabinet wasn't very big, so it wouldn't take long to go through the contents. I opened it and started rifling through papers. Everything inside was really boring: credit card and bank statements, passports and birth certificates, house and car insurance bills, information about the animals' vaccinations… I scoured all the paperwork, but I wasn't finding anything of interest until I came across a folder full of check stubs. I flipped through a month of check stubs and bingo. There was a stub for a check to Brookside Assisted Living for six thousand dollars. I went through a whole year of check stubs and each month there was a stub for a check to Brookside for the same amount. Six thousand dollars a month was a lot of money. Why on earth was my mother giving Brookside so much money? I couldn't wait till they phoned me and okayed my pet therapy visit. A desire to figure this all out was burning a hole inside me.

I locked up the cabinet and put the key back in the desk drawer and started out of the den. I was almost to the door when I noticed a large, black spider crawling across a bright green book. My mother, who was practically a Jainist, had taught us to return all insects to the great outdoors. I grabbed a tissue, stood on my tiptoes, and attempted to nab the spider. But my hand slipped, the spider skittered away and the green book fell to the floor. I picked up the book and gasped as I looked at the title. It was a collection of Dylan Thomas poems. Dylan Thomas! The poet who wrote the stanza Ben had copied onto his binder. This couldn't be a coincidence.

The book was dusty, and the spine cracked as I opened it. I read the inscription on the first page: "To Jane Rose, my lovely little flower, on your third birthday. Ten or twenty years from now you'll read this book and, hopefully, find the poems as transcendent as I do. Love, Dad." The book burned in my fingers as I burst into tears. "I'm here, Dad," I whispered. "I'm sorry it's taken me this long to find this book. I'm sure I'll love it just like you did."

I checked out the stanza of the Dylan Thomas poem that Ben had written on his folder: *"The force that through the green fuse drives the flower Drives my green age."* The force. The life force. The power surge that I could feel electrifying every atom inside my body. Of course.

I read the poem over and over, enjoying it. Enjoying a poem wasn't normal for me. Stella was correct when she told Ben that I disliked poetry. My problem with poetry was that I'd read a poem and love how it sounded and love what it meant to me—my interpretation. Sometimes I'd even feel a real connection with a poem. Then, sure enough, a teacher or a textbook would explain what the poem really meant, which was something I didn't relate to and/or wasn't interested in. The poetry police had let me down one too many times. But, maybe the problem was the poetry police and not the poetry. Maybe poetry was just another casualty of a high school education.

I shut the Dylan Thomas book and set it on the desk. As I left the den, an image floated through my mind. The image was of Ben and the fallen expression that crossed his face after I'd turned him down for a date. I'd disappointed him and stomped out something joyful inside of him. Stomped out something joyful inside of me.

Twenty minutes later, I was driving in my car with two dogs in the backseat and a jar of peanut butter resting on the passenger seat. I reached Ben's house, which was easily six miles from my house, in minutes and parked the car. I silently thanked Tiffany for the gift of Ben's address, which I hadn't properly appreciated on my birthday, and stepped out of the car. It was very late and all the windows in his house were dark. The house looked smaller than I remembered it being, but I had been so horrified when I found out where I was then that I hadn't studied it closely. I wasn't horrified to be in front of Ben's house now. I was fired up. Thrilled.

A tall, sturdy oak tree stretched the height of the house; one of its branches leaned up against the window that Tiffany had specified was Ben's bedroom window. I kicked off my shoes, grabbed the peanut butter, and scurried to the tree. It was the perfect climbing tree, with plenty of long, thick branches layered on top of one another.

I tucked the peanut butter under my sweater, climbed onto the trunk of the tree, and pulled myself up, swinging branch by branch, until I was just inches from Ben's bedroom window. My palms got clammy just thinking about how close I was to Ben – mere feet away from him snuggled up in blankets, asleep. I debated over what message to leave. I settled upon the most honest, basic truth I could think of. On the window, in peanut butter, I wrote, "I like you, but I'm goofed up." Backwards, in da Vinci's mirror style. Then I dropped the peanut butter onto the lawn, climbed down the tree, jumped into my car, and sped home.

# FOUR

SATURDAY MORNING, I woke up before the sun did, my new norm. Crew practice wasn't until noon, so I decided to give myself a good scrubbing. I'd read about all the toxins and bacteria in the air and on surfaces; I was starting to get paranoid that an illness or infection was out there waiting for me, and I couldn't afford it—not when I had so many important things going on.

I showered, using a loofah to exfoliate every inch of my body. After toweling off, I examined my left foot, which had been itching all week. I noticed that there was a small crack in the skin between the big toe and the second toe. Without hesitation, I phoned Maya, who wasn't pleased to be awakened at five a.m. on a weekend, and told her about my toe. At first, she thought I'd cut myself, but when I explained that I hadn't so much as scratched my foot she concluded that I had athlete's foot, a fungus one usually catches in locker room showers. She instructed me to buy medicated foot powder and hung up.

Because I shared the locker room at the boathouse almost daily with the girls on my crew team after rowing practice, I was positive that one of them was spreading the fungus, or maybe several of them were. I started to fret. What if bacteria snuck into the crack in my toe and swam up my bloodstream, spreading an infection that could make me very ill—deathly ill—and keep me from accomplishing great things?

Socks. It started with socks. Socks were where the fungus was hiding.

At ten a.m. I was standing in front of a sporting goods store waiting for it to open. I had already swung by the pharmacy and purchased a few containers of athlete's foot powder. Finally, the store manager, wearing a nametag that read "Irma," arrived and opened the door. I explained to her that I needed women's white athletic socks. And I didn't just need a few pairs. I was prepared to buy every pair of women's white athletic socks she had for sale. I asked her for a shopping bag and headed to the sock racks, dropping pairs of white socks (of all sizes) into the sack.

After emptying the racks, I asked Irma if there were more socks in stock. She eyed me skeptically and asked what I was going to do with all the socks. Instead of answering, I handed over my American Express. She asked for my i.d., saw that it matched the name on the card, and disappeared through a door at the back of the store.

Soon, Irma wheeled out a dolly that contained three large, brown boxes. "That's it," she said. "There are no more women's white athletic socks in the store." After she tallied up a price for the socks, I signed the bill—without looking at the total.

Irma helped me pack the socks into the back seat and trunk of my car. When we were finished, I reached out to shake her hand. "Thank you for your help."

She reached out her hand and gave mine a lifeless jiggle. "I have to get back inside," she said. I climbed into my car and sped to the marina for crew practice, confident that I had what it took to nip this potentially dangerous Athlete's Foot in the bud.

As my teammates arrived at the beach for warm ups, I dragged the boxes of athletic socks from my car and onto the sand. I announced my plan: "A top-notch rower needs strong, healthy feet to push on the foot-stop. Presently, our feet are compromised by athlete's foot. To stop the spread of the fungus that threatens to destroy our feet and our health in general, we are all going to shake foot powder into these clean white socks and change into them before stepping into the shell." The girls claimed to already be wearing clean socks and not one admitted to having athlete's foot, but I knew better and insisted they wear the socks. Slowly, maybe just to shut me up, they all changed socks. But my plan had a part two: "Sweat makes the fungus multiply, so we're going to change socks every ten minutes so our feet stay cool and dry."

Claire was the first to speak up. "We put the socks on and that's all we're doing. Now we're starting practice."

Claire led the other eight team members into the boat as I gathered socks from the boxes. "Don't come crying to me when your feet are gangrenous," I sneered as I hopped into the stroke seat with an armful of socks.

"Get out of my seat," Devon said.

"I'm going to play stroke today," I said.

"You're not," Devon argued.

"Move," Claire shouted.

"I will not," I insisted. "My butt is stuck to the seat and I'm not moving. I deserve to spend one measly practice in the seat." This time I really meant it. I wasn't budging. I was going to get a chance to show my stuff for once.

"She's right," Audrey said. "Just for today, let's try it."

"She's not taking your seat, Devon," Ella, another teammate, said. "It's just one practice. What could it hurt?"

Devon grumbled as she lowered herself into seat seven.

"This is not permanent, Jane," Claire said as we pushed away from the dock. "I'm only letting you stay put because I don't feel like wasting our time arguing. Let's get into the harbor. We're doing an easy workout today – coach's orders."

I was quiet as we plowed through the water, way too slowly. But, after a spell, I just couldn't take the sloth anymore. I drove my blade through the water hard and got the boat moving faster. "On one we go all out!" I shouted. "Three, two, one . . . go!"

"Wait for my command!" Claire shouted.

"Go, go, go," I shouted, rowing faster and harder. "Our oars are our wings. Fly!"

"Jane! Stop!" Claire yelled. "We're not sprinting today!"

"Don't stop! Faster!" I shouted. "Look alive!"

After about twenty strokes I shouted, "Stop! Time for sock change." I dug my oar in, slowing the boat, and quickly removed my shoes, wriggled out of my socks and tossed them into the water and then slid on a fresh pair of socks.

"You can't just throw socks into the water," Claire said. "That's littering. And none of us are changing socks. Now cut it out with all this goofiness and switch seats with Devon."

I picked up my oar and drove it through the water. "Back to work, girls! Do you want to paddle uselessly around the marina, or do you want to win South Coast and get recruited to row for Oxford or Cambridge at the Henley? We're here to win races! To show everybody how awesome we are!"

The girls whined, struggling to keep up with me as I set the pace faster and faster, not heeding Claire's instructions to "Knock it off or you're going back to the dock and getting out of the boat."

Suddenly, I noticed one of the boys' boats about a hundred yards beyond us. I squinted, trying to make out who was in the boat, and saw what had to be the back of Ben's head. I'd studied every part of him so closely that I could recognize his hairline and his shoulders. "Let's catch the boys' boat!" I cried, picking the pace up even faster. "Let's show them who's faster!" (I left out, "I want to impress Ben!")

"My lungs are burning," Audrey panted.

"Burn baby burn!" I was pushing my legs so hard against the footplate and driving my blade through the water so furiously that I was starting to feel out of control. The whole boat was feeling out of control.

Suddenly, I pushed my legs so hard that my butt came up off the seat; the seat slid out from under me and off the rails and my butt landed on the rails with a powerful thud.

"Jane's seat jumped the slide!" Claire shouted.

I swung my oar out, trying to get up off the slide. I wasn't intending to put the oar in the water, but I leaned hard and fell sideways and the oar dug into the water and got stuck and I couldn't get it out of the water fast enough and . . .

"Slow! She's going over the . . !" Claire shouted

And just like that, I toppled over the edge of the boat and into the water. Then my teammate, Pilar, was ejected, followed by Devon. We thrashed around the cold water and one by one pulled ourselves back into the boat.

"That's it," Claire said. "You're out of the boat. I'm telling Coach Beverly and you're going to be in trouble."

We turned the boat around and headed back to the dock. I felt guilty watching Pilar and Devon shivering. Tossing them into the drink wasn't in my plan for the morning. "What's happened to you?" Pilar asked me. "You've gotten really strange."

"And not only in the boat. She's doing weird things at school, too," Devon said.

"Can't you go back to the way you used to be and act normal?" Ella asked.

"You mean go back to a scaredy cat B person trapped in averageness and sleepwalking through life? No, thank you," I said. "You may be content with mediocre, but I want more."

When the boat reached the shore, Claire ordered me out. "Whatever it is you're trying to be or trying to do is hurting the team. I'm going to recommend to Coach Beverly that you sit out until you behave more sportsmanlike."

I quietly removed myself from the boat, wondering why I was working so hard trying to mold these ungrateful, second-rate athletes into something better—and whether I should even continue. Maybe rowing a single and winning big regattas on my own was the way for me to stand out and get recruited by a college with a top team.

I gathered the unused socks and exited the beach parking lot in a hurry. I had a busy day ahead.

Around two, after showering off the muck from the contaminated marina water, I headed to the grocery store to shop for food to match my mood. I blazed through the aisles, searching for products with merry names and tossing them into my cart: beer nuts, Fruit Loops, Crackerjacks, jellybeans, Twinkies, Cheese Whiz, Rice Crispies, a coconut. Then there were the foods I pulled off the shelves because I liked their colors: lemons, lime green Jell-O, bright pink bubble gum, American Cheese.

The checkout line was long and I was restless. My cell phone was dead, so I couldn't text anybody or read my e-mail. The covers of the various magazines hanging around me were all plastered with photos of stars of reality shows that I'd never watched. I had no choice but to stare at the customer waiting in front of me. He was African American with long, espresso-colored dreadlocks. I'd always liked dreadlocks. I'd even tried once, unsuccessfully, to make dreadlocks of my own hair. I tapped him on the shoulder and he turned around. "I like your dreads," I said, smiling.

"Thanks," he answered. He pivoted around, and I studied the dreadlocks for a couple more minutes. I tapped him on the shoulder again.

"I've never touched dreadlocks before," I said. "May I touch one?"

"Go ahead," he said, and he bent his head down toward me. I ran my fingers down one dreadlock, then another and another.

"Thanks," I said.

"You're welcome," he said, and he turned around. I continued examining his dreadlocks, wishing that I could touch them again. But I didn't want to bother him. I did my best to keep my hands on my shopping cart and off his hair, but his hair was tempting me so badly.

I scanned the shelves across from the magazine rack. In between the gum and batteries were packages of razors and razor blades. I grabbed one of the packages, ripped it open and yanked a razor blade from the plastic. I reached out and sliced through one of the dreadlocks. It took only a second and the dreadlock was cut and in my hand.

The guy looked over his shoulder and saw his dreadlock in my hand. "What the hell are you doing?" he yelled. "What did you do to my hair?"

The cashier, along with everyone in line, was staring at me. I abandoned my cart and sprinted out of the store and into the parking lot. I reached my car but couldn't find the keys in my giant bag. As I nervously shook the purse, hunting for the keys, the dreadlocked dude appeared. He stood close, pushing beyond the boundaries of my personal space and wedging me between him and the car door. I started panicking. He was a lot bigger than me. What if he was mad enough about his hair to hurt me?

"I'm sorry. I'm so sorry," I stammered. "I didn't mean to bother you. I've just always wanted dreadlocks and you have so many that I didn't think you would miss one. I didn't mean to upset you." I placed the dreadlock in his hand, praying this would chill him out. "Here. Maybe somebody can weave it back into your hair."

He stared at me and then broke into subtle laughter, shaking his head in disbelief. "You are one crazy chick," he said. "You know that?"

"If you say so," I answered. He backed away a few inches and I sighed with relief that he wasn't going to beat me up or call the cops.

He dropped the dreadlock back into my hand. "You're right. I do have a lot of dreads," he said. "I apologize for yelling at you and scaring you. You just surprised me. That's all. Consider this dread a gift from me."

"Wow. Thanks. I'll take good care of it," I said, petting the piece of hair.

"What's your name?" he asked.

"Jane," I stammered.

"I'm Jared," he said, shaking my hand. "And the only thing I ask in return is that you let me take you out to lunch." He handed me his business card. "Call or text me and we'll make a plan."

"I will," I said.

"Promise?" he asked.

"Promise," I answered as I fished the keys out from my purse. I dove into the driver's seat, started the engine, and peeled out of the parking lot and headed home. I had dodged a bullet. I needed to be more careful.

Late that afternoon, after falling down the stairs to the basement because our housekeeper, Blanca, hadn't warned me that she had just mopped them, I realized that I hadn't fallen down the stairs randomly. The universe was tripping me, causing a minor accident to let me know that if I didn't protect myself I could have a major accident.

Soon after, I was shopping for safety supplies at the drug store. If I did get hurt, I wanted to be prepared. I bought a tube of topical antibiotic, bandages in every size and shape, latex gloves, an emetic to induce vomiting in case I was poisoned, a splint and a first aid kit. After a fruitless search for a hazmat suit I returned home—prepared for the worst.

At eight I left my house to pick up Tiffany, making a detour on the way to pick up a wild card. We were going to a party at our classmate Jason's house. Jason, like me, had little in the way of adult supervision; his parties were legendary for being a parent's worst nightmare and for keeping kids out way past their curfew.

I reached Tiffany's house and sat on the horn until she walked through the front door. "Do you know how obnoxious that was—honking so loud for so long?" she spat as she climbed into the car. "My mom is fuming."

"If you had left your house faster, I wouldn't have had to honk for so long, would I?" I replied.

Tiffany checked her makeup in the sun visor mirror and then gave me the onceover. "What are you wearing?"

"What does it look like I'm wearing?"

"It looks like you're dressed to lounge around a resort."

I was wearing a straw hat, a bikini, a sarong, and flip-flops. "Jason has a pool and a hot tub," I answered.

"This isn't a pool party," Tiffany said. "It's a party party. A regular party."

"What's a regular party?" I asked. "Who decides what regular is?"

"You look ridiculous," she said. "And Ben might be there. And Tal. I can't have him thinking I'm friends with a . . . lunatic."

"I hope they're both there," I said. "There's a full moon out—the perfect night for us both to make a move."

"I don't recommend making any kind of move dressed like that," she said. "Unless you first tell Ben that you thought tonight was a costume party."

"No. Ben should know that I'm bold," I said. "I don't join the herd—not where dressing is concerned. Not where anything is concerned."

"Fine, but you're not wearing the sun hat," she said, plucking it from my head. She turned to toss the hat into the backseat and gasped. "Dickens?"

"Hello, Tiffany. I'm so glad you could join us this splendid evening," said Dickens, who was sitting in the backseat, tipping his top hat to her.

"Join *you*? Jane and I had plans. Were you even invited to Jason's party?" she asked.

"Don't be rude, Tiffany. Of course he was invited. I invited him," I said.

"It's not your party, so you don't do the inviting," Tiffany growled. "Whatever. It's your social funeral."

When we reached Jason's house, Tiffany insisted she enter the party by herself and that Dickens and I wait ten minutes before going inside. She didn't want to be seen with us, which would have been insulting without the realization that Tiffany was shallow. Cute and sweet, but shallow. I didn't know why I'd never noticed it before.

An eerie hush fell over the living room when Dickens and I finally entered Jason's house. Ariana and Alexis were the first to notice us. They did a double take and then both screwed up their faces in confusion as they looked us up and down.

Tiffany took off for another room, dodging us. We wandered through the house and reached the bar. "What spirits are you offering?" Dickens asked Jason, who was serving the drinks. Jason, speechless, pulled two beers out of a minifridge. "What about a mint julep or a gin gimlet instead?" Dickens asked.

Jason remained silent as he used a bottle opener to pop the caps off the beers. He slid them across the bar to us.

Dickens smiled as he took the beer. "On second thought, the stout will be fine," he said. "Cheers, mate."

Dickens left the bar and headed off to the den to see if there was any "literature to read" while I made my way through the house. "WTF?" I heard from behind me as I stepped into the dining room for snacks. I flipped around and was face-to-face with Stella. She aimed her phone at me and laughed while she shot a couple photos. "Don't stay here too late, Jane, or you'll miss your flight to Club Med." Before Stella could say anything more, Tiffany grabbed my arm and led me through the crowd and outside, where Jason's pool was waiting for me, the water glittering.

"You have to slow down, Jane," Tiffany said. "People are starting to think you're a head case."

I moved to the pool and dipped a toe in the water. It was chilly, invigorating. "If they think I'm a head case then I think they're head cases," I said. "Two can play their game." I shrugged off my sarong and dove into the water.

"It's like you've gone off the deep end," Tiffany said.

I climbed out of the pool and marched around the deck until I was standing over the deep end. "Hey, watch me go off the deep end!" I laughed. Down I dove. I reached the drain and then swam back up to the surface.

"You're going to regret all this, Jane," Tiffany said. "It's gotten out of hand. Don't say I didn't warn you when nobody will talk to you anymore." She threw her hands up, turned on her heels, and headed back into the house. Tiffany really didn't get it. I couldn't have cared less what anyone thought of me – except Ben. If somebody didn't like me or thought I was weird that was their loss.

After some freestyle laps and underwater handstands, I climbed out of the pool and wrapped my sarong around my hips. I was dripping wet when I stepped back into the house and headed to the bar for another beer. After I'd gotten a beer, I searched the crowd for Ben—while getting lots of confused looks. Once I'd checked every room and closet and determined that Ben wasn't around, I found Dickens, alone in the study reading *Jane Eyre*, and told him I was ready to split. I'd had enough of the conformists.

Dickens was happy to depart. "They don't make parties the way they used to," he said. "No waltz. No tea sandwiches. Not even a parlor game. A round of blind man's bluff would have done wonders for the crowd."

"What's going on with you, Jane?" Jason asked as I reached the front door. "As your friend, I need to tell you that you seem really . . . off lately. Kind of mental. Not at all like your normal self. Are you okay?"

"You're just not ready for who I really am," I told him. I guzzled the beer in giant slugs, handed Jason the bottle, and strode out the door with Dickens beside me.

# FIVE

$I$T DIDN'T TAKE LONG till I was on a driving, superclear high. It was meth with a crack chaser, nirvana mixed with the excitement of Christmas morning, the pride of a straight-A report card, and the joy of a new puppy—plus the thrill of crossing the finish line first, the soaring ego trip of performing for one hundred thousand adoring fans, and the adrenaline rush of a roller coaster ride. It was every best feeling I'd ever had all squished together and multiplied by a thousand. It was like falling in love for the first time . . . with everything.

I had the inhibition of a pole dancer and the fearlessness of a NASCAR driver. I'd won the mood lottery. I could feel my synapses firing with the force of a machine gun. My senses were heightened—as sensitive as those of a panther or a lion stalking a gazelle. I could hear a cicada buzzing from the neighbor's yard and the peaches molding in the fruit basket in the kitchen. I could smell the fish in the sea all the way from the hills. I could feel my breath tickling my lungs and taste the nitrogen in the air. I could feel my hair growing.

The universe had unzipped itself and dropped at my feet the answers to all its mysteries. I had broken through the fourth wall—I knew why the earth rotated instead of sliding back and forth. I understood why a story could be told in only three acts and what was lurking at the bottom of a black hole. I remembered where I was when the big bang burst and I could hear the giant explosion reverberating inside my head. I may have been asleep and in the making for three-and-a-half-billion years, but I was awake now. Fully awake.

I arrived at school early Thursday morning to address discriminatory parking practices. I'd found the parking practices at West Hills outrageously unfair for years, but I'd never had the guts to do anything about it. I parked my car in Stella's prime A spot and walked to the center of the parking lot to direct traffic. Behind me were the entrance to the B lot, the entrance to the A lot, and the entrance to the back lot—the C lot. Coincidentally, Nell and Tiffany showed up at the parking lot first.

"What on God's earth are you doing?" Nell asked, stopping in front of me.

"Directing traffic," I answered, waving her in the direction of the B lot. "You two can park in the B lot as usual, so you don't have anything to worry about."

"We have a lot to worry about," Tiffany said. "You. You need help. Get in the car. You could get into a lot of trouble for doing this." Tiffany stepped out of the car, opened the back door and pointed inside.

"I'm warning you, Jane," Tiffany said, once it became clear I wasn't budging. "I'm going to call Maya if you don't cut it out!" Maya? Maya didn't have the control over me that she used to have. I loved Maya, but I was done with her being my keeper. I certainly wasn't going to leave the parking lot because *she* said to.

Just then another car pulled up, and I waved Tiffany and Nell forward. "Get going, please. We don't want to hold up traffic."

"Don't say we didn't try to help you when you have nowhere to go to school," Nell said, shaking her head in frustration as she accelerated and headed into the B lot.

Cars continued driving into the lot. I sent some of the Bs I didn't like (including my crew teammates, who had been so creepy to me) to the C lot, but most of them I let stay in the B lot. Plenty of drivers grumbled and wanted to know "what the hell" I was doing and "who the hell" I thought I was. A few tried to frighten me into moving by driving mere inches from me, but I knew they wouldn't run over me, so I stood my ground.

Fiona, a tenth-grader with a stuttering problem, was the first C to show up. I directed her to the A lot. "I c-c-can't go in there," she said. "I'm n-n-ot an A."

"The Atrium lot doesn't have designated spots like the teachers' lot. It's for everybody," I said. But poor Fiona was so programmed for loser treatment that she refused to park near the Atrium. I finally talked her into parking in the B lot.

Stella was the first A to arrive. "Why are you in my spot?" she asked, pointing to my car. "What are you thinking?"

"I'm thinking I'm tired of having bird poop on my car. There are a lot of birds in the B lot, did you know that?"

After threatening to call the principal, Stella started backing down. "At least move so that I can park in B. My backpack is stuffed with books today. I can't walk all the way from the back parking lot."

"It'll be good exercise for you," I said. She called me a string of choice words before heading into the back parking lot, which was a first for her.

It took a lot of cajoling, but I got Dickens and Zeke to park in the A lot. There was still a long line of cars filing into the parking lot when I left for class. But I figured I should abandon my post, given that Principal Hodge had probably caught wind of what I was up to and was on his way to deliver a punishment.

I wasn't in the mood for war, since I'd spent the morning fighting a battle of my own, so I skipped history and hid in the bathroom until chemistry. On my way to chemistry, I decided that I didn't want to be around toxic chemicals and possibly be poisoned, so I headed to my car and hid out there through midmorning break.

I was bored in my car when it came time for English, so I headed out. Class had already started when I slid into my seat in the front row. "Sorry I'm late," I told the teacher, Miss Jackson. "I got here as soon as I felt like it." I handed her my overdue essay on Ernest Hemingway's *Old Man and the Sea*. My essay, typed sdrawkcab in daVinci's mirror writing, was one page long and focused on how to improve this classic story of a fisherman trying to catch an enormous marlin. My suggestion on how to make the manuscript really pop was to change the hero from the man to the fish—and have the marlin use a rod with a hundred-dollar bill attached to the line as bait to catch the old man. *Old Fish and the Sea* would be the new title. Done. The end.

Miss Jackson handed out a vocabulary pop quiz that I hadn't studied for. I wasn't doing much studying in general. I didn't have the attention span for it. I filled in the answers to the quiz as best as I could, stumbling over the meanings of "pusillanimous" and "temerity." After we'd all handed in our quizzes, I raised my hand. I kept it raised until Miss Jackson finally asked me, "What is it?"

"This vocabulary quiz got me thinking about our English language and how there are all these words out there and they all mean something that we're supposed to remember," I started. "It seems kind of unfair that our ancestors got to decide what everything would be called and now we have to use their words, even if we don't like them. Why should they be allowed to hog up all the fun of naming things? Can't we have a say in what a few things are called? Like eggplant, for instance. It doesn't much resemble an egg. Its more striking feature is its purple color. How about purpola? 'Tulip' could use some reworking, since it doesn't have a lip."

"Jane . . ." Miss Jackson tried to cut in.

Just then the bell rang and everybody started rising from their seats. I gathered up my books and raced for the door, paying no heed to Miss Jackson, who asked me to stay behind so we could "talk." I didn't mean to be rude, but this "talk" she wanted to have was bound to be an indictment of me that I didn't feel like hearing.

I dragged myself kicking and screaming to trigonometry, which I seriously considered cutting for good, since I didn't think studying the ins and outs of triangles was useful unless I was aiming for a career in making tortilla chips or "yield" signs. I took my uncomfortable spot next to Miss Disapproving Nell. She started in again about how I was out of hand and needed to check in with my shrink and could she take me to visit him; I plugged my ears. She was such a broken record that I couldn't even listen anymore.

The teacher, Mr. Okoro, arrived and asked us all to swap our homework with our "next-door-neighbor" so that we could grade each other's papers while he went over the answers. Nell placed her homework on my desk and then held out her palm to me. I reached into my bag, retrieved a piece of gum and placed it in her hand. "What's this?" she asked—loudly, so that the class turned to look at us.

"Don't you like gum?" I asked.

Mr. Okoro marched over to my desk. "Did you do your homework, Jane?" he asked.

"Affirmative," I answered.

"Then where is it?" he asked.

I pointed to my head. "It's in here. And I did a really good job. I got all the answers right, so Nell doesn't need to grade it."

"That's not amusing," Mr. Okoro said. "I won't let you turn this class into a circus. I want you to leave and go to the principal's office – immediately."

I happily popped up from my chair. I was glad to have an excuse to leave a class that was no doubt going to bore me into a coma. I wandered down the hall, heading toward the parking lot, and noticed Mr. Beal, the guidance counselor, rounding the corner. I made a beeline for the girls' bathroom, but I was too late. He had already noticed me. "I've been looking for you," he bellowed. "Why aren't you in class?"

I lied that I had a throbbing headache and that I was sick to my stomach. He prattled on about my behavior in general and about the parking lot "antics" specifically and said he was calling my mother in for a conference with Principal Hodge to determine whether to suspend me or even, possibly, expel me. I couldn't believe how uptight and closed-minded everyone was.

I placed my hand over my mouth, summoning an about-to-vomit face. "I think I'm going to throw up." I raced into the bathroom and hid in a stall until enough time had passed that it was safe to slip back into the hallway and escape to the parking lot and spirit myself away in my car.

I stayed off campus through lunch, but I made sure I returned in time for Spanish class. In time to see Ben. I reached class early and took my seat. I had stared at the boring white board at the front of the classroom daily for months. I had grown weary of it. There was a window at the back of the classroom, which faced a grove of sycamore trees, a far more pleasing sight. I scooted my desk around so that I was facing the window and watched the leaves of the sycamores blowing with the breeze.

As students filed into the classroom, I heard snickering and whispering. I couldn't see any of the students, since I was facing the back of the room, so I had no idea if Ben had arrived yet. Then I heard Señora Flores: "Jane? Janelle Flynn? What are you doing? Please turn your chair around." I didn't move. "This prank of yours isn't amusing," she said.

"It's not a prank," I said. "Yo am just sick of looking at the white board when the trees blowing in the breeze is such a beautiful sight."

She moved toward me and hit her fist against my desk. "Get up and go to the principal's office—now!"

I rose and slowly ambled past the rows of desks. Ben was chuckling softly as I passed his desk. I winked at him. I was glad I'd gotten a laugh out of him – the first one yet.

"And bring your backpack with you," Señora Flores commanded. I grabbed the closest backpack and held it up, examining it. "Wait. This isn't my backpack. I don't have a polka-dotted backpack." I dropped it and picked up Stella's backpack. "This one can't be mine," I said, scrutinizing it. "It's chartreuse. I hate the color chartreuse."

Stella grunted as she pulled her backpack from me.

"Stop it and exit now," Señora Flores said.

Tiffany leapt up from her seat and grabbed my backpack. She took hold of my arm and whispered into my ear as she walked me to the door. "You can't do this, Jane. You're going to get kicked out of school. Go home. Say you're sick. I'll make an appointment with your doctor."

We reached the door where Señora Flores was waiting. "Olé!" I shouted as she opened the door and shoved me out of the room.

I dashed down the hall, not stopping as I flew by the administration office and into the parking lot. I jumped inside my car, locked the doors, and sped off.

I reached my house and pulled into the driveway, parking my car behind my mother's car. As soon as I turned off the engine, my mother bounded out the front door and onto the porch. She did not look happy.

"The school just phoned me," she hissed. "You have been expelled. Expelled."

"Well, that's their loss, not mine," I said. "I've been trying to breathe life into that stale institution, and clearly the administration is intimidated by me. That's the reason they're kicking me out. They're afraid of change."

"West Hills Prep doesn't need changing. It is one of the best schools in the city. You need changing!" she screeched. "You're grounded!"

"Grounded?" I didn't think my mother knew the meaning of a parenting term like "grounded." She'd never bothered with disciplining me before.

"Why are you making such a big deal out of this?" I asked. "It's not like I was learning anything at West Hills. I already know it all. Now you can take the money you were spending on tuition and put it to good use. Donate it to Furry Friends."

"Dr. Rice called. You lied. You haven't been to see him. I made an appointment for tomorrow morning, and you are not leaving here until then. There is something very wrong with you. You've gone bananas."

"How would you know if something was wrong with me?" I asked. "You barely know me."

"Of course I know you," she said. "I'm your mother."

"In title only," I answered.

"You can't talk to me like that. Go to your room," she said, wagging a finger in my face. It only had taken seventeen years for my mom to start acting like a mom. Ironically, I had no use or desire for a mother at this particular point in time.

I'd just gotten to my room when my phone rang. It was Brookside Assisted Living. "Sorry it's taken so long for me to get back to you regarding your pet therapist application," the director said. "I've okayed you for volunteering. When would you like to start?"

I scheduled a visit for the next day and promised to bring proof that my dog had been vaccinated for rabies and to make sure he didn't have fleas. If my mother was going to keep me "grounded" for more than a night then I'd have to figure a way to sneak out of the house. I was *not* missing this appointment and the chance to start unlocking the riddle of my mother. All I had to do was figure out which dog to bring with me...

I spent the rest of the afternoon and evening in my room, as directed. I texted Tiffany with questions like: Is it a teeny bit possible leprechauns are real? If you constantly travel back and forth between different time zones, losing time and gaining time, do you maybe shave some days off your age?

I sent a text to Nell asking where one could buy a llama and how much one might cost.

I phoned Maya in her dorm and rattled off my theory on how to create peace between the Muslim world and America. We convert to Islam. From what I'd learned in my Middle Eastern studies class last semester, Christianity and the Islamic religion were pretty similar at base, so nobody would have to radically alter their belief system. Ramadan is the same month as Christmas, so we could throw in some presents and nobody would even notice they were celebrating a different holiday. Santa isn't Christian, so he could still stick around—ditto on Christmas trees and lights and parties. For the Jesus part, maybe we could call him Mo-hesus and keep him on the cross but have him dying as a martyr instead of being crucified for our sins. A fortnight after our conversion, gas would be down to five cents a gallon, a fortune would be made selling designer burkahs, and we wouldn't need to remove our shoes at the airport or have our hair gel confiscated. Problem solved.

Maya interrupted me several times and, when I was done, informed me that I sounded manic. Because Maya was studying psychology, she thought she was an expert on the mind. I accused her of not having studied the brain long enough to know what she was talking about and of using psychobabble.

I googled the word "manic" and read up on it. In the view of psychiatry-expert Maya, I had earned myself a new code: "MANIA DSM 296.3: Unstable emotional state characterized by a markedly elevated mood . . . Symptoms include: . . . extreme excitement, elation, hyperactivity, agitation, impulsivity, talkativeness, decreased need for food and sleep, disconnected thoughts, fleeting attention, feelings of invincibility, hyper sexuality, inappropriate social behavior." And, apparently, I might become "violent and destructive" and "engage in reckless and self-destructive behaviors, such as wasteful expenditures of money and sex with strangers." How about this for a code instead: "JANE DSM INFINITY: a mental state caused by being the two-thousand-years-awaited Messiah. Symptoms include: major awesomeness."

Later, I googled quotes from revolutionaries and artists (the ones I'd missed in my earlier visit to the den) and wrote them on my bedroom walls for inspiration. When I was finished, I stepped to the center of the room and turned in a circle to admire all four walls—and tripped over my Spanish book. What was my Spanish book doing in the center of the room and why had I tripped over it? There were no coincidences. What was the book trying to tell me? I glanced up at a van Gogh quote: "What would life be if we had the courage to do anything?" I glanced back at the Spanish book and back up at the quote and back at the Spanish book again.

# SIX

*I* ARRIVED AT BEN'S HOUSE at the stroke of midnight and parked my car at the bottom of his driveway. As I'd suspected would be the case, there wasn't a light burning in any of the windows. So, the question was how to awaken him. I couldn't ring the doorbell, because I'd wake up the whole family. I could climb the tree again and knock on the window, but Ben might freak out if he opened his curtain and saw a face staring back at him. He might think I was a prowler and scream or shove me and knock me from the tree and send me tumbling to the ground where'd I'd break my hip or collarbone. What if he owned a gun? Then, too, there was the chance that he didn't want to see me. How humiliating would it be to have to climb back down the tree, like a squirrel or a raccoon, ashamed and with my tail between my legs? I wished I knew his cell number so that I could text him and ask him to open his door.

I remembered that I had a can of beer nuts in my car. I dug around and found it under the backseat. The can was more than half full, which, hopefully, would be enough to get the job done. I started in. With careful aim, I was able to hit Ben's bedroom window. I continued throwing beer nut after beer nut at his window. I had plowed through almost all the nuts when the curtain finally parted and the window slid open. Ben stuck his head out the open window.

"Who's out there?" he shouted, not loudly, but loud enough for me to hear. "What's going on?"

"Hi," I answered, waving. "It's me. Did I wake you up?"

"Jane?" he yelled back. "Is that you?"

"Yah, sorry it's so late," I said, not sorry at all.

"Hold on a minute," he said. I waited and waited at the front door, wondering what was taking so long. Was he showering? Flossing his teeth? Or maybe he had fallen down the stairs or back to sleep. Just as I was about to begin tossing nuts again, he opened the front door—shirtless and wearing boxers, scratching his bed head. Looking oh so inviting.

"Come in, but be really quiet," he said as I walked through the doorway. "My mom has these intense ears that can practically hear a car starting in the next area code."

We reached his room, and I saw why it had taken him so long to answer the door. The bed was made and the room was neat as a piecrust. There was a dim light shining, and I could smell minty toothpaste on Ben's breath. He held my hand and led me to the edge of his bed, where we sat down. My heart was fluttering faster than a hummingbird's. This was the first time we'd touched one another. "I didn't expect to wake up to this," he said, smiling slyly. "So that note the other night was from you, wasn't it?"

"Afraid so."

"I was hoping it was you."

"Really?" I asked.

"I asked you out last month, if you don't remember." He was examining the carpet, looking uneasy.

"I wanted to go out with you, but . . . Last month was . . . It was just so . . ."

"Don't sweat it. You're here now. By the way, that move in Spanish today was awesome."

"I'm glad you liked it. Not everybody is down with how I've been acting lately. There are plenty of people who are calling me strange—and worse. I was kinda nervous that you might be in that camp."

"Don't worry about strange," he said reassuringly. "I'm down with strange. Strange is cool with me. It's boring how everybody is the same... Was that you who got ejected at crew practice the other day?"

"Yah, but it wasn't my fault," I answered. "It happened because the girls were rowing so slowly—I'm convinced that they're afraid of success—and I was rowing so fast that I couldn't stay in sync with them and then one thing led to another . . . and I jumped the slide and the rest is history. Uhm . . . So, are you going out with anyone?"

"Nah," he said. "You?"

"No. Definitely not," I said. "High school guys are a drag. Not one I've ever gone out with has been interested in knowing the real me. And, before I came to my senses, I worried the real me would probably turn them off anyway, so I always ended things before they went anywhere serious." I felt so comfortable telling him the truth, holding nothing back. I was finally letting somebody see inside my head and heart.

"I'm not going to be turned off by the real you," he said.

"And then there's the fooling around thing."

"You don't like it?" he asked. He wrapped his arm around me and began rubbing my shoulder.

"You've never made out with a teenage boy," I said. My shoulder was tingling as he massaged it. "They grab and squeeze. You practically need an ice pack afterwards. And I have this theory that if someone can't kiss, then everything after that is gonna suck, so why bother?"

"I'll try not to suck," he whispered, his hickory-smoked voice sounding even sexier in the dark. Then he kissed me. My forehead, my eyelids, each cheek, my neck, my chin. He reached my lips, kissing them tentatively at first and then more insistently. This was a real kiss, way better than I'd even imagined it would be—charged and seductive. His lips were creamy and pillowy and he tasted like X-rated movies and See's candy—ambrosia.

We spent a lot of time breathing hard as we shed our clothes and explored each other's bodies. It was a lush and blissful alchemy of lust and liking. Then Ben said softly in my ear, "I have some condoms. Do you want to go for it?"

"Uh, sort of," I answered. Was I really going to try this again? "I've only slept with one person once and it was . . . bad. . . . I'm nervous."

"If it makes you feel any better, I am too." He opened his nightstand and pulled out a small square package.

"No offense, because I think it's cute, but you're so shy that I wouldn't have pegged you as a guy with a box of condoms at his bedside."

"My old girlfriend, Gabriella, and I were together for a year and a half," he said as ripped open the condom. "And I'm not usually so . . . frozen and . . . stupid around a girl as I am with you."

Seconds after Ben lay on top of me, my focus shifted. My brain began buzzing with chatter. I tried to concentrate on how sublime it had felt to be with him just minutes ago, but I couldn't. I was leaving my body and moving into my head.

I examined the framed photos hanging on the wall next to Ben's bed. There was a photograph of a homeless person huddled under a tarp. Adjacent to it was a photo of an apple tree. Apple. Homeless person. Apple. Homeless person. Why were the photos hanging there? What were they telling me?

My mind had taken over, and I could feel nothing except blood pounding against my forehead and boiling in my veins, so hot it was making me itch. I had left the stage. I was gone from Ben. But he was so lost in how good he was feeling that he didn't notice he was acting out a scene all by himself.

The photos were coming into sharper focus. Homeless person. Apple. Homeless person. Apple. Homeless people. Apples. Homeless people. Apples. The photos were there to guide me. To tell me that there were starving homeless people who needed food. I had to help them. I needed to get apples to homeless people. They were hungry.

I pushed Ben off of me and leapt from the bed. "I have to go," I said as I struggled into my clothes. "Homeless people need apples."

"I'm sorry," Ben said, jumping up from the bed and trying to hug me. "I got carried away. We can just talk. We don't have to do anything you're not ready for."

I shoved him hard and he reeled, his face registering horror and disbelief. He let out a whimper.

"I told you, the homeless people need apples." I bolted out of the bedroom and down the stairs, slammed the front door behind me, and raced for the car.

As I backed down the driveway, a light flicked on in an upstairs bedroom window, where I saw Ben's mother pull back the curtain and peer down at my car.

The surface streets were nearly empty, so it didn't take me long to reach downtown. Around Third and Alameda Streets, I came smack up against Tent City. The homeless were everywhere—with shopping carts and cardboard boxes, wearing blankets and tattered clothes. I had found the transients. Now I needed the apples. I searched for a market and finally found one. The lights were on, but the front door was locked. I pounded at the window until a tiny Asian woman appeared. She opened the door. "We're closed," she said.

"I'll only take a minute. I need apples. All the apples you have."

"We're closed. I'm cleaning the store."

"I'll pay big money for your apples. You can charge me five times what you normally charge. Ten times. I promise I'll be out of here fast," I assured her. "Even faster if you bring me some boxes."

She let me inside the store and checked her watch and then slid me a couple crates. "You have three minutes."

I moved as quickly as I could, tossing apple after apple into the crates. "Do you have any more?" I asked after I'd torn through the pile. The storekeeper pointed underneath the table, where two more boxes of apples rested.

I stacked the apples outside the front door and pulled out my mom's Visa. She had cancelled my American Express for "irresponsible and extravagant spending," but she hadn't been swift enough to hide her own credit cards. "How about $100? Does that sound fair?"

The storekeeper shuffled to the cash register. She ran my credit card, handed it back to me, asked me to sign the bill, and then moved to the front door.

"Out," she demanded. I left and she locked the door and cut the lights.

One by one, I hoisted the crates into the trunk, the back seat and the front seat of my car. Soon, my car was full of apples. It smelled like a Fourth of July bake-off.

After several wrong turns, I returned to Third and Alameda and parked my car at the curb, directly in front of dozens of people sleeping in make-shift beds, wandering in circles and inspecting garbage cans.

"Apples for everyone!" I announced as I swung open the doors of my car and trunk and began unloading the crates. I walked up the street with a handful of apples and handed them out. Nobody looked too cheered up or appreciative, but they took the apples nonetheless. I returned to my car, and a group of homeless persons gathered around the trunk as I continued handing out apples. I'd expected a "wow" reaction, but mostly everyone was quiet save a few "thank yous" and some muttering about topics like where the devil was hiding and their plans for world domination.

I had depleted about half of my apple supply when a patrol car pulled over and a Goliath-sized officer stepped out and walked slowly toward me. He had a porcine face and was chewing on a toothpick. "What are you doing?" he asked, shining a flashlight into my eyes.

"I'm giving apples to poor people," I said. I had a hunch that he was going to cease and desist my business, so I quickly slid another crate out from my car.

"Do you realize that you're parked illegally?" he asked. He pointed the flashlight into my car and then into my trunk.

"I'm sorry. I'll move as soon as I've finished handing out the fruit," I said, chasing down apples that were rolling away.

"No," he said firmly. "You'll move the car now unless you want a ticket." This supposed officer of the peace looked about as interested in harmony as a velociraptor.

"Just give me another minute to finish with the apples. I'm only trying to help out and…"

"Get in that car and drive away now or I will have your vehicle towed and impounded." He was chewing harder on the toothpick—as if to say he could crush my legs just as easily as he was pulverizing the toothpick. I was no match for him. He was the first person who had scared me in weeks. I quickly shut the trunk and jumped into the driver's seat and took off.

I returned home and decided I should get some rest, although I wasn't tired. I thought about all the pressing issues I'd begun tackling at school, but there was still so much more to be done—and so much wider to go with it all. How was I going to continue with my mission and carry it out countrywide if I'd been expelled, like my mother said I had been? I needed to remain a student at West Hills, at least for now. I read and reread a quote of Lincoln's on my bedroom wall as I dozed off: "Some-day I will be president."

I woke at six and sprang out of bed, not having intended to sleep in so late. It was imperative that I leave the house before my mother woke up. What I had to do wouldn't take long. Afterwards, I would return home and face the allied enemy forces of Minute Rice and Mommy Dearest.

I chose my outfit carefully and took time with my hair and makeup. It was important that I look the part. I put on thigh-high brown suede boots, orange polka dot leggings, a brown mini skirt, an orange leather jacket, and plenty of bling. My hair was piled on top of my head in a coif that resem-bled an ice cream sundae—with a tiara in the maraschino cherry's spot.

I shut my eyes and tried to center myself and envision success. This was a historic morning. I needed to display confidence and the ability to think outside the box—a female George Washington with Einstein's smarts, Cleopatra's guts, Elvis's flair, and Mona Lisa's smile. Once I was satisfied with how I looked, I scrambled downstairs and into my car.

I arrived at school at eight twenty-four, just six minutes before the election was slated to begin. Even though I'd been kicked out, the student council and kids who were gathered to hear speeches from next year's student body president hopefuls didn't know that. And once the administration heard my ingenious plans for the school, they would quickly realize their gross error in expelling me and open their classroom doors to me once again. Being on the student council wasn't something I was avid to do. But the students needed and deserved a good president, and they weren't going to get one if any of the sorry candidates who were running won. Plus, being president would formalize me as a leader and stamp legitimacy on my mission.

Once inside the auditorium, I found Isabella, the current student body president. "Please add my name to the roster," I said to her. "Jane Flynn."

"I know your name," she said. "We've gone to school together for six years. What are you doing here? What are you wearing?"

"Running for president," I said.

Isabella looked down at her paperwork and then up at me. She frowned. "Is this a joke? Because if it is a joke, I don't have time for it. The election is about to begin."

"No joke," I answered.

"But you haven't campaigned," she said. "You haven't hung posters or held any meet-and-greets or sent out e-mails or handed out flyers or buttons. You aren't even on the ballot." If she was trying to scare me off it wasn't working.

"I'm running as a write-in," I said. "Write-ins are allowed, right? So be right and write me in right now. Alright?"

Isabella chewed on her pen. "Write-ins are allowed . . . but, nobody has done it... because... how could you win as a write-in?"

"Where do you think we'd be if 'nobody has done it' had stopped the Wright brothers from flying or Benjamin Franklin from tying a key to a kite and harnessing electricity?"

"Okay," she said. "You can give a speech, but I think you're wasting your time." Isabella shook her head and copied down my name. "You'll go last since you only just announced your candidacy."

I waited at the back of the auditorium. There were three others running for school president, but I knew I would win. Not just win, but leave the others as roadkill. I was the super Buddha, third coming, bodhisattva on steroids, and the top ten boldest revolutionaries of all time wrapped neatly into one fajita burrito and smothered in happy sauce. I wasn't Jesus. No. Jesus was working for me.

"Our next presidential candidate is uhm . . . Jane Flynn," Isabella stammered into the microphone attached to the podium onstage. "Remember when you are voting that she is not on the ballot. She is a . . . write-in. Will you please come to the podium, Jane?"

I strutted to the stage. "Thank you for showing up here, I'm Jane Rose Flynn and I'm running for student body president," I said, speaking into the microphone. "I only decided to run this morning, but I've spent 1,987 hours in this school, so I know what goes on around here."

"You should know that I'm not running for me. I couldn't care less about being president. I'm running for you. I care about you, and I want all of you to be happy and succeed in life. If elected president, I'm going to shake up not only what and how we're learning or, more accurately, not learning, but also the unbearable social scene. I have a dream that one day there will be no A, B, or C people. We will all just be students. That people who eat food from our cafeteria will be welcomed when they bring their sandwiches and stews into the Atrium. That B people will understand that the middle of the road is where you find dead cats and yellow lines and step out of their comfort zone and take a stand for what they believe in. That persons of the A persuasion will get over themselves."

"To all of you, A, B, C, or independent, I say this: Enough with the labels. Don't let anyone define you and tell you who you are or that you're not good enough—not your peers, your parents, or your teachers. You can be whoever the hell you want to be and do whatever the hell you want to do if you put your mind to it."

"Moving right along to our education, which is what we're all supposedly here for. Here's what we're learning—things that people have already learned and stuff that has already happened. Is that all we want to do? Learn the same things everybody older than you already knows and then take that knowledge and go out in the world and use it to do the same thing everybody else is doing, which, judging by the state of the planet, has gotten us nowhere?"

"The curriculum could be much fresher and more amusing. Maybe we could write our own textbooks and design our own classes. I'd love to see a class called 'How to Do Bold Things' or 'Invent Something Really Cool.' Wouldn't it be great to learn about the future too, instead of just the present and the overanalyzed past? I know the teachers at West Hills work hard and care, but they're lulling us to sleep."

The door to the back of the auditorium swung open and Principal Hodge marched into the room. Time was up for me.

"My vision is to make this place a model of how cool high school can really be. To start a revolution that will cause a ripple effect and spread to schools everywhere. If a bunch of uneducated, poor French peasants surviving on tack could overthrow a four-hundred-year-old monarchy with more money than God, then surely we can overthrow the stale and repressive high school experience. We don't have to go with things because that's just the way they've always been done. Let's change the course of our destiny. It's in our hot little hands. Band together with me and let's rock the roof off this school!!!"

I swaggered off the stage to thunderous applause. I had cinched the election. I marched past Principal Hodge and into the parking lot, where my mother and sister were waiting by my car. They weren't smiling.

# SEVEN

"How could you let it get this bad? She's completely psychotic," Maya said. She and my mother had been arguing since we left the parking lot.

"Psychotic is a strong word, Maya," my mom said. "I wouldn't call Pumpkin psychotic."

"I would. Have you seen what she's posted online or read her e-mails?" Maya asked. "Have you heard from Nell and Tiffany what she's been doing at school? Have you seen her room?"

"I locked the door. Nobody's allowed in there," I said. Of course there was no response. They were talking about me like I wasn't there—like I was preverbal and propped up in a car seat.

"How could you let her out of the house like this? Can you imagine the damage she's done to her reputation? What the kids are saying about her?" Maya asked. "And how do you get into college when you've been expelled from high school?"

"I don't care about college. I . . ."

"Quiet, Jane," my mom ordered. She turned back to Maya. "I told Jane to tone it down after the principal called."

"Tone it down? That's like telling a rabid wolf to take a nap."

"You're getting overly dramatic, Sweet Pea," my mom told Maya.

"Dr. Rice says it sounds like she's had a complete nervous breakdown."

"I'm not nervous . . ."

"Stay out of this, Jane," Maya said. That I was to "stay out" of something that had everything to do with me seemed preposterous, but they hadn't listened to a word I'd said since we'd left school.

"Dr. Rice hasn't seen her yet," my mom said. "I'm sure he'll be able to give her something that will cure her. There are dozens of psychoactive drugs out there."

"You don't just segue out of psychosis overnight. Why wasn't she in his office sooner?"

"She told me she'd visited him," my mom answered.

"And you believed her?" Maya asked. "She told her history teacher that she'd unearthed dinosaur bones."

That wasn't entirely true. I told Vegas that I'd dug up something in my backyard that I was pretty sure dated back to the Triassic period and asked why we hadn't studied the Triassic era in class. He didn't give an answer, but I already knew the answer: Because there weren't any wars fought during the Triassic era!

"She told Nell she's been talking to Dad," Maya said.

"I knew this was about grief," my mom said.

"It's not about grief! She's mentally ill!"

"I'm in college," Maya said. "I live in Santa Barbara. I have a boy-friend. I have an internship. I can't hold her hand anymore."

"I don't need anyone holding my hand." I would have thought Maya had figured that out by now. I'd only called her twice in the last couple weeks.

"Stop interrupting, Jane," Maya said.

"Who taught her to tie her shoes?" she asked my mom. "Who helped her with her homework? Who made her breakfast? Who does she call when she's confused about what to do with a boy?"

What to do with a boy? Like I'd unwrapped him and needed to know what voltage batteries to insert? It was all so insulting. I was finally my own independent person and Maya was talking about me like I was a baby. She was probably just frustrated that I wasn't under her thumb any longer.

"Calm down, Maya," my mom said. "You're shouting. You're fright-ening Jane."

"No, she's not," I said. "But I wish I could say some . . ."

"Shut up, Jane," Maya hissed. Wow. Shut up. This was getting ugly. "That you can't own up to the fact that your daughter is in seriously bad shape and haven't been able to find the time to help her is pathetic. You are a horrible mother. We would have been better off as orphans," Maya said.

"I'll second that. And she's keeping secrets, too," I said. "Secrets I am going to get to the bottom of."

"Quiet. Both of you," my mother hissed. I'd never heard her so heated up before. "You're being disrespectful."

"We're being disrespectful because we don't respect you," I said. "And why should we? What have you ever done to gain our respect?" I'd never spoken so rudely to my mother, but these were probably the most honest words I'd ever said to her.

"Stop talking, Jane," my mother shouted. "I don't want to hear another word."

I put a lid on the hostility that was bubbling up to the surface and shut up while she and Maya got into it again, squabbling over me like I wasn't there for the remainder of the ride to the doctor's office.

I'd never thought I'd be happy to return to Minute Rice's office, but when the minivan pulled into his parking lot, I rejoiced. I couldn't listen to Maya and my mom getting it all wrong about me any longer. It was now my chance to speak for myself and explain to Minute Rice what was really going on. Once he'd heard me plead my case, he would either kindly tell them to butt out and leave me to my doings or I would kindly tell all three of them to butt out and I would return to my doings.

We reached Minute Rice's office, and Maya checked in with receptionist, who told her off for being tardy, which brought about more bickering between her and my mother—each blaming the other for arriving late. Mentally, I prepared what I would say. I was certain Minute Rice wasn't going to allow me much time, so I had to be brief and concise. I'd hit the bullet points: genius, student body president, crew star. Revolutionize high school. Done.

Minute Rice opened his door and requested that Maya and my mom step inside. I rose to enter the room with them, but Minute Rice held his hand out, blocking me, and told me to settle back down on the couch and wait.

"But, I need to explain what's going on," I protested. "Those two don't know anything. Maya hasn't seen me in weeks and my mom and I only bump into each other in the hallway or the kitchen every now and then."

"Take a seat, Janelle," Minute Rice ordered as he closed his office door.

When the receptionist slid his counter window shut, I moved to Minute Rice's door and tried the knob. It was locked. I put my ear against the door trying to hear what was being said: "Bipolar . . . blah blah . . . Mania . . . blah blah . . . Out of control . . . wah wah . . . Expelled . . . blah blah yada yada . . . Hospital!" Alarms blared in my head. I was going to be locked up. I had to do something fast!

I frantically searched my bag for my phone and then remembered that I'd left it at home. I dashed to the receptionist's window and banged against it. He slid it open slowly. "You have to call my friend Tiffany! They're going to lock me up! Please help me!"

The receptionist stared at me blankly. "Please! Pick up your phone!" I pleaded desperately. "Give it to me so that I can call her. Tiffany's number is 310 . . . ." He slid the window shut. I banged on it. "Open up! I have to get a hold of somebody who can rescue me!" I smacked my fist against the window, trying to break the glass. But it was constructed of some industrial-strength material made to survive Armageddon. I tried to slide open the window, but my palms were sweating so much from nerves that I couldn't get a good grip.

Suddenly, Minute Rice's office door swung open. I raced inside, nearly knocking over Maya, who was standing in the way. My mother was sitting slouched on the couch sobbing (which I'd never seen her do over anything related to me), and Minute Rice was standing beside his enormous desk.

"We've decided what's best for you," Minute Rice said.

"How can you know what's best for me when you have no idea what I'm thinking or feeling?" I lunged for Dr. Rice. I was so gunned up that I was practically frothing at the mouth. "Listen to me. I have to talk. None of you know what's in my soul and what I'm on this earth to do. You haven't heard what I have to say . . . ."

Dr. Rice stepped back, looking legitimately terrified of me—a barely 110-pound teenager. "You're invading my personal space, Janelle. Stand back!"

"I won't! Not until you've heard me!" Maya grabbed my arms and pinned them behind my back, tugging me away from Minute Rice.

"Where are they?" Minute Rice shouted out the door to the receptionist. "What's taking so long?"

"Who? What?" I asked. "Who's coming here?"

Two security guards arrived. A man and a woman. The man took hold of me and clamped a set of handcuffs around my wrists while the woman lingered in the waiting room. The female guard held up my purse. "Is this hers? It was on the couch in the waiting room."

"Give it back!" I kicked my legs, trying to break free.

The woman unzipped my purse and searched through it. "No weapons," she announced. Weapons? What would I be doing with weapons? Why were they treating me this way? I wasn't a criminal.

The guards each took one of my arms. I continued kicking and screaming, "Let go of me! Stop!"

Maya had tears in her eyes as she watched them haul me out of the room. "They're going to lock me up! Do something, Maya! Don't let them take me away!" But, Maya turned away from me. Maya, my guardian angel for all these years, was just standing there doing nothing to save me. I wouldn't expect my mother to help me, but Maya was abandoning me, too? The one person I'd always counted on? It was so unbelievable that it was almost surreal.

I kicked and screamed and cried as the two security guards escorted me out of the office building and into an elevator. "We're not going to hurt you," the woman purred. "We're taking you to the hospital where you can be helped."

"I don't need help," I insisted. "Go help a sick person. I'm fine."

When the elevator opened, I went limp and refused to move my legs so that they had to tow me inside the hospital next door and into another elevator. "You don't need to be frightened, Janelle," the female guard repeated over and over as we exited the elevator, waded through a waiting room, and then entered an examination room. I wasn't frightened. I was terrified.

Once inside the examination room, the female guard departed, and the male guard stayed behind with me and took off the handcuffs, which brought me down a few notches. At least they weren't treating me like an inmate anymore. I took a couple deep breaths. It was time to get a grip and find my way out of this situation. "I want a lawyer," I told the guard. "I have rights."

"A nurse is coming," the guard told me as he sat me in a chair.

"I don't need medical attention," I explained tersely. "I need to be set free."

A few minutes later, a nurse with a clipboard arrived and checked my blood pressure and heart and took my temperature. I explained that I wasn't sick and told him that I was being unjustly detained and asked him to please let me leave. "Somebody from the PET team is coming," he answered as he made some notes.

"I don't want animals," I told the nurse. "I have enough at home. I want legal help if you won't let me go. And I need water. I'm thirsty."

"I'll have somebody fetch water for you," he said as he finished making notes and disappeared out the door.

"I need to use the bathroom," I told the guard. I was suddenly dying to pee.

"You'll have to wait for a female to escort you to the bathroom," he said as he positioned himself in the doorway, filling it with his girth—presenting himself as a cinder block wall.

The guard pulled out a bag of potato chips from his pocket and began eating one after another—excruciatingly slowly. I was a raw nerve, and my ears were so sensitive that I could hear his molars biting against one another as the chips were turned to paste inside his mouth. It was like a classroom of children all scratching their nails against a chalkboard simultaneously. I asked for earplugs to help bring down the crunching sounds, but the guard paid zero attention to my request. I took some more deep breaths, trying my hardest not to start screaming.

Soon, a middle-aged woman holding a folder arrived. She introduced herself as a county social worker from the PET team. But, social she was not. The only party she could have ever planned was a wake. And she didn't arrive, as one would expect from the term "PET team," with a litter of puppies or a petting zoo. PET stood for Psychiatric Evaluation Team, and she was there to evaluate me.

"Evaluate me for what?" I asked.

"What's your name?" she asked.

"Jane," I answered. "Can I have a glass of water?" My mouth, due to a side effect of the medication I was on and of my not having had anything to drink for hours, lacked enough moisture to even lick a postage stamp. "And I really need to use the bathroom."

"When the nurse gets here, you can use the lavatory," she answered. "Do you know where you are?"

"St. Joan's Hospital."

"Do you know why you're here?"

"Because my mother and sister drove me here," I answered.

The third degree went on and on. How long have you felt like this? Are you hearing voices? After the questions were completed, she flipped through a bunch of papers in her folder, checking off boxes and initialing paragraphs. Finally: "That's all. I'm done with my evaluation."

"Did I pass?" I asked, trying to smile at her in the hopes I'd win her over. She said nothing. "I would like to know what I'm being charged with."

"You're not being charged with anything. You are psychotic and need help," she answered.

"I would like the DSM code and definition of psychosis. I have a right to know what you're diagnosing me with," I said. It was getting increasingly difficult to keep it together. My insides were roiling.

The social worker refused to provide me with info regarding my new label. She said my doctor could talk to me about it. I whined until she finally found a copy of the mental manual and read me my latest code. I had been upgraded to PSYCHOSIS DSM 293.81: "Loss of contact with reality . . . abnormal condition of the mind. Symptoms include: paranoia, hallucinations, delusions such as belief that strange occurrences and coincidences are happening or that one is God . . . disintegration of personality and thoughts . . . bizarre behavior . . . difficulty with social interaction and carrying out daily life activities . . . might become violent and danger to others and self."

"I haven't 'lost contact with reality,'" I told the social worker, feeling big, red hot anger igniting somewhere deep inside. "It's this diagnosis that has no basis in reality."

The social worker stuck her pen in her pocket, gathered her papers, and moved away from the examination table.

"The bathroom?" I asked, but she didn't listen.

"She'll be in here a while longer," the social worker told the security guard as she vanished through the door. "They're waiting on authorization from her health insurance company."

Health insurance company? I didn't like the sound of that. If they were talking to the health insurance company that meant they had plans for me. Why weren't they going to let me go? I'd answered all the social worker's and nurse's questions right. I wasn't yelling or making trouble anymore. Please, *not* the hospital. "The bathroom?" I asked the security guard. I was so desperate to use the bathroom that I was squirming.

"I'll send over a woman to bring you," he answered. "Hold tight." But, I couldn't hold tight.

"I can't wait anymore," I said.

"Well, you're going to have to," the security guard said. "I can't let you go alone and I can't escort you."

There was a loud shriek coming from the hallway. The security guard took a step back to see where the noise was coming from, freeing up space in the doorway – just enough for me to squeeze through. I jumped up from the chair, charged past the guard and into the hall. I saw a restroom sign ahead and sprinted for it. Just as I reached the door, the guard grabbed me from behind and pulled me from the door.

"You let me use the bathroom now or I'll pee down your leg." I warned, trying to break free. I kicked my leg out behind me and got him in the stomach. Immediately, I knew I'd made a mistake. This was not how you acted if you were trying to prove how sane you were. But, I couldn't help it. My bladder won out over my rationality.

"Oomph," he coughed, letting go of me.

As I disappeared inside the bathroom and into one of the stalls, I heard the nurse screaming to the guard, "Do your job!"

"I tried!" he yelled back. "She pulled herself out of my arms!"

I peed as fast as I could and exited the stall to face a female orderly. She led me from the bathroom and to the security guard. "Hold her tight," she told him.

The security guard dragged me back into the examination room. "We need restraints," he snarled. Another guard arrived, and the two lifted me up and wrestled me onto the examination table, placing straps around my ankles and wrists and then attaching them to the table so I couldn't move. "No! Stop!" I screamed. "Let me go!" I started hyperventilating, feeling like I was being held underwater. I couldn't hold it in anymore, and what was the point. Cool and collected had gotten me nowhere with these ogres.

A nurse appeared with a syringe, lifted up my skirt, and jabbed it into my upper thigh. "This will calm you down," she said.

"Stop I don't want to be calm!" I shouted at her. I continued wailing and begging for water. A nurse finally arrived with a tiny cup of water and lifted my head up and helped me drink it. Minutes later, a psychiatrist, Dr. Prateek, arrived.

"I gave her the tranquilizer, but it hasn't done anything," the nurse reported.

"Can I see her file?" Dr. Prateek asked. She handed Dr. Prateek a folder thick with papers. "Let's give her another injection," Dr. Prateek ordered the nurse after he'd flipped through the folder. The nurse pulled out another syringe, and I unleashed it. "No! No more of that! You're trying to poison me! Get away from me! I want a lawyer!"

Dr. Prateek poked the needle into my thigh, right near where the nurse had injected me before. "Give her fifteen minutes and then inject another one if she's still agitated," he said. "I'm going to see what beds they have available."

I started crying and shrieking louder and louder – getting more revved up and out of control. I told the security guard and the nurse that I would have them arrested for holding me against my will. I told them that I would put them behind bars for what they were doing to me.

After ten minutes of my howling and threatening, the nurse disappeared briefly and reappeared with Dr. Prateek, who was holding yet another syringe. "It hasn't been fifteen minutes! It's only been ten! Check the clock!" I demanded between choking sobs.

Dr. Prateek injected me again, this time into my arm. "Let's get her out," he said.

Dr. Prateek had used the word "out." I prayed that meant they were bringing me to the lobby floor and were going to set me free. The security guard unshackled my wrists and ankles and he and the nurse and Dr. Prateek shoved me into a wheelchair and pushed me up the hallway and into a waiting elevator. We went down, down, down.

When the elevator opened, a large Latino guy greeted me. "I'm Alfredo and I'm going to show you to your room." My stomach dropped.

"She's had a lot of sedatives. She'll want to sleep soon," Dr. Prateek said. But I wasn't a bit sleepy. I was as charged up as I'd ever been and this was my last shot at freedom. When Alfredo motioned for me to stand, I leapt up, punched him in the stomach, and ran for it. Within seconds, two sizeable orderlies appeared. Each took an arm, and my escape plans were done for. I was one hundred percent at these strangers' mercy and there wasn't a thing I could do about it.

"Isolation," Dr. Prateek ordered. The orderlies pulled me down a long hallway into a dark room and shut the door. Inside was nothing but blackness. I couldn't see anything, not even my own hand. It was quiet, too quiet—I could hear the blood running through my veins and my jagged, labored breathing. If this was supposed to calm me down, it wasn't working. I could feel an anxiety attack rising. I dropped to my knees and started gasping for air.

Once the anxiety attack had passed, I got up and moved along the walls, pounding them with my fists, trying to figure out where the door was. The walls were surprisingly soft and felt like they were upholstered.

After banging my fists around the perimeter of the cell, I hit what felt like a hinge. I moved my hand a few inches to the side of the hinge, guessing that this was where the door was. I knocked and knocked, but there was no reply. Why were they being so cruel to me? Why had they locked me in here? Maybe there was a secret knock I needed to give—one that meant I was ready to be released. I tried slow knocks. Fast knocks. Soft knocks. Loud knocks. Staccatos. I rapped my fist with steady and unsteady rhythms. I drummed my fingers against the door one by one. I slapped the door. Slugged the door. I tried every combination of sound and tempo I could make. But nobody answered.

# EIGHT

$\mathcal{I}$ WOKE UP in a twin bed in a small, windowless, rectangular room with a blue linoleum floor and beige walls. The bed was lumpy and felt like it was filled with sand, and both my sheet and blanket were that dull, greyish shade that white laundry gets when it's been washed too many times with the darks.

I felt like I'd spent the night in a ditch. My back and legs were sore and my wrists and ankles were stinging. I was dizzy and disoriented and my head throbbed and my thoughts stuttered.

Inside a tiny closet across from my bed, I found some of my clothes. I shed my nightgown and set it in on a shelf. As I slipped on a pair of jeans and a T-shirt, I looked down at my ankles and wrists. They were red and chafed and there were black-and-blue bruises on my thighs and scratches across my arms.

I stepped into the hallway and wandered into the room next door that had a name card hanging on the door that read "Dominga." The room was identical to mine except for a stack of books on the bedside table and a pair of slippers resting on the floor in front of the closet. I slid my feet into the slippers, which fit perfectly, and shuffled back into the hallway.

Next to Dominga's room was a room with a placard that read "Ebony." The room was larger than mine and had two bulletin boards on the wall, both of which were covered with pictures. There was a long shelf where more pictures, books, magazines, and toiletries rested. I squeezed some rose-scented lotion into my hand and spread it over my neck and arms.

At the other end of the hallway was a doorway with an office next to it where a large African American woman (with a name tag that read "Effie") sat behind a desk. "Morning, Janelle. Ready for breakfast?" Effie asked. There it was—the dreaded "Janelle"—harbinger of bad things ahead. She pressed a button on her switchboard and the door buzzed.

I pushed the door open and found myself in what looked like the lobby of a ghetto housing project. The carpet was brown and stained, and there were stray marks on the off-white walls. None of this looked familiar to me.

I didn't see any bars, so I wasn't in prison. There wasn't any medical equipment or people wearing scrubs, so I couldn't be in a hospital. Where the heck was I and how did I get here? At the far end of the lobby was a set of glass doors.

I headed to the doors and tried to pry them apart, but they were locked tight and wouldn't budge. An alarm sounded, and a tall Latino man, who introduced himself as Manuel, arrived. He seized my arm and informed me that if I couldn't follow the rules and settle down, I would be confined to my room again. Maybe I was in prison after all. "Who's keeping me here?" I asked, an uneasiness washing over me. "What is this place? Why can't I leave?"

"Why don't we get you some breakfast," Manuel suggested. Maybe that was a good idea. My stomach was rumbling from hunger. I'd get some food in me and then get to the bottom of what was going on. Manuel guided me to a cafeteria filled with round tables where about ten teenagers, who looked vaguely familiar, were eating and chatting. A pretty, light-skinned African American girl with large, round eyes and braided hair waved to me and pointed to the empty chair next to hers. "I saved you a spot," she shouted. "Go get your tray."

To the side of the room was a counter where a twenty-something guy wearing a baseball cap was serving food. I picked up a tray and slid it in front of him. He handed me a glass of orange juice and a plate containing a sliced apple, a piece of wheat toast, a fried egg and two sausages. "I'm a vegetarian," I said, pointing to the sausages.

"Since when?" he asked.

"Since always," I answered. "Can I give the sausages back to you?"

"You didn't specify vegetarian on your menu request form, so you'll have to talk to your nurse about changing your meals to meatless. I don't have that authority," he said.

I took a seat next to the African American girl. Across the table sat an African American guy wearing sweatpants, a long-sleeved T-shirt, and a watch cap—a strange outfit considering it was May in Southern California – if I was still in Southern California.

"Everyday with the glass doors," the girl remarked. "When are you going to learn that you're not getting out of here?"

Suddenly I remembered her name. "Where am I, Autumn?"

"It's Ebony," she snapped. "Ebony. Ebony. Ebony. I've told you a billion times. Look at the color of my skin. It's black—Ebony. Got it?"

"Where am I?" I repeated.

"You still don't know, or are you messing with me?" she asked.

"I don't have a clue where I am."

"You're in Saint Joan's Hospital Psychiatric Unit," she answered. "Acute Level I, where they store the major crazies."

"Who's crazy?" I asked.

"You're crazy," Ebony said. "We all are."

"What defines crazy?" I asked, anger stirring in me. I wasn't taking on this label.

"Ask the doctors," Ebony said.

"You can't just lock up people who aren't criminals," I said. "They have to let us leave if we want to."

"There's no leaving here without a security guard—and they'll only let you leave if you need to visit the regular hospital for some kind of serious medical issue—like a seizure where your eyes roll back in your head," Ebony said.

"But we have rights!" I said. "What about the constitution?"

"They don't keep a copy in here," Ebony said.

As I picked at my breakfast, blurry images swam through my mind: the crowded school auditorium, my mother and Maya fighting over what was wrong with me, Dr. Rice's office, security guards and nurses. So, this is where they'd stuck me. The loony bin. The place was giving me the creeps. It had to be a mistake that I was here – a mistake to be fixed.

"Do you want my sausages?" I asked Ebony. "I'm a vegetarian."

"You haven't been a vegetarian for the past three days," she said.

"I've been here three days?" I asked. "That long?"

"That's nothing," Ebony said. "I've been here three weeks."

"I've been here six weeks," the guy wearing all the clothes told me. "My name is Reggie. I'll eat the sausages. I'm part vampire, and vampires like meat."

Ebony surreptitiously snatched the sausages from my plate and tossed them onto Reggie's plate. "They better not see me doing this," she said. "They want everybody eating their own food."

"Who are they?"

"The nurses and doctors."

Ebony began sniffing, edging her nose closer and closer to me. "You used my lotion again, didn't you," she asked.

I nodded.

"Stop going in my room and using my things," she said. "It's not cool." She peered down at my shoes. "You're wearing Dominga's slippers, too. Do we go in your room and use your stuff?"

I had no idea if they went into my room and used my stuff. I couldn't remember seeing my room before this morning.

Ebony grabbed her tray and stomped off. I'd never seen someone get so upset over something as inconsequential as a tablespoon of lotion. I hoped the others weren't going to be as touchy as she was.

"Don't worry. She gets over it every morning," Reggie said.

"Why are you wearing all those clothes?" I asked him.

"Vampires need to protect their skin from light," he answered. "You could almost pass for a vampire, you know. Your skin is almost as white as mine." His skin was as dark as licorice.

"You really believe you're a vampire?" I asked. I for sure didn't belong in a place where people were crazy enough to think they were vampires.

"The government transformed me into a vampire so that I could work for them—kill terrorists," he said. "My family brought me here so the doctors could get the vampire out of me and make me fully human again. Don't worry. I won't suck your blood. I don't even like the sight of blood anymore—now that I'm returning to a human state."

When we finished breakfast, we were directed to stand in a medication line. At the front of the line was a tall, slender man wearing the expression of someone who had just pulled a slug out of his sock. One by one, the patients reached him and received a small cup with pills inside and another cup filled with water.

I arrived at the front of the line and studied my cup of pills. There were four of them. Two were the same yellow color, one was blue, and the other one was white. I had to be careful. Most likely these pills were meant to overmedicate me and dull my mind—squelch my initiative.

"What is this stuff?" I asked, pointing to the pills.

"Ask your nurse," the man with the meds barked. "I only dispense the pills. Please swallow them while I'm watching or I will have to get a member of the staff to help you." That sounded ominous. I swallowed the pills and stepped into the next line—the nurse's office line.

The nurse checked my blood pressure, drew blood, listened to my heartbeat, and then read over my chart. "Do you know why you're here?" she asked.

"All I've done is try to help society," I explained, trying to speak slowly and act like I had it together. If the medical staff had stuck me here then it would be the medical staff who would let me out. I had to impress her. "But, clearly some small-minded people out there view me as a threat and they've conspired to stick me here. Since there's obviously nothing wrong with me that requires medical attention, I would like to leave. I will give you the phone number of somebody who can pick me up."

She smiled. I felt a twinge of hope. "It is the opinion of the hospital staff that you need medical attention," she said. "You are not due to be released yet." In an instant, the hope was replaced with doom. This nurse obviously wasn't even listening to me. Between her, the locked doors and the guards it was going to be tougher to get out of here than I thought.

"The other patients here might accept being locked up, but I don't. I want a lawyer," I told her.

"Miss Flynn, there are other people waiting in line to see me," she said. "Please step outside." So that was it. No rights. No voice.

I glared at her for a few seconds beyond a normal glare and stood up. Just as I'd stepped out of the room, I remembered that I hadn't asked what drugs I was on, but it was too late. Another patient was already inside her office.

The next hour was free time. I felt grubby, so I decided to clean up. I returned to my room and collected what I needed for a shower: soap, comb, shampoo and conditioner, and some toothpaste and a toothbrush—but there was no razor. I returned to the lobby and asked a chubby white guy named Paul if I could have a razor to shave my legs. "I am not your nurse," he said. "I am your social worker. You will need to speak to your nurse regarding bathing."

I asked a crabby blonde if she was my nurse, and she told me, with an "I don't do windows" attitude, to find Autumn. It seemed Autumn was my day nurse. So that was where I'd gotten the name. It was so aggravating to have lost my memory. It was like I'd blacked out for several days – or been in a coma.

I asked two staff members if they were Autumn and then, on try number three, I finally found her. Autumn moved back at least three paces when I approached her—like she was going to catch crazy if I got too close. The name Autumn brings up the pleasant image of lovely orange and red leaves and a crisp but not too cold climate. This thoroughly unpleasant Autumn should have been named Arctic Winter or, better yet, Polar Bear Attack.

"I'd like a razor to shave my legs, please," I told Autumn.

"I think you have a razor," she answered, and we marched down the hall to a locked closet. Inside the closet was a shelf marked "Janelle." Stored on my shelf were earrings, a couple necklaces, a candle, my phone, headphones, and nail clippers.

"Ooh," I said, grabbing for my belongings.

"Ah, ah," Autumn said, waving my hand away. "These are items your sister brought that have been confiscated." So, Maya had been here? And she'd left me here? I felt betrayed enough that she'd let them stick me here. Now that I knew she hadn't even taken me out when she had the chance the betrayal felt worse.

"Why?" I asked. "I need them."

"They're suicide hazards—the necklaces can strangle, nail clippers can cut skin, and the earrings are sharp. The candle is useless because we don't allow matches. You'll be allowed to use the phone to listen to music, but only when supervised because the headphone cord could be used for strangulation." She finally dug out a razor and handed it to me. "Let me lock up the closet, and then I'll take you to the bathroom."

"It's okay," I said. "I know where it is."

"You can't use a razor unsupervised," she said. "I have to watch you while you shower."

Yuck. I didn't want her watching me take a shower. I handed the razor back to her. "I'll pass," I said. "Now let's get to the business of me leaving. I've been voted president of my school and the students are probably very confused as to why I'm not around."

"Interesting," she said. "Your doctor will decide when you are ready to leave. Why don't you go take that shower."

Later in the morning, the patients gathered in the dayroom—a dark and dreary cave with two loser couches that needed to be taken out to pasture, a television set (the old-fashioned, clunky kind that is deeper than it is wide), sagging bookshelves, and a few forlorn chairs. Paul arranged the patients into a semicircle and announced that we were going to be telling our stories today, explaining to the others why we were here in the hospital. Some of us had already shared our stories, but he liked to cover this particular topic once a week so that newcomers could get to know those who had been in the hospital for a while. Paul spoke in a singsong voice that reminded me so much of a kindergarten teacher that I was waiting for him to break into nursery rhymes.

Reggie was first to speak. He repeated the same information he'd given me in the morning about his being a vampire. "I'm getting less and less vampire," he announced. "I think I'll be able to get out pretty soon and go back to being a regular kid."

"I'm here to judge the living and the dead," explained a white skinhead. He stared at the rest of us with disdain and spit on the floor. Paul told him to use a tissue next time.

Ebony cried when she was called upon to speak. Leopoldo, a slight white guy with blonde hair, said that he had jumped out a window trying to save his life because he thought there were people chasing him. Now he realized that there wasn't anyone after him and that he was just having a delusional episode. A boy named Joel, who looked about fourteen, said that he had checked in because his dad wanted him there and then started laughing. He laughed through the rest of group; I'd heard him laughing at breakfast.

I introduced myself as Janelle because I had a feeling that this place wasn't going to leave me with good memories, so I might as well use my bad memory name. "I am being held here against my will by those who weren't happy with me shaking up the status quo." I stood up. "Take a stand with me. They can't just lock us up here!" Joel, laughing, slowly stood up. Skinhead uncrossed his legs and started rising to his feet.

"That's enough, Janelle," Paul said. "All of you sit down."

Joel and Skinhead quickly sat down, but I stood my ground. "You too, Janelle, or you're going to your room," Paul said. "Now."

Slowly, I sat. "Just because I'm sitting doesn't mean I'm giving up," I said.

Dominga, a very young, thin Latina girl whom I hadn't seen before, arrived just as group was ending. She displayed her upper arms and thighs, which were covered in scars, and explained that she had been cutting herself for three years and that a few of her cuts had gotten badly infected—so infected that she had to be on IV antibiotics for days. She was in the hospital to learn how to stop hurting herself. I studied Dominga's face. Although she was Latina, she looked a lot like my sister. They had the same strong jaw line and high forehead, identical almond-shaped eyes, and similar long, curly, light brown hair. The main difference was that Dominga wore glasses.

I turned to Dominga. "You look like my sister Maya," I told her. "But Maya doesn't wear glasses." I pulled the glasses off her face. "There. Now you look more like her." I tossed the glasses back to Dominga, but she missed catching them. The glasses hit the linoleum floor.

"Unacceptable behavior, Jane. Unacceptable behavior," Paul said. "You'll apologize and then you'll leave." I apologized and then I was given a shot of tranquilizers in my upper arm and sent to my room for the remainder of the day. I moped, feeling like the most misunderstood person in the world. I was certain that I shouldn't be in the hospital, but nobody would agree with me. And I seemed to be rubbing everyone the wrong way even though I was trying to be nice. It was like the whole world had turned against me.

I jogged in place until my energy flagged and I was able to be still, and then I sat on the floor in a cross-legged position with my arms at my sides—a pose you see chubby Buddha lawn statues sitting in; a pose that I'd heard brought on peace. I shut my eyes and tried to quiet my mind enough to envision Ben. It seemed like forever since I'd thought of him. I knew we'd spent a night together—or at least part of a night—and I could remember the delicious feelings, but I couldn't remember the details. Slowly, Ben came into focus. First his eyes, then his smile. Then I saw him sitting on the edge of his bed —his head facing the floor while his eyes looked sideways at me and his lips curved up ever so slightly. Then the image of him began pulling away—his face muddy and out of focus. I struggled to stay with him, wanting more, but he faded out and vanished.

Eventually, a tray arrived with my dinner (a meat entrée because I'd forgotten to ask Autumn to change my menu request). I ate alone, and lonely, picking beef out of a stroganoff, and went to sleep early after being force-fed a pink pill with Propofol-like superpowers.

# NINE

THE NEXT MORNING, I vowed not to do anything that might get me banished to my room again. My energy level, even when medicated, was still so high that being caged inside one hundred square feet was excruciating. And it was boring. I had only a pad of paper, a pen, and the book *The Hunchback of Notre Dame*, which we'd been assigned to read in English class.

I ate all of my breakfast, except for the meat. I took my medication from Med Man, thanking him several times for handing my pills to me, though he still acted like I was one giant bother. I went to the nurse for my daily checkup and smiled while I answered all her pointless questions, again forgetting to ask what cocktail of pills I was being forced to take, and then headed out to the rooftop yard.

All the patients filed outside except Reggie, who explained that he was still vampire enough that the sun could kill him. The yard, covered in cracked asphalt and devoid of shrubs, trees, or flowers, was one of the most unsightly outdoor spaces I'd ever beheld, but I was overjoyed to be moving my body in the fresh spring air. I sprinted around in circles while listening to music through my headphones. Ebony was listening to music, too, and dancing. Skinhead was smoking. Paul organized the others in a kiddie game that looked like Duck Duck Goose.

I sized up the space. The rooftop had a six-foot brick wall surrounding the yard. It looked just short enough for me to climb—and if there was a ledge below or a fire escape, it might be a way to break out. I skipped to the wall and leapt up as high as I could and grabbed the ledge, struggling as I tried desperately to hoist myself up and over.

"Don't! You'll get caught again!" Ebony shrieked, racing to my side and tugging me from the wall. "You already climbed the wall three times. Do you want to be stuck in your room again?"

"Paul isn't looking over here. We could make a climb for it," I said.

"There's nowhere to go once you get to the top of the wall—unless you want to jump off the building," Ebony said. "You're the one who told me that after you climbed up there three days ago."

"So that's a 'no' on the wall?" I said.

"A 'no' on getting out of here in general," Ebony said. "There are no windows that open and there is only one door out—one locked door with an alarm on it. And don't forget the guards."

"People tunnel out of maximum security prisons," I said. "What about a mass exodus? We could all march out together."

Just then, Paul blew his whistle, signaling the end of outdoor time. We sauntered into the dayroom for what was billed as "free period," where we were allowed to do whatever we wanted to do, which would have been fine if there was anything to do.

I browsed the bookshelves. There were wrinkled magazines from when Michael Jackson was still alive, tattered novels missing either their front or their back cover or both, a row of Bibles, an entire shelf of books in Spanish, *How to Survive the Loss of a Loved One*, and some Nancy Drew books. Nancy Drew books? Just because we were supposedly mad didn't mean we couldn't read past third-grade level.

I investigated both the dayroom and the lobby and, sadly, had to concur with Ebony. St. Joan's Psych Unit was sealed pretty tight. But if I could organize the others, maybe we could all storm out together. I studied my fellow patients, except for Ebony and Leopoldo, who had taken off for their rooms. Reggie was playing solitaire, Joel was doing a puzzle; Dominga was reading and Skinhead was asleep on the couch, snoring.

I started with Reggie. "I've got a plan for busting us out of here," I told him.

"Where are we going?" he asked.

"Wherever you want to go when we get out," I said. "It's called freedom."

Joel heard us talking and moved closer, laughing (of course). "Where are you guys going?"

"Shhh," I told him. "I'm planning an escape."

"It's not safe for me to go anywhere," Reggie said. "Not while I'm still part vampire."

"I wouldn't mind going to Game Stop and getting an Xbox," Joel said. "I have a credit card. Do you think an Xbox would work with that old TV they've got here? Do you think they'd even let me use it?"

"He might want to leave," Reggie said, pointing to Skinhead. "I don't think he's happy here. I've never seen him smile. Not even on Monopoly night."

I moved to Skinhead and whispered in his ear: "Wake up. Up. Up." He opened his eyes, shut them, and then rolled onto his other side and started snoring again, louder than before.

These poor souls were even more beaten down than the C class at my school. They needed to get a life before they could get a spine—or vice versa. I would do what I could while I was in the hospital, but I might not be able to see all these sad little urchins realize their greater glory.

I left the dayroom and headed for the lobby. The pay phone was in the lobby, and I badly wanted to talk to Maya and Tiffany or Nell. I had to get at least one of them on my side to begin Operation Get Jane Out of Here. Maybe I could even get one of them to find Ben's number for me. I wanted to hear his voice. I asked Paul for quarters, and he told me to ask Autumn if I had any quarters in the supply closet. I found Autumn, who seemed tickled to inform me that Maya had not brought me any quarters, so I wouldn't be able to use the phone.

"Is there a rowing machine here? I'm on crew team and I'm going to be taking over the most important seat in my boat, so I need to stay in shape," I said.

"You can walk and run during outdoor time and do calisthenics during free time," she answered.

"What about school work? Could we call West Hills Prep and have them send over my lessons? Otherwise I'll get behind. I have to keep my grades up or the administration will take my student body office away from me."

"In Acute Level I, we don't allow schoolwork," she continued. "Your energy needs to be directed at recovery." She commanded me to clean my room and make my bed, both of which, she said punitively, were supposed to be completed before breakfast every morning. Something I didn't remember being told.

I tidied my room, which took five seconds since there was barely anything in it, while the Nepalese maid, Kamala, mopped the floor. She couldn't speak English well, but she was warm and smiley. She was the first nice employee I'd met in the hospital and the first who'd made me feel anything akin to being taken care of. All the others just made me feel like I was being punished.

Once Kamala left to clean the bathroom, I meandered into Dominga's room. Stacked up on her bedside table were a book about cutting, the third in the Harry Potter series, and *The Lion, the Witch and the Wardrobe*. The books were for such a juvenile audience that I guessed she was even younger than she looked.

I nabbed the book about cutting (I'd always been curious why people cut themselves) and ducked into Ebony's room, where I flipped through her magazines and photo albums, which were mostly filled with baby pictures. I borrowed a couple magazines and a few sheets of stationery and sprayed some of her musky-smelling perfume on my wrist.

I arrived at lunch late, and the surly guy behind the counter served me a roast beef sandwich and bowl of chicken noodle soup. I had to get the meal change request in today or I'd starve. I sat with Ebony, Dominga (who was taking out her cutting obsession on a black bean enchilada—slicing it into tiny cat-food-sized bites), Reggie (who was trying to eat chicken wings wearing plastic fangs), and Leopoldo. Ebony immediately started sniffing in my direction. "You're wearing my perfume again, aren't you?" she asked curtly.

"I only used a quick squirt."

"My boyfriend, Anton, gave me that perfume and it was expensive. It's his favorite scent. He likes to smell it on me, but if you use up the perfume I'll have to just smell like soap because I'm not rich and I can't afford to buy another bottle."

"I'm sorry," I said.

"Didn't I ask you not to go into my room and move things around?" she spat. "I feel like I'm losing it when I leave something in one place and I go back and it's somewhere else. What's wrong with you?"

"If you believe the staff here—a lot," I answered. I couldn't understand why she was getting so worked up over a dab of perfume – even more worked up than she got about the thimble of lotion I'd used—but I was sorry I'd upset her nonetheless.

"Dominga says you're messing with her crap, too," she said. Dominga looked up and nodded in agreement. "I'm telling Autumn if you go in my room again."

Memo to self: Stay out of Ebony's room – and Dominga's.

Leopoldo semi-chilled out Ebony and got me to give my word not to use her perfume ever again. He told me that he was bipolar and that he had rapid cycling, which is where you yo-yo a bunch of times in a day or a week. He tried to wean himself off his medicine because he couldn't afford it anymore; three weeks into going cold turkey, he landed in the ward. He committed himself voluntarily. "I was trying to save my life when I checked in here," he said. "A big part of me believed there were people trying to kill me. Another part of me thought maybe I was having one of my psychotic episodes. Either way, I knew I needed help. I've been committed to St. Joan's twice, for suicide attempts, so I knew I'd be safe here—be taken care of." Leopoldo added that he wanted to live next to a fire station or police station when he moved out of his mom's house. "I'll feel safe knowing that if I make a mistake and slash an artery or down a bottle of shoe polish, I can rush next door and there will be somebody on duty who will keep me alive."

Ebony predicted that Leopoldo would be out of the hospital soon because he made sense. "I wish I could get out," she moaned. "I miss Anton so much it hurts. In the two years we've been together I'd never spent more than twelve hours away from him until I got here." I asked Ebony why she was in the hospital and she said that it was for depression, "and don't ask for any details because it's private."

When Leopoldo asked me why I was at St. Joan's I realized that I had no answer. Unlike them, I wasn't buying what the staff was telling me about my "condition." I wasn't buying that there was anything wrong with me medically. I wanted to forge a bond, since they seemed like okay people – and since I might be stuck with them for a while – only it wasn't going to be by telling them that I had a mental disorder that I didn't think I had. So, I just answered, "I was put here mistakenly." They all looked at me blankly, like they didn't believe me – just like the staff. There I was. Misunderstood by yet more people.

I complained about not having quarters for the pay phone, and Ebony told me the quarters wouldn't help much in the communication department. "The phone is janky," she said. "It cuts out and sometimes you can't get a dial tone."

"You're only allowed eight minutes a call," Leopoldo said. This place had more rules than a Catholic school.

"I poked around this morning, looking for ways outta here, and you're right," I told Ebony. "It's not on. I didn't just want freedom for me, I wanted to help everyone here get out and on with their lives. I can't imagine this wretched place is helping anyone."

"Most of these kids don't want out anyway. And the ones who do probably couldn't survive fifteen minutes on the street," she said. "You can't change things here. This is a hospital for mentally ill folks. It's not fun and it's not pretty, and it's not changing—at least not for us."

"Well, they could at least make the conditions nicer," I said. "The place looks like it needs a flea bath. And I'm tired of everybody who works here being rude to me."

"They're rude to everybody—in different degrees," Ebony said. "It's like how prison guards get sick of the inmates. These folks are sick of the mentals."

"You say that so matter of fact," I said. "Doesn't it make you angry? Why are we all standing for it?"

"Welcome to the lower-archy," she said.

"The lower-archy?" I asked.

"Now that you've been officially documented as nuts, you're part of the lower-archy," she said. "We are only one level above convicts in the eyes of society."

"So, if there's a lower-archy, I'm guessing, from how mean the staff is to me, that I'm on the bottom," I said.

"You're on the bottom because you gave the staff a hard time your first days here," Leopoldo said. "You were *off the chain*."

"What was I doing?" I asked.

"Scratching, screaming, punching, and hitting the security guards," Ebony said. "Way out of control. And you wouldn't shut up about being a 'chosen one' who was going to change the whole world. That kinda talk makes everyone think you're a snob."

"What exactly did I do? Can you be more specific?" I asked.

"Let it go," she said. "The details won't help you recover. Trust me."

Not knowing the details wasn't going to help me recover either. It was an acutely uncomfortable feeling not to recall what I did during three days of apparently out-of-bounds behavior. Why couldn't I remember?

After lunch, I returned to my room and shut my eyes and tried my darnedest to work my way backwards to my first days at the hospital. But there was a gaping hole between being evaluated to be admitted to the hospital and the near present. Even the prehospital memories were spotty at best. In fact, the past few weeks were murky.

As much as I disliked poetry, I decided to try to write a poem for Ben, since it seemed to be one of his passions: "The whole world turned bright and glittery the first time I glanced at your face. Your smile collapsed time and space. My heart skipped then jogged then danced. We kissed and . . ." I squeezed my eyes shut and pictured Ben's face and zoomed in on his lips. His lips moved toward my face, and I remembered his butterfly kisses that tickled my eyelashes, flirty Eskimo kisses, delicate soft kisses, nipping nibbling kisses, harder kisses that made me shiver and . . . nothing. His kiss turned cold and his face vanished. So we'd made out and it had been luscious and steamy, but then what?

Visiting hours were from four to six—smack dab in the middle of rush hour and before many people had left work. Clearly, the schedule had been designed to further punish the detainees by keeping away family and friends. Surprisingly, a fair number of visitors showed up. Reggie's mother and sister, whom Ebony said visited everyday, rain or shine, sat with him, holding his hands and rubbing his back, looking worried. Ebony's brother brought her a couple magazines and a bag of snacks. Josh's father, who looked exactly like him, sat with his son, who couldn't stop laughing long enough to utter more than a few words. Leopoldo's sister arrived late and gave him lots of hugs and a cappuccino.

I asked Autumn if I was going to have a visitor. "I don't think so," she answered. "Your sister said she could only make it up here on weekends when she's home from school."

"My mother?" I already knew the answer to that one.

"I haven't met your mother," she said.

It wasn't a great surprise that nobody came to see me. Who would come here by choice? The place was as grubby and grim as an abandoned coal mine.

As I peered around the visiting room, I realized that nobody sends you flowers or balloons when you're in the psych ward. Balloons are probably a choking hazard and flowers could be poisonous. But I hadn't seen get well cards or heard the pay phone ring much or watched a singing telegram being delivered. There had been no cookie baskets or boxes of candy in the mail. It was like we weren't worthy of being fussed over or we were in hiding. I mostly felt like I'd been forgotten. Ebony was right. We were viewed as the lower-archy. We were the D people—disenfranchised, demented, done for, damned.

When lights went out at ten o'clock, I was way too wired to settle into bed. I rarely fell asleep earlier than midnight, and for the last month I hadn't hit the pillow before three or four in the morning. Reading might have lulled me to sleep, but I couldn't read in the dark and flashlights weren't permitted. Also, I was used to sharing my bed with a dog or two.

Making sleep more challenging was the lopsided, sprung mattress that belonged in an alley waiting for a dump truck. I fumbled with the control panel on the side of the bed, which emitted a loud groan—and that's all it did. The busted clunker of a bed was further proof that the mentally ill were viewed as being entitled to only the worn-out hand-me-downs and discards of the sane patients.

I pulled the bed off the frame and slid it onto the floor, hoping that by bypassing the box spring the mattress might be slightly more bearable. The mattress wasn't on the floor for longer than a blink when Rufus, the nighttime security guard assigned to the girls' wing, notified me that (surprise, surprise—another no-no) the beds weren't to be tampered with and that I would have to put my mattress back the way it was.

I hoisted the mattress back on the frame, lay down, and pulled up the covers. I tossed and turned and tossed and turned like I was spinning on a rotisserie.

Rufus pulled a chair into my doorway and said that he was required to stay there until I fell asleep—hospital policy. I told him that I couldn't sleep with somebody watching me. "You've fallen asleep every night but last night with me in your doorway," he answered. "We've talked about Ben and your dogs. We talked about my old girlfriend and how we patched things up."

Ben? What had I told him about Ben? And why was Rufus using the phrase "patched things up"? Did that mean that there was a problem between me and Ben that needed patching? Now I was worried *and* restless.

I tried lying still, but it was unbearable. Every part of my body wanted to wiggle—even my eyebrows. I invented excuses to get out of bed. I visited the bathroom to brush my teeth a second time and returned to use the toilet and later went back to blow my nose. I fetched a cup of water and then another cup and one more. I said that I was cold and pulled a blanket out from the closet. I said I was hot and folded the blanket and tucked it back into the closet.

All the while, Rufus was urging me to sleep: "The nurses want you getting a minimum of six hours of shut eye." I stalled some more, mentioning that my back hurt. Rufus said he'd get me something for it. Med Man arrived and asked me how bad my pain was on a scale of one to ten. I reported a six, and he left without offering me anything.

"Please stay in bed," Rufus urged after my fourth visit to the bathroom. "Watching those sweet little cheeks of yours through your pajamas is driving me crazy. Don't make me do something I shouldn't."

"Out!" I screeched. "Get out!" I threw a pillow at him and then a book. He ducked and told me that he was just trying to compliment me—that he didn't mean any harm.

"Get away from me or I'll give you a black eye," I threatened. I raced down the hall, so repulsed that I felt like throwing up, and asked the night receptionist to please get Rufus out of my sight immediately. She informed me that I would have to take up the matter with my night nurse. I asked a woman in the lobby if she was my night nurse, and she told me that Gemma was my night nurse. "You were briefed repeatedly on who your staff was on your first few days here. You should remember them by now."

"News flash," I hissed. "All this stuff I supposedly learned during the first few days I was here is impossible to know because I can't recall my first few days in this place and the pills I'm taking have messed up my short-term memory." Seconds after the outburst, my night nurse, a handsome British woman named Gemma, found me in my room. "I will not sleep with Rufus in my doorway," I declared. "He's slimy and gross and I'll howl all night like a wolf at a full moon and keep everyone awake if you leave him here."

"Rufus is here to protect you," Gemma said.

"It feels more like he's here to molest me," I said.

Rufus pulled up beside Gemma. "You misinterpreted what I said, Janelle," he lied.

"You commented on my ass," I said. "What is there to misinterpret about that?"

"You've got it all wrong," Rufus said, looking anxious. I wanted to slap him. If Gemma took his side I was going to raise hell until someone took me seriously.

"We're shorthanded tonight," Gemma said after deliberating. "But tomorrow I promise I'll find another staff member to look after you while you fall asleep."

"Could you check on me while Rufus is out there?" I asked.

"I'll swing by every fifteen minutes," she promised. Gemma had a soft, sweet voice that reminded me of a fairy princess and made me feel like she was actually interested in my well-being. The sight of Rufus made me gag, but there was something about her warm way that made me believe that she truly would try and protect me.

Gemma recommended I take sleeping medication, because once I was asleep Rufus would be gone. Med Man, who seemed to work twenty-four hours a day (a possible explanation for the grudge against the universe he seemed to be nursing), returned with a green and white capsule that I washed down with a cup of water that he had probably spit in. I changed out of my pajamas and into two pairs of underwear, a pair of jeans, a bra, and a T-shirt. I wanted some layers of protection in case I woke up with Rufus under my blankets. I rolled onto my side so that I was staring at the wall instead of at Rufus and pretended I was asleep long enough to finally fall asleep.

The next morning, Ebony wasn't around for breakfast or group, but she showed up for lunch. (My request for meat-free meals finally went through, so now I had something to eat. Unfortunately, the food tasted like it had been marinated in room temperature urine for twenty-four hours.) Ebony had been at her hearing. Pretty soon she was going to have lived out the number of days she had been involuntarily committed to the hospital. If the hospital administration wants to keep you in the hospital longer, you have the right to a hearing with mental health professionals, where you plead your case, explaining why you should be checked out. She had already failed two hearings, but she was certain this hearing had gone better than the others and that she would be sprung sometime soon. I told Ebony that she slurred her words and if she didn't pass this hearing, maybe she could take a few less pills before her next hearing and see if she could cut down on the gummed-up words.

"Thanks, but I don't take advice from fellow crazies," she said. "If any of us had the sense we were born with, we wouldn't be in here, would we?"

Leopoldo was angry when I related the hellacious experience I'd had with Rufus the previous evening. Ebony didn't even raise an eyebrow.

"He's a pervert," she said. "But he's harmless."

I didn't think the words pervert and harmless went together.

"He mentioned my booty a few times," Ebony said. "Told Dominga she looked tasty in a camisole. It's just what Rufus does. Get over it." Ebony seemed like a strong person. I couldn't believe she was settling for this kind of treatment. Maybe the hospital had beaten her down so sufficiently that she no longer had a voice. I wasn't going to let that happen to me.

"It's not right. He shouldn't be checking us out or talking about our bodies," I argued. "We're in a hospital, not a strip club."

"It may not be right, but guys can be like that. You need to get into the real world," Ebony snapped. "Here's a dose of reality for you, Janelle: I've been raped. Raped. I bet nothing like that's ever happened to you, has it?"

Since when had being raped become a rite of passage, like taking the training wheels off your bike or getting your first period? I stared at Ebony, shocked.

"What?" Ebony asked. "You've never met somebody who's been raped before? Do they even have rape where you're from?"

Now rape was about diversity?

"And I wouldn't bother complaining about Rufus," Ebony added. "Nobody will believe you because you're supposed to be too lulu to know what's what."

"Just because the world sees us as people who don't deserve rights, doesn't mean we have to. You're only as oppressed as you allow yourself to be," I said.

"And what, exactly, do you know about oppression? A private school white girl from the Westside?" Ebony asked. "I'll tell you what you know—nothing."

"Give her a break," Leopoldo said. "Rufus got into her kitchen and rattled her pots and pans."

"Yah, well she's rattling my pots and pans," Ebony said. She crumpled up her napkin, tossed it on her plate, and stomped off.

It hadn't been my intention to piss off Ebony, and I immediately regretted everything I said to her. I was actually starting to like her and wanted to get to know her better. I hoped she would cool off enough to see the wisdom in my words and come around.

After breakfast, Dominga appeared in the lobby with a scratched-up suitcase. Her mother and grandmother arrived and walked out with her. She disappeared through the glass doors without a good-bye or a wave to anyone. I stared at the doors, sadly wishing they would open for me. The doors were a constant and sobering reminder that it was us against them. But did society think they were protecting us or being protected from us?

# TEN

$\mathcal{M}$Y FAVORITE PART of the day was art therapy, where we worked on crafts projects. The therapy room was filled with pastels, paints, clay, colored pencils and pens, yarn, tissue paper, glue, shellac, shells, clay and beads. Art therapy was the one place where I stopped obsessing about how much I wanted out and stopped devising doomed plans to make it happen. It was the only time of the day where I was able to sit still. During art therapy, it was like somebody pulled the plug on my motor.

The therapist, Miss Brandstein, was kind in a grandmotherly way. She called me dear and marveled at everything I did – even though I wasn't doing anything particularly marvelous. It made me feel warm and fuzzy inside. She played jazz and blues and had cool, colorful paintings hanging on the walls.

Leopoldo and I were sitting together in the art room—deep into beading. I was working on a beaded necklace for Ben, in earth tones to complement his olive complexion. Beading was tricky because my hands shook so badly (nobody was able to tell me why), but it was gratifying to watch the necklace grow longer with each session.

"I wish Ebony could understand what I'm doing," I told Leopoldo. "I'm only trying to help people in here rise to their abilities." It had been a few days since Ebony had gotten angry with me and she was still acting prickly.

"You gotta cut Ebony some slack," Leopoldo said. "She's had it rough. She grew up poor and neglected. She sees a more advantaged white girl and she doesn't think you get it. To her, it's condescending when you tell her how to change her life and stand up for herself when you don't know her world. She likes you, but she thinks you're full of yourself."

"You don't have to be poor to be neglected," I answered. "And I'm not full of myself, and I do get it."

"I know your heart is in the right place and I like you, but you don't know as much as you think you know," Leopoldo countered. "You think you're going to transform the hospital—save everyone in here. But that's not possible. The staff might be creepy and the place is dingy, but they really are trying to help us. We're all here for a reason."

"There you go with victim mode," I said. Leopoldo and I had been growing closer, but it was comments like this that made me wonder if we'd ever get to a place where we were truly in sync.

"It's not victim mode," he said. "It's reality. I've watched you improve since you arrived. When you landed here, you made no sense. You were psychotic. You're on the road to being well, and I don't want you to get shot out of the sky when you're through your episode and you realize that you're not as almighty as you think you are. Your ego is too big for your britches. Classic mania."

A pang of betrayal pierced me in the gut. Leopoldo may have though he was helping me, but it felt more like he'd gone over to the other side and was, along with the rest of them, trying to pour me into the cuckoo box.

Luckily, before Leopoldo was able to expand on his critique of me, Dr. Prateek arrived and asked me to come with him for a checkup. All it took was a quick glance at his face to stir up disturbing images of being shot full of tranquilizers and shackled to a table.

Dr. Prateek ushered me into the nurse's office and flipped through a bulging file. He checked my pulse and blood pressure, listened to my heart and lungs, and told me that he was sorry he hadn't visited me earlier, but he'd been at a seminar in Houston. While he was gone, the nurses had kept him abreast of my condition. Dr. Prateek asked me how I was feeling. "I feel like leaving," I said.

"Besides that," he said. I paused a minute, not knowing exactly how to convey how wired and festive I felt. There was a magazine on the table between us. I leafed through it and showed him a couple photos of the sun and the Northern Lights, to illustrate how bright my brain felt. To describe my energy level, I did some fast-paced jumping jacks.

"Still with the manic energy level . . . Talking fast, moving a lot," he said, taking down notes. "We need to get you sleeping more. You're up to five hours, but I'd like to see you at seven. That's our goal. Bipolar persons need strict sleep schedules."

I explained to Dr. Prateek that I didn't belong in the psych ward. It was possible that I was a little bipolar, but I was smart and stable enough to tend to the condition on my own, and I *certainly* wasn't as far gone as the others in the hospital. I was a visionary and had a streak of genius; there were persons on the outside depending on me to help change their lives.

"Grandiosity still present," he commented, making more notes. What? Like I wasn't grand? I'd spent my whole life thinking everybody was better than me. Now I knew how truly great I was, and he wanted to take that from me? "You'd be surprised how many 'geniuses' we get in here," he said. "Plenty of Jesuses and Mohammeds too—the occasional Allah and even a God or three. It goes with the mania." He sounded like he'd been talking to Leopoldo.

"Well, I'm sorry for those misguided people, but I'm nothing like them. I'd like to take off tonight," I told Dr. Prateek. "I was just voted president of my high school."

"Actually, you've been expelled from school," Dr. Prateek informed me. "You won't be discharged from the hospital for several days."

Expelled? Seriously? How could that be true? What could I have possibly done to get expelled? "I'd like to know on what grounds you people were able to store me here," I demanded.

Dr. Prateek pulled a couple of papers from the file and allowed me to flip through them. "You were initially held here under a 5150," he said. I read the certification paper. There were checks inside the boxes marked "danger to self," "danger to others," and "gravely disabled." Now I was being called "dangerous?" I'd never even killed an insect – literally. I didn't want to ask what I'd done that had endangered anyone. It was all too horrifying. For a moment, I was actually *glad* my memory was shot.

He explained that a 5150 is where a person who is established as being seriously mentally ill is hospitalized against their will for seventy-two hours. "Then what the heck am I still doing here?" I asked. "It's been well over seventy-two hours."

Dr. Prateek pulled out another paper. "You are now here under a 5250," he said. "An involuntary hold for up to fourteen days." He explained that after the seventy-two hours were up, I was still manic and delusional enough for he and my family to have me detained at the hospital for longer.

"How much longer?" I asked.

"Until you are well," Dr. Prateek answered. This was highly distressing news. There was no release day yet set for me. I was stuck in this hellhole for the foreseeable future. "I know you don't like it here, but this is where you can be safe and nursed back to health."

"I don't feel like I'm being nursed to health. I feel like I'm being warehoused," I grumbled. "I don't fit in here."

"I'm sorry you feel that way, but you do fit in here," Dr. Prateek said. "You're not better than the other patients."

"I don't think I'm better than them," I said. "I just don't think I'm sick like they are... Whatever. If I'm not going to be discharged, then I would like to go on an outing. Maybe a walk or lunch at a café?"

"Not yet," he answered. "Level Two, upstairs, the patients have more freedom. Level One is like intensive care for your brain. Eventually I'll be able to move you upstairs."

I demonstrated for Dr. Prateek my trembling hands and a rash that had erupted on my back a few days earlier and asked what he could do for them.

"They're side effects of the lithium you are on," he said.

"Then I need to get off lithium," I said. "It's making eating and beading and writing too hard. It's tough to even zip my jeans. And the rash is itchy."

"Lithium is the gold standard for mania—and bipolar disorder in general. It's a mood stabilizer that's been used for decades. Nothing will even you out faster," he said, adding that I might just be on lithium for the rest of my life. (I guess, if he had it his way, I'd have to chuck those dreams of a career as a vascular surgeon or an embroiderer.) Dr. Prateek informed me that I was on two other drugs, whose names sounded like tub and tile cleansers, and said he'd prescribe a cream for my rash.

Before Dr. Prateek left, I asked him why I couldn't remember my first few days in the hospital and why even the past few weeks were so fuzzy. "Dissociative amnesia," he answered. "After a trauma like you've been through, it's not uncommon to be unable to remember the details. It's like your brain is protecting itself from memories that might disturb you." What disturbing things had happened that I couldn't remember?

I hoped and hoped that nothing disturbing had happened between Ben and me.

I was ticked off when I discovered that my too-long visit with Dr. Prateek had eaten into my treasured outdoor time. Outdoor time was already too brief. When I reached the blacktop, Ebony was listening to music and dancing, Skinhead was smoking, and Paul was playing tag with the others. I was surprised they weren't playing pin the tail on the donkey—without the pin.

I took a few laps and then ran to Ebony and told her that I didn't like fighting with her and asked her if we could be friends. "Shut up and dance with me," she answered, seeming much warmer than she had been lately. Maybe Leopoldo had intervened on my behalf and had a talk with her.

"I'm sorry I insulted you," I told Ebony. "I was just trying to be helpful."

"It's okay," she said. "But, please stop being helpful. You know nothing about my life and what would help me."

"Well, then maybe you could tell me about your life," I said. "Maybe even tell me how you got here."

"I got here because I was really depressed," she answered. "Something you wouldn't know anything about, since according to you there's nothing wrong with you."

"I know about depression," I said. "A month ago, I could barely get out of bed." I hadn't thought about my depression in weeks. Those feelings of deep unhappiness were so foreign to me now. I couldn't access anything remotely related to depression.

"Wow, little Miss 'I Have No Mental Problems' admits to depression," she said. "Maybe you're coming out of denial."

"What's that supposed to mean?" I asked.

"It means that you might be ready to drop the act and admit that you need help like the rest of us," she said.

"Let's just dance and talk about all that later," I said. I was burnt out on defending my sanity after my visit with Dr. Prateek. It would be so easy to just give in and agree with everyone that I was a mental case. I could admit defeat and offer my brain up to be deemed flawed. It's what everybody seemed to want me to do. But, that would just leave me back where I'd always been – thinking there was something wrong with me and that everyone was better than me. I didn't want to go back to that place.

As Ebony and I danced, I studied the depressing outdoor yard. If I wasn't going to be able to break out of this wasteland, maybe I could at least improve the conditions—for everyone.

When Paul blew his whistle, I still had enough energy in me to power an urban sprawl. I begged to stay outside, but he wasn't having any of it. "When you're not so manic, outdoor time will feel long enough," he promised. If I heard the word "manic" one more time, I was going to scream.

"I have a brilliant plan for the outdoor yard," I told Paul. "And we patients could do all the labor, which would keep costs down and give us good exercise." My plan was to excavate the asphalt and plant a lawn, trees, and bright-colored flowers in its place. "Can you imagine how much less gloomy your suicidal patients would be if they could look out at something beautiful?" I asked.

"I'll think about that," Paul told me, with the enthusiasm of a person who has just been given a pot holder for Christmas.

As visiting hour approached, I tried not to get my hopes up that someone would come to see me. At four on the dot, I took a seat in the back of the visitors' lounge and faked reading a magazine so that I wouldn't look as desperate as I was to see friend or family. Reggie's mother and sister arrived at four-ten, and Ebony squealed with delight when Anton showed up. He didn't stay long, but she was glowing the rest of the night.

By four-twenty, it wasn't looking good for me. I was about to leave for my room and drown my sorrows (and burn off my energy) in handstands and push-ups when I heard "Jane!" from the other side of the room. Maya ran to me and hugged me tightly. I was so happy to see her and know she hadn't forgotten about me and to finally have a visitor. But, right away I could sense a divide between us that had never been there before. She had helped commit me. It was hard not to see her as something of a traitor.

We sat at a table, and she opened a giant shopping bag and began handing me things: bottles of vitamin water and peach iced tea, a bag of cookies, magazines, a couple books, stationary, sweatpants, more jeans, a sweatshirt and more and more...

"Thanks for visiting me," I told her. "I'm sure it's hard coming here and trying to understand the new me. Well, actually, the me that I was all along but was too scared to be."

"We can talk about all that when you get home," Maya said dismissively. Clearly, she hadn't come around yet and accepted who I'd become. Hopefully, she'd see the light once I was home and she'd spent some quality time with me. Maya rummaged around in her purse and pulled out photos of the dogs, photos of her and me skiing, and some pix of my friends. She studied my face for a second. "This place is agreeing with you, I can tell. How's it going?"

"Great if you like being locked in a dungeon," I answered.

"As soon as you're better, I promise I'll get you out," she said. "Right now, this is where you belong. Trust me. You need the care and attention of hospital employees."

"I'm already better because there never was anything wrong with me. And what care and attention are you referring to?" I asked.

"All the group therapy and classes on dealing with your emotions," she said. "The medication education, the one-on-one counseling, the bodywork and exercises. It actually sounds kinda nice here. Like a spa."

"A spa?" I asked. "Look around. Does this place look at all like a spa to you?"

"It's a little rundown, but your room is nice, isn't it?" she asked. "I heard you got your own private room in the suite."

"The only positive thing I can say about my room is that it doesn't have rats," I answered. "Or cockroaches—or maybe I just haven't seen any. Where'd you get all the misinformation about this dump?"

Maya pulled an envelope from her purse and handed it to me. Inside was a folder that resembled a travel brochure, with a picture of a colorful garden with a waterfall on the front and the words "Welcome to St. Joan's Hospital Psychiatric Unit—Where Healing Happens."

According to the brochure, filled with photos of smiling nurses and good-looking doctors, I was in a facility designed and maintained to create "optimal mental health for all our patients." Apparently, we were being looked after by committed medical experts with training in all aspects of psychiatry. We were staying in comfortable, well-appointed rooms and enjoying customized meals, counseling on a variety of subjects, and classes on goal setting, stress management, time structuring, and interpersonal relationships. The fibs continued. Each of us was receiving the highest quality care available—tailored to our specific needs. (I must have been in great need of the cold shoulder.)

The roof yard was described as "a sun-drenched terrace where games are played and fresh air is abundant," and the accompanying photo was of a view of trees from the ledge of the yard—a ledge that was too high for us to see over. Whoo hoo! I was at the Four Seasons Flew Over the Cuckoo's Nest.

Included in the folder was a list of restaurants that delivered takeout to the hospital should guests get hungry while they were visiting our palace—like anybody stayed in the visitors' lounge long enough to eat a meal, let alone wait for one to be delivered. I handed Maya back her folder. I considered telling her that it was filled with pages of lies, but she probably wouldn't believe me. I was also considering telling her about my mom and Brookside Assisted Living, but she'd probably think it was some manic delusion. I didn't get the feeling that Maya was on Team Jane, and that hurt. But, there wasn't time for her to hear me out, so I'd have to leave it for now.

"Are you aware that my own mother hasn't come to see me?" I asked.

"She said it would be too upsetting for her," Maya admitted. "She said that besides Dad dying, this is the most difficult thing she's ever experienced."

"She's experienced?" I said. "But, this isn't her experience. It's mine."

"You know Mom. It's always all about her," Maya said. "Anyway, you don't want her here. She wouldn't be any help."

"What about Nell and Tiffany?" I asked. "Are they going to visit?"

"I just told them yesterday where you are," Maya answered. "Mom is spreading the word that you are in the hospital for a kidney problem and that the doctors don't want anyone disturbing you. I figured that your two best friends were entitled to the truth."

"Does it sound better to have kidney failure than it does to be in a psych ward?"

"She claims she's saving you from embarrassment," Maya said. "I know. I know. She's weak."

"What about the other kids at school? Or my crewmates? What do they know?" I asked. Maya didn't know.

Maya, who excelled in the field of guilt, spent the next hour empathizing and sympathizing and apologizing. It didn't mean as much to me as she probably thought it did. If she hadn't helped stick me in the hospital then she wouldn't have had so much rectifying to do.

When time was up, she handed me a Ziploc bag filled with quarters. "Please only call me, Mom, Nell or Tiffany—and be courteous," she instructed. "And no late night or early morning calls."

"You got it," I answered as Maya stood to leave.

Maya was still visible in the hallway beyond the glass doors when Jude, my alternate nurse, grabbed the bag of goodies that Maya had delivered and dumped the contents onto the table. Ever since I had commented on the large, red birthmark that covered half of Jude's face, she had been curt with me and displayed resentment at even the most modest requests—like where to find detergent for the washing machine or if we could turn down the air conditioning. And I hadn't even said anything creepy about her wine stain. I had complimented her, saying that the splash of color brightened her face and that it set her apart from evenly complexioned people. She misinterpreted what I said and told me that I needed to show more respect to the staff.

Jude sifted through my supplies. I was allowed to store only one bottle of iced tea and one bottle of vitamin water in the cafeteria refrigerator because other patients needed room to stash their perishables and cold drinks. (Never mind that the refrigerator was empty, save a moldy tub of yogurt.) She confiscated a Lakers T-shirt that she explained could antagonize people who might not be fans of the team and set aside more than half of the other clothes in the bag because "We don't want to make others jealous that you have more than they do."

"What if I share?" I asked, but Jude was too busy taking away nail polish and hair spray (both poisonous if drunk) and the two belts that were strangulation hazards. She left me with two dollars in quarters and reminded me of the eight-minute limit on phone calls.

That night, Leopoldo asked me if I wanted to watch TV with him, and for the first time I said "yes." I had stayed away from TV because I knew it would be hard to sit still for the duration of an entire show, but I was feeling a little less antsy, so I decided to give it a try. Unfortunately, the group voted to watch some dopey reality show that Leopoldo and I weren't interested in, so we just sat and talked quietly instead.

While Leopoldo gave me a world-class back massage, he described his far-from-perfect childhood and said that he had early-onset bipolar that had its unveiling when he was only eleven. He had thought he wanted to be a teacher when he was younger, but he'd chucked that idea, since he didn't think he could hack college. "I can't trust my mind to get through all that schooling," he said. His current plan, once he'd graduated high school, was to work for FedEx because they had good benefits and he liked the Zen of lifting things and moving them to another place and then looking back at the empty place where the object had previously been. I told him not to waste his whole life ruining his back. "Aim for what you really want," I said. "You don't have to rely on your mind. It's your mind that relies on you. Tell that brain to buckle down because you're going to college to become a teacher."

"It's not that easy," Leopoldo said.

"It isn't easy if you listen to the quacks who work here," I said. "They think they're going to break my spirit and drive my plans off the rails, but they won't."

Leopoldo again urged me to start accepting the fact that I was in the hospital for medical reasons. There was no conspiracy against me, no teen revolution that I was leading, and although he found me intelligent, I most likely wasn't a genius. He'd seen me with Maya at visitors' hour and told me that he'd talked to her the last time she visited. He wanted me to let go of my resentments toward Maya and try and understand that her helping to put me in the hospital came from a place of love and caring and was the best thing she could have done for me.

The last time Leopoldo had talked like this, I'd felt mildly betrayed, but this time I felt like I'd been kicked in the teeth. Maybe it was because I had just seen Maya and been reminded of how she betrayed me and had earlier listened to Ebony accuse me of being in denial. It was coming at me from all sides. My jaw clenched and my throat constricted as he continued, telling me that while I might be able to make some positive adjustments to my school, it was highly questionable that I'd be able to make the reforms I dreamed were possible—particularly where classes and the curriculum were concerned. He even said that some of my notions sounded a little . . . silly and "off the coast of Pluto." And, unlike me, he didn't think school was the devil and that kids weren't learning useful things, although he did agree that the social hierarchy at my school sounded like a drag. But he said that the social scene at most schools was a drag because lots of teenagers are a drag in general. Then he reiterated how the hospital wasn't the devil either.

I started grinding my teeth, feeling anxious. What did he know about anything? I wanted to tell him to shut up, but the look on his face was so sincere. "I've been where you are, Janelle. I know the syndrome. I know how intensely real and true it all seems, but it's not. You wouldn't still be listening to me if you really believed I was wrong. You're starting to get it—a little more everyday."

It had been a long day of people lecturing me and my stamina was wearing thin. For the first time, I caught myself doubting that I was really as powerful as I thought I was. I felt like I was selling myself short, but I was having a hard time formulating a rebuttal to Leopoldo's analysis of me. Over the past couple days, my brain had been slowing down. I wasn't as sharp as I'd been. I missed the boundless energy and racing thoughts. Where had they gone? Was the medicine stealing them from me? I didn't want to see myself through Leopoldo's eyes, but I had to admit that lately, when I thought about some of the stuff I'd done before the hospital (what I could remember, anyway), portions of it did not make sense. Why had I bought all the white socks in the sporting goods store? Who had I thought I was, cutting a dreadlock from a stranger's head? Was it even possible to learn about the future—like I'd suggested the students at my school do? Was I seriously mentally ill like everybody said?

"Don't tackle it all at once," Leopoldo urged. "Just little by little open up to it."

Next morning, Paul was off and Jude was in charge of group therapy. "We'll go around the circle and each of you will share with the group what makes you smile," she instructed. It was an odd request coming from Jude, whom I hadn't seen smile once.

Reggie said that his bat collection made him smile. Skinhead said he'd smile the day he could judge the living and the dead. Joel just laughed. I wanted to say that the vision of Jude and Autumn being fired made me smile, but instead I said that the thought of Ben made me smile. Ebony said that her baby Imani made her smile. Wait. What? Ebony had a baby? And she hadn't told me?

"How could you keep you being a mom from me?" I asked Ebony when group was over. She led me down the hallway of the girls' wing and into her room and shut the door.

"Listen," she said. "I haven't even known you for two weeks, and I wasn't sure I liked you until recently. It's something private. I don't even know why I shared it at all today."

"So, you and Anton have a baby together? Why wouldn't you want to tell me about it?" I asked. "You're so wild for him. Aren't you proud? Thrilled?"

Ebony agreed to tell me the story of Imani, but only if I turned away from her because she was too ashamed to recount it face-to-face. Imani wasn't planned, but she was wanted, and the day of Imani's delivery was the best day of Ebony's life. The day after her delivery was one of the worst days of Ebony's life, and each day after that was even worse, as Ebony sunk into postpartum depression that left her barely able to feed Imani a bottle. It got so bad that Ebony decided that Imani would be better off without her, and she left her baby alone, in her crib, and went to the drugstore, where she bought bottles of different over-the-counter drugs and downed them. Somebody found her in the parking lot, barely alive. Ebony was sent to St. Joan's and her grandmother moved in with Anton to help with the baby, since he worked long hours. She had been slowly crawling her way out of the blackness for weeks now.

The story brought tears to my eyes. I realized that Ebony had suffered even more than I had when I was depressed. She'd actually tried to kill herself. The fact that she had admitted her plight to me made me feel like we'd busted down a barrier. There was a closeness growing between us that I'd never experienced before. Nobody had ever shared something so deeply personal and difficult with me. It was like peeking inside someone's soul. I wanted to share something deep with her, but words wouldn't come.

I flipped around and hugged Ebony. "You have nothing to be ashamed of. One day Imani will be so proud of her brave, strong mother."

"Thank God nothing happened to Imani," Ebony said, tears dribbling from her eyes. "Thank God Anton stood by me. I got so lucky when I met him."

"And he got even luckier when he met you," I said. "I hope someday I can be together with Ben, the way you are with Anton," I told her. "I hope whatever was starting up between us isn't all being ruined by my having to be away like this."

"If he's the right guy, he'll wait," she promised. "And he'll understand. Like Anton."

I hugged Ebony again and we both cried. I wasn't sure what I was crying about – maybe being stuck in the hospital, maybe remembering how depressed I'd been, maybe the sadness over being, basically, parentless for so many years. Whatever it was, I cried and cried with her as we hugged each other tighter.

I arrived in the crafts room early. I wanted to finish my necklace so that I could start in on another present for Ben and maybe something for Leopoldo. Considering how badly my hands were shaking, it was amazing I was almost finished with the necklace. "Mind if I try it on you for size?" I asked Leopoldo when he arrived. He bent his head and I wrapped the necklace around his neck. Just a few more beads and the necklace would be the perfect size. I slipped it off Leopoldo, who was crocheting a hat for his sister, and got back to the business of beading.

I'd probably have to wait until I got out to give the necklace to Ben, unless I could talk Tiffany or Nell into delivering it to him—if they ever visited. I'd show up at Ben's door with the necklace—maybe at night to make it more romantic—and gently clasp it around his neck. I shut my eyes and pictured the necklace around Ben's neck. I saw him in his room, sitting on his bed with the necklace dangling over his bare chest. Then I started travelling back. His arms were wrapped around me, and we were laughing about something and he squeezed my hand. Then we were lying down together and I had goose bumps and . . .

"Earth to Janelle. Earth to Janelle," Leopoldo said.

I opened my eyes. "Were you in Ben land?" he asked. He'd seen me several times daydreaming about Ben.

"Affirmative," I said, wanting to add, "And I still would be, if you hadn't interrupted me when I was just about to remember juicier details of our night together."

"I'm not saying this to be mean or freak you out, but I don't want you setting yourself up for heartbreak," he said. There he went again with the disappointment angle. "It's happened to me and I've seen it in other people when they cycle. Sometimes, during the madness, you create a relationship in your head that is a bigger deal than it is in reality. Please don't put all your eggs in his basket—especially since you remember only part of your night together."

Always with the pessimism. He and Nell would do great together. He put doubts in my head about being a genius and starting a revolution.

And now, because of him, I was "opening up" to the idea that I was mentally ill, which wasn't fun. But he wasn't taking Ben from me. The excitement of seeing Ben when I was discharged was the only thing that was making the hospital bearable. Before I was able to give Leopoldo a proper retort, Skinhead jumped up and started projectiling paper and pens and glue around the room, screaming, "You're all going to hell. All you dirty, evil people will be burnt up!" along with some choice four letter words—including the f-bomb.

I dropped from my chair and hid under the table. Quickly, Manuel and Alberto were at the table and pinned Skinhead's arms behind his back. As they dragged him away, Jude raced up. "This is why you can't go up to Level Two where Jesus wants you to go," she told Skinhead. "You must be able to behave better."

Skinhead had been gone for over ten minutes before Leopoldo was able to coax me out from under the table. I was quivering when I sat back down, making beading nearly impossible.

I was still trembling when we rose from the table to leave. Miss Brandstein noticed how badly I was shaking and pulled me aside. "I hope you aren't going to judge him for what he did," she said. "Caleb is schizophrenic and the doctors are having a hard time stabilizing him. The poor kid is in very bad shape." She bit her lip, her eyes misty. "With the proper treatment, the rest of you should be able to enjoy normal lives—at least much of the time. He will always have it rough." Miss Brandstein told me that Caleb had been in the hospital before and that he was actually a sweet guy underneath it all – not the angry racist one would expect from how he looked and acted.

I felt guilty that I'd judged Skinhead so harshly without knowing anything about him. I had thought he was lazy, sleeping all day on the couch, and that he was a white supremacist, undeserving of sympathy. I guess it bothered me to be around somebody so ill, because if I belonged in the trenches with him then that meant that there was something seriously wrong with me, too – and that wasn't a pleasant thought.

At visiting time, I was surprised by both Tiffany and Nell. Tiffany, all smiles, immediately took a shine to the unit. "OMG! I've never been in a mental institute before," she said. She wore a fascinated expression as she took in the surroundings—like she had just arrived on an exotic tropical island inhabited by endangered species. She wanted to know my exact routine and what illness each patient suffered from.

"Check out the dude at eleven o'clock!" she said, smiling across the room at Reggie. "I'd let him help me with my homework."

"He thinks he's part vampire," I told her.

"Excellent," she said. "You couldn't make this stuff up."

Nell's eyes filled with tears. "I've never been anywhere so heart-breaking and grim in my whole life," she said. "I'm beyond sorry that it came to this. I wish I could have helped you. I feel guilty all day, everyday."

"We both feel so bad," Tiffany said. "I mean, I knew something was way off with you, but I didn't realize you were truly sick. We didn't have your back. Can you forgive us?"

"Apologies accepted," I said. "But please stop talking to me like I'm in a cancer ward. I might be sick, but I'm not *all* that sick. I might just be a little . . . bipolar. It's not that big a deal."

"Sometimes I feel like I belong here," Nell continued. "I get it. Life is hard. It's one big struggle and then you die of some horrible disease."

"Stop it," Tiffany said. "You're going to bum out Jane. Anyway, I bet this place beats school. You're so lucky you got out of finals, Jane."

"Don't be a moron," Nell said. "She's not getting out of finals. She'll have to finish her classes next school year and take the finals."

"I will?" I asked.

"Of course," Nell said. "How else would you graduate high school?"

Up until now I had assumed I'd just take a few tests I'd missed (which I'd ace) when I got out of the hospital and continue with business as usual at West Hills (after they realized their mistake in expelling me and readmitted me.)

"You really know how to be a downer, Nell. At least Jane doesn't have to go back to West Hills—though I'm gonna miss you," Tiffany said. "I wish I were going to a different school next year."

"I still can't believe they expelled me after I was elected student body president," I said. "But I think they'll change their mind when fall rolls around."

"You weren't elected president," Nell said. "Principal Hodge had you removed from the running."

"I didn't hear your speech, but there are some kids who said it was awesome," Tiffany said.

"There are many others who would disagree," Nell said. From the pained look on her face, I guessed that Nell wouldn't have voted for me if I'd been on the ballot.

"Have my crewmates asked after me?" I asked. "I was just about to take over the stroke seat when they trapped me in here."

"Only thing I heard about crew is that you were kicked off the team," Nell said.

The world outside was sounding so harsh and judgmental – more than even the hospital. Was I going to have to move to a different country – or a different planet – to be understood?

"Subject change," Tiffany said. "Tal has started getting food from the CEA and bringing it to the Atrium. I haven't made my move yet, but I will as soon as my bangs grow out and my forehead doesn't look so vast. And Zeke is making Stella nuts because he's been parking in her space."

"That's great! I'm glad that what I started didn't come to a screeching halt," I said. "What about Ben? Did you tell him where I was? Has he asked after me?"

Tiffany and Nell glanced nervously at one another. "Uhm, not so much," Tiffany said. "We didn't know what you'd want us to say. So, we've kind of left that alone and kind of . . . not really talked to him."

"Oh . . . Well . . ." I stammered, feeling disappointed. Why hadn't Ben approached them? "I've got something I need you to deliver for me." I scurried to the art room and got Ben's necklace from Miss Brandstein. I returned to the lounge and handed it to Nell.

"That's a necklace for Ben," I said. "If you could slip it to him, that would be great."

"I don't get it," Nell said, waving the necklace. "Why are you sending Ben a necklace? You haven't even dated, have you?"

"There isn't time for me to get into the whole deal, but . . . we've started up something," I said. "It's only been one night so far. I don't remember all the details, but I know it was a really intense night. Trust me when I say that he's into me."

"One night does not make a relationship," Nell said.

Tiffany snatched the necklace from Nell's hand and shoved it into her bag. "I'll take care of it." She turned to Nell. "Will you cut it out with the negativity?"

"Okay. You're right. I'm sorry. I've got a good one to lighten things up," Nell said. "Would you rather eat a bar of soap or drink a bottle of dishwashing liquid?"

"That's not lightening up anything. That's gross. I've got the perfect thing to brighten the mood," Tiffany chirped. She dipped into her purse and pulled out six airline-sized bottles of vodka. "Thought we could have our own private party. Two bottles each."

"What have you been smoking?" Nell asked her. "She can't have alcohol. They're trying to fix her brain, not sauté it in cocktails."

"Sorry, I thought it would be fun," she told Nell. "Have you ever heard of fun? F-U-N?"

"Get those back in your purse," I told Tiffany. "They don't allow booze here." But it was too late.

Jude appeared and scooped up the tiny bottles. "I'm going to have to ask you two to leave. No alcoholic beverages are allowed in the unit. It's against hospital policy."

Nell gave Tiffany a tongue-lashing as they got up to leave. "They won't be permitted to return," Jude told me as she marched away with the vodka, which I hoped she'd drink. Maybe it would improve her bitter state of mind.

I watched Nell and Tiffany as they moved through the glass doors and disappeared down the hallway. I was happy that they'd visited, but I felt like I was living in an alternate universe from theirs. They had no idea what it was like to be in a psychiatric ward. No idea what it was like to go through what I was going through. Two weeks ago, I'd never met anyone remotely similar to the kids at the hospital. Now I felt closer to Ebony and Leopoldo than I did to my best friends since third grade. We were sharing an experience that wasn't enjoyable, but it was real and bonding in a way that gossiping and going to parties and doing homework together wasn't.

# ELEVEN

HE NEXT DAY, a dark-haired girl with a sunburned face and an outfit that hugged her every curve and dimple was wheeled into the unit, and Joel was discharged. His exit surprised me because I hadn't noticed that he'd progressed or changed a smidgen from the time I'd entered the hospital. But I was glad to see him depart. His laugh was grating and he stunk up every room he entered with his chronic gas.

After the medication line and nurse visit, Paul pulled Ebony and me aside. "I want you two to give our new patient, Yasmine, as much space as you can today," he said. "When you go back in the wing, don't try to engage her in conversation or enter her room. She's had a long couple days."

Effie buzzed Ebony and me into the girls' wing, and I could hear Yasmine from the end of the hall. "I need somewhere to put my flat screen TV and stereo when they're delivered this afternoon," she boomed. "A table or a console."

Ebony and I crept down the hall to spy on Yasmine, who had moved her mattress across her room and was sliding her bedside table next to it while Autumn supervised. "And I'd like somebody to bring me a mocha," Yasmine said.

"We don't have room service or designer coffee drinks," Autumn said. "It's outdoor time in five minutes. I'd like you to change into your scrubs and get out to the rooftop yard."

Ebony and I fled to our rooms to change for exercise before Autumn caught us spying.

Yasmine arrived on the blacktop wearing her scrubs. She ran up alongside me while I jogged. I still had the energy to run for the whole forty-five minutes of outdoor time, but I wasn't moving as fast as I had been, and now when the break was up I was plenty ready to head inside.

"Do you have some clothes I can borrow?" Yasmine asked. "I only have the one change of clothes I came here wearing, and these scrubs aren't my style. Three people could fit inside here."

"You can try some of my clothes," I said. "But I think we have different body types." That was my polite way of telling her that my clothes would never fit her. She was at least thirty pounds heavier than I was.

"I like tight clothes," she said.

At free time, Yasmine followed me into my room, pulled off her scrubs, and headed to my closet. Without asking permission, she plucked my jeans and T-shirts off the shelves and tried them on—or, more accurately, attempted to try them on. She couldn't yank the tops over her chest or zip the jeans. She left my discarded clothes on the floor and told me that I needed to pack on a few pounds for curves. "You have the body of a boy."

Yasmine left my room and flagged down Autumn. "I need scissors and a needle and thread," she told Autumn. "These scrubs are huge. I can't see my own body. I need to make them smaller."

"Scissors and needles aren't allowed," Autumn informed her. "And you can't alter the hospital clothes."

Yasmine stepped back into my room. "I need help moving the big table in the hallway into my room. My TV and stereo are being delivered later this afternoon and there's nowhere to place them."

"There's no point to bringing electronics in here," I told her. "There aren't any electrical outlets in the rooms. They're suicide hazards."

"We'll see about that," she said. "C'mon."

I followed her down the hall to her room, where she searched the floor and walls for an outlet. "There are wires behind these walls," she said. "I'll punch a hole and tap into them. They can't stop me." She started pounding on the walls with her fists. "Help me with this and I'll get them to release you when I leave. They won't get away with keeping me here for long."

For courtesy's sake, I tapped on the wall a few times, but I knew that what Yasmine was doing was futile. Watching her was making me feel prickly and nervous. There were lots of things that the kids in the hospital had said and done that struck me as loony, but nobody until now had struck me as totally bughouse—not even Caleb when he yelled about

Satan. Nobody's brand of nuttiness had made me this uncomfortable. She reminded me of something or someone, but I couldn't put my finger on what or who it was.

Luckily, I soon had an excuse to exit Yasmine's room. Autumn returned and told Yasmine to leave the wall alone. Then she told me that she needed to speak to Yasmine privately and ordered me to leave.

The rest of the day followed the predictable routine. At dinner, Yasmine sat with Ebony, Leopoldo, and me. She polished each piece of "filthy silverware" before she used it. After three bites of food, she dropped her fork onto her plate. "This meal tastes worse than sperm. I'm getting something else." She lifted her tray and stood up from the table.

"Don't bother going to the counter," I told her. "The guy back there won't give you another meal."

"Why can't he give me what you have?" she asked. "You're eating something different. Maybe it's better."

"I requested the vegetarian meal plan," I told her. "You have to tell your nurse you want a different meal plan. They won't change your food without a formal request—something in writing. They're hard-ass about it. And the vegetarian food is just as bad as the regular food."

Reluctantly, Yasmine sat back in her chair and picked at her dinner. "I guess I'll be on a diet while I'm here," she said. "If I lose some weight in my thighs, this visit won't be a total bust." Yasmine looked up from her tray and eyed Ebony's food. "Can I try your French onion soup?" Ebony slid the bowl to Yasmine, who started slurping it down.

"Quit it," Ebony said. "You're eating all my soup."

"Don't worry about it," Yasmine said. "I'll buy you Paris. You'll eat all the French onion soup you like." She slid the nearly empty soup bowl back to Ebony and then picked up my oatmeal raisin cookie. "Do you mind?"

"All yours," I said.

Gemma approached the table and instructed Yasmine to put down the cookie. "You're not supposed to be eating sweets," she said. "You have borderline diabetes."

"Oh, really?" Yasmine said. She smiled, waved the cookie at Gemma, and then gobbled it down in three big bites.

"Fine. It's your health," Gemma said.

"It sure is my health," Yasmine said as Gemma turned and stomped off.

I was secretly happy with the way Yasmine was treating the staff because I now had somebody under me on the lower-archy. Yasmine had been in the unit barely a day and she had already pissed off a long list of people. Nobody seemed to like her—not even Miss Brandstein.

Yasmine turned to me. "The brain-donor doctors and nurses in this Laughing Academy claim I have a busload of things wrong with me," she said. "I don't have diabetes. I'm not manic. The only thing wrong with me is my thyroid. Sometimes it gets overactive and hypes me up."

Yasmine asked Ebony and me why we were in the hospital. I had dropped the genius revolutionary rap—my new reason for being locked up was that I was a little bit bipolar and had been a little manic. It was getting easier to admit to my diagnosis, though I still wasn't enjoying verbalizing it, and part of me wasn't there in terms of believing it.

Yasmine, according to her, was at St. Joan's because of the unjust and pig-headed police force. Here goes her story: "My boyfriend, Boris, and I were heading to Vegas. I was driving his Mustang—superfast because I love to go fast, almost a hundred miles an hour. Boris wigged out because I was way over the speed limit and he didn't think it was safe. He was acting like a grandpa and throwing a wet blanket over my fun. So, I dropped him off in the center median and sped off for Vegas."

Then, to make a long story short, Yasmine was pulled over by the police for reckless driving and speeding—and they had witnessed her abandoning Boris on the freeway. She got into a "little tussle" with the cops and tried to run away and resisted arrest. They cuffed her and carted her off in the patrol car, but they didn't drop her at the station. They brought her to the hospital. "I'm going to sue the police force," she said. "They stole my romantic weekend with Boris." It wasn't clear how she was going to spend a romantic weekend with Boris when he was standing in the middle of the freeway waiting to be run over.

Once Yasmine started talking, she didn't shut up. We heard about the Porsche she was going to buy when she got out, how she was an Olympic-caliber volleyball player, how two famous heartthrob actors (their names couldn't be divulged) had asked her out, and how she was a genius even though she only used fifty percent of her mind. "Imagine how smart I'd be if I used my whole brain," she said. If that meant she would talk more than she already did, then I was all for her keeping a lid on her smarts.

As we finished dinner, Skinhead walked past our table. "Look at that disgusting guy," Yasmine growled.

"He's schizophrenic," I told her.

"He's a sicko," she said. "I'm Persian. He'd assassinate me if he could." She stuck her spoon in Ebony's pudding, scooped up a healthy dose of the creamy dessert, and popped up from the table. She rushed to Skinhead and overturned the pudding onto his head. He turned around and stared at Yasmine, dazed and speechless as pudding ran down his face.

"To hell with you and your prejudices," Yasmine said.

Ebony raced to Skinhead with a napkin and wiped the pudding from his face. "That's not okay," she told Yasmine. "You can't do that to him. You can't dump food on his head."

"Why are you defending him?" Yasmine asked. "He doesn't even like you. He's a white man who hates anyone who isn't white. If you haven't noticed, you're black. He'd go KKK on you if he got the chance."

"Don't talk about him like that. It isn't right," Ebony said. "He is my brother—and your brother. He's ill like us. Don't you get it? We're the same. All of us here. We're a group."

"If you want to stick up for an evil white supremacist, that's your problem," Yasmine said as she left the cafeteria. "I'm not a part of any group but the group called Yasmine. You people are not me."

I watched Ebony as she dipped a napkin in a glass of water and gently wiped the remains of the pudding from Caleb's neck and the dabs of it that were on his clothes. "It's okay now," she told him in a soft, assuring voice.

"We really are the same—all of us here—aren't we? We're a group," I whispered to Ebony as she sat back down next to me. She nodded her head. "That was out of line, what Yasmine did," I said.

"Take a good, long look at Yasmine, girl," Ebony said. "That's how far you've come in less than two weeks. You're a nicer person than Yasmine, so you weren't obnoxious in a mean way, like she is, but you were for sure in the same place."

I could hear Yasmine shouting at someone in the lobby and I got that prickly feeling all over again. Was that who Yasmine reminded me of? Myself?

"It's true, isn't it. I'm bipolar. I was manic—even psychotic." I couldn't believe I was uttering the words.

"Yes, but you're the one who said it—just because we're ill doesn't mean we're less than. I'm starting to think I might not be as worthless and broken as I thought. Maybe I have you to thank for that." Ebony smiled and squeezed my hand. "Keep going, girl. You're getting there."

She was right. I was getting there – thought I didn't know where exactly. There was a shift going on inside. It was like my brain had started rotating in a different direction. It was a little scary, since I didn't know where it would stop, but I couldn't resist it. Whatever they were doing to me in the hospital was slowly changing me.

# TWELVE

HE NEXT MORNING, I awoke early from a dream about Ben. In the dream, we were having some kind of conflict, but there were no words. There were anger and outrage in his eyes. I shoved him away. He didn't shove me back. I ran—out of his room, down the stairs, out the front door, down the walkway, and to my car. The dream left me with the heavy, remorseful feeling you get after a fight with somebody you care about.

I squeezed my eyes shut and there was his face again—his eyes wide, his mouth hanging open, his brows furrowed and creased. He looked sad, mad, and so bewildered. He stepped aside and mouthed some words I couldn't hear. I tried desperately to rewind further—before the outraged face, before the shove. But my brain wouldn't let me back up an inch further. Had we had an argument? About what? Or was it just a bad dream?

I was quiet all morning, haunted by the scene in my dream. I was worried that maybe I'd somehow taken a sledgehammer to the budding romance between Ben and me. Also, I was downbeat because Leopoldo was being discharged in the afternoon. I was waiting for him to pack up so that I could talk to him about Ben and my dream, when his mother and sister appeared in the lobby. I was bummed. They weren't supposed to arrive until three. They were taking Leopoldo away from me two-and-a-half hours early. I ran to the art therapy room and retrieved the crocheted keychain I'd made for him.

"All that work was for me?" he asked, beaming as I dropped it in his palm. "I thought the keychain was for Ben."

He wrapped his arms around me and squeezed me tightly, not letting go. "Are we gonna stay in touch?" he asked. "Be friends?"

"I've got your e-mail address and phone number in my room," I said.

Leopoldo kissed me on the cheek. "You're doing good, Janelle. Just keep leaning into the truth about your disorder."

"And you remember not to sell yourself short," I told him. "You're smart and you can do anything you set your mind to. Go back to school and start studying to be a teacher."

Leopoldo turned away from me, picked up his bags, and followed his mom and sister through the glass doors into freedom. I choked up watching him go and thought about how bizarre it was that I was already badly missing someone I'd known for such a short time.

I spent the afternoon moping about Leopoldo. "What's wrong?" Paul asked. "Are you dipping down?"

I told Paul that I missed Leopoldo. Paul said that he didn't miss Leopoldo. I wouldn't miss Paul when I left.

Ebony's brother came calling for her at visting time and told her that her doctor confirmed that she was for real getting out the next day. "Right on!" Ebony squealed. "Yes! Thank you, God!" Ebony turned to me (uselessly waiting for a visitor to arrive and pretty much knowing that one wouldn't) and shouted, "You hear that? I'm out tomorrow!"

"Excellent, Ebony," I said. I was happy for her, but I felt sorry for myself. Now there'd be nobody left to talk to besides Yasmine, who was grating on me more and more. It was increasingly uncomfortable to look at her and know that I had been that far gone and that full of myself.

Gemma gave me a few of my quarters; I called Maya and told her that she had to get me out of the hospital ASAP. Maya assured me that she and my mom were working with Dr. Prateek to hammer out a discharge plan. "Well, hammer it out already," I told her.

"Dr. Prateek doesn't think you're quite there," Maya said. "He still thinks you're a little too sped up." She took a long pause. "Do you still think I'm a traitor? You called me that the first time I visited you in the hospital."

I took a while to answer. It had happened slowly, probably because of all of Leopoldo's urgings, but I wasn't pissed off at her anymore. In fact, her soft voice sounded soothing to me. The sincerity in her words left no doubt that hurting me hadn't been her goal. "No. Don't worry about it," I said.

After I hung up with Maya, I called my mom. I asked her to put in a good word for me with Dr. Prateek, and she said that she'd been putting in good words regularly. "If it were up to me, Pumpkin, you never would have been checked into the hospital to begin with." She put each dog on the phone one by one, including Hollywood, the cocker spaniel she'd just adopted from a Hollywood shelter. I listened to dogs panting for about ten minutes and then hung up after my mom's "XOX."

Before bed, Gemma let Ebony, Yasmine, and me use my nail supplies to give ourselves manicures. Ebony wanted to look as h-o-t hot as she could when Anton picked her up in the morning. Rufus sat in the doorway "keeping us safe" while we painted our nails. I tried to pretend he wasn't there.

I asked Ebony for pointers on how to get out of the hospital. Without giving Ebony a chance to answer, Yasmine said that it was all about wooing the staff. "Start telling the dudes how handsome they are. Make presents for the women. Compliment them. Volunteer to vacuum and answer the phone." This was strange advice coming from a girl who did everything but projectile vomit on the staff. "If none of that works you could say you have smallpox or T.B. They don't want you in here if you're contagious with something nasty."

"Or you could just try and act well," Ebony said. "Fall asleep early. Sit still. Talk slow. Eat your meals. Stay in bed till eight."

I faked falling asleep early that night and tried my darnedest to stay in bed until eight, but every minute past five felt like I was wearing restraints. The rest of the day, before every move I made or word I uttered, I asked myself, "What would a sane person do?" I also asked both Yasmine and Ebony to tell me if I did anything nutty.

During outdoor time, I played the stupid dodge ball game that Paul organized. I chewed each bite of food I ate fifteen to twenty times and tried to finish my breakfast and lunch. I sat quietly doing puzzles during free time. I smiled at the staff. I worked hard to tone all my wiggles down to flinches. I kept my voice at library level and spoke only when spoken to.

Dr. Prateek visited me later in the day. He asked the usual questions, and then I brought up the touchy subject of leaving. "Unfortunately, I can't keep you here after the end of the week," he slowly admitted. "Your

5250 will be up. I have to fight to keep patients in here for lengthy stays, and you're well enough that I wouldn't win the battle at your hearing. That said, I'm urging you to stay here voluntarily. You're not leveled out yet."

"I'm outta here Friday," I told him. The thought of leaving the hospital was making me downright giddy, but I tried not to look too happy because he might mistake the exuberance for evidence of mania.

"What if I sent you upstairs to Level Two?" he asked. "You'd have more freedom. You could use your computer and phone. You could leave the hospital for a couple hours a day. You'd fit in better. The patients are mostly white upper-middle class. It's less dingy, too. The furniture's newer."

"Do you have any idea how screwed up that sounds?" I asked him. "You just described Level Two as more high class. I didn't know there were class distinctions and segregation in hospitals." I would be sure to keep this segment of our conversation from Ebony because I knew it would infuriate her – and rightly so.

"It's reality," he said. "Just think about it. You'd be better off if you went upstairs for a week to ten days." Dr. Prateek handed me a card. "This is the new psychiatrist you'll be seeing once you're out. It doesn't sound like Dr. Rice was a good fit, so I'm recommending Dr. Fontaine. She's an excellent adolescent psychiatrist."

"I won't be needing her," I said, handing him back the card. "I'm done with psychiatrists and psychiatry." One of the things I was most excited about was that once I left the hospital I wouldn't have medical staff tending to me everyday. I wanted people to stop monitoring my brain and fiddling with it. I wanted my brain back to myself.

Dr. Prateek shoved the card into my hand and wrapped my fingers around it. "You're just beginning a lengthy and fruitful relationship with the field of psychiatry. You'll probably be seeing a psychiatrist for the rest of your life. I've diagnosed you as bipolar one. Persons with bipolar one disorder need constant and consistent oversight by a professional. It's a serious mental condition."

"But I'm well now," I insisted. "I don't need a psychiatrist. It's a psychiatrist who got me sick to begin with."

"It's a psychiatrist who got you well," he said. "And it's a psychiatrist who will keep you well. Somebody needs to supervise your moods and medications. Dr. Rice didn't give you bipolar disorder. He unearthed it.

It was unfortunate that the antidepressants made you so manic, but you would have become manic at some point regardless. The medication just sped up the process. You're lucky in a way. You got diagnosed early." (With luck like mine I'd be sure to hotfoot it to the slot machines upon discharge.) "Some people bumble around sick for years not knowing what's wrong with them—wasting their lives. Trust me, you'll love Dr. Fontaine. And you need her."

The truth was that I had nobody on the outside who would understand or be able to relate to what I'd been through. I was going to be all alone in my experience, but I couldn't imagine that a psychiatrist was going to make me feel any less alone.

Dr. Prateek stood and we shook hands. "I'm not saying this in a mean way because you've been good to me," I said. "But I hope I don't see you again."

"I hope I don't see you either," he said. "Not in a mean way."

Knowing I was being set loose soon made Ebony's departure tolerable. At visiting hour, Anton arrived with an entourage—Ebony's brother, stepsister, mother, and grandmother, who had the precious little poached egg that was Imani in her arms.

As soon as Ebony laid eyes on Imani, it was like nobody else existed. She grabbed Imani in her arms and rocked her, covering her with kisses. "My baby, my baby," she cooed. "Mama has missed you so, so, so much. I'm never leaving you again, baby. Never never ever."

Ebony let me hold Imani for all of one second. She felt like a loaf of freshly baked bread, and her smile was otherworldly adorable. When I tickled her foot, she let out a tinkling little jingle bell of a laugh.

Before Ebony left, she high-fived me. "I left my e-mail address and phone number in your room," she said. "We're sisters for good, right?"

"Always," I told her.

Watching Ebony march out the glass doors was as sad as it was watching Leopoldo leave. Who knew I would have so much in common with someone whose life outside the hospital I had nothing in common with?

Seventy-two hours later, it was discharge day for me. I woke up at five, sooo pumped that I was going home. I couldn't wait to sleep in my own bed and see my friends and check my texts and e-mails and shave my legs and contact Ben and go where I wanted to go without the fun police following me. I made sure I stayed in bed until six. (I didn't want to sound any alarm bells and get slapped with another 5250.) Then I got out of bed and wrote thank you/good-bye notes to Kamala, Miss Brandstein, Dr. Prateek, and Gemma. The rest of them could rot.

Yasmine was all up in my business the entire time I packed. "Can I have that?" was her mantra. I gave her all my bath and beauty products, my pajamas and bathrobe, my sweatpants and sweatshirt, T-shirts, jeans (which she claimed would fit her after she lost weight in her thighs)—even my underwear. The only things she didn't want were my bras, which she proudly announced were two cup sizes too small—and she definitely wasn't losing any padding up there.

"I need things to remember you by," she kept telling me. I was so happy I was leaving that I didn't care that she was stripping me bare. Also, I felt sorry for her. She still refused to take medication, and it didn't take an m.d. to notice that she was getting more and more loco and out of control by the day. "Won't you stay another night?" she asked. "We'll tell each other all our secrets. We'll stay up late and watch the stars. I'll point out the Big Dipper and Orion's Belt." I didn't remind her that our rooms had no windows and that it wasn't dark enough to see stars at four-thirty in the afternoon, when we came back inside after our last outdoor visit for the day.

After Yasmine had cleaned me out, I headed to the lobby with a suitcase that was so empty that you could hear my toothbrush and quarters rattling around inside it. Autumn followed behind me with my sack of forbidden items.

Maya and my mother were waiting in the lobby. Well, Maya was waiting. My mother was standing behind the glass doors waving at me nervously.

"What's with the woman behind the glass?" I asked Maya.

"She says she's coming down with something and doesn't want to infect the patients," Maya said. "I know. It's totally lame. Don't get me started." She picked up my bag. "Wow, this is light. What happened to all your stuff?"

"Her," I said, pointing to Yasmine.

"Be sure Janelle calls me as soon as she gets home," Yasmine told Maya. "She's going to help me find a lawyer."

"I can't promise that," I told Yasmine.

"You have to help me," she said. "Boris is too wimpy to stand up for me and nobody in my family believes me. The police fooled them."

"I'll try," I told her.

"Take me with you," she begged. "I shouldn't be here." She pulled on Maya's arm. "Can't you talk to someone for me? They'll listen to you." For once I was glad to see the likes of Autumn. She was a pro at what needed to be done. She pulled Yasmine aside and told her to wave good-bye and get back to her room and change for outdoor time.

I watched Yasmine walk away and felt like a part of me was walking away with her. Everyday I moved farther from the girl who had landed in the hospital. She was becoming more of a stranger to me little by little, to the point that I didn't know if she lived inside me at all anymore. I missed her, but I no longer completely understood her.

When the glass doors opened, I didn't look back. I ran past my mother and down the hall shouting, "I'm free. I'm free. I'm free," all the way into the parking lot.

# THIRTEEN

WHEN WE ARRIVED HOME, Maya followed me upstairs to my bedroom. The walls had been painted bright white, my bulletin boards were gone, and there was a new, large desk made of blonde wood against the wall across from my bed. The room wasn't even recognizable.

"The place was a mess—writing all over the walls and the desk," Maya explained. "I thought it might be good for you to start fresh—wipe the slate clean." I wanted my old room back – the one I was used to – but Maya looked so pleased with herself over what she'd done that I didn't want to burst her bubble.

"Is that a new computer?" I asked as I moved toward the shiny aluminum laptop resting on the desk.

"Your computer was thrashed," Maya said. "It looked like you'd dismantled the innards."

"I think I thought it was bugged—or that somebody was spying on me through the computer," I said. I switched on the new laptop, excited to plug back into my life.

"You won't find any of your files on that computer," Maya informed me. "And you're not allowed to contact anyone—via computer or phone."

"Why?" I asked.

"You need to adjust first," she said.

"Adjust to what? And where am I going to school?" I asked.

"We'll talk all about that later," she answered. "Why don't you clean up and relax a while before dinner?"

I shuffled off to shower and was delighted to see that I had "adjusted" enough to have a razor in the bathroom. I took a good long time shampooing and rinsing and repeating and conditioning and shaved my legs and armpits. Then I blow-dried my hair, clipped my nails, sprayed perfume on my wrists, put on a couple necklaces and a belt with my jeans and lit a candle. If only Autumn could see me now.

I felt like the choke collar had been lifted from my neck as I wandered around the house and yard without a schedule or a set of beady eyes trained on me, waiting for me to slip up so that someone could chew me out.

After I'd played with the dogs for a spell, I returned upstairs to unpack the few items that were in my suitcase. I removed Ben's necklace (I had made two for him) and held it up to the light to admire it. I wondered how long I'd have to wait to give the necklace to him—or to even talk to him. I shut my eyes and pictured Ben's face. He was smiling at me in the dark. Then I heard his voice: "I won't be turned off by the real you." Until then, my memories of Ben had no sound track. This was the first time I had remembered dialogue, and the dialogue was encouraging. He didn't know that the "real me" had just left St. Joan's psych ward, but if he was true to his word, that wouldn't turn him off.

I heard Maya shouting from downstairs. Dinner was ready.

Maya had cooked my favorite meal—spaghetti with soy meatballs and a Caesar salad—and I was eating like a starved refugee, savoring food that tasted like it was made in a kitchen and not in a sweatshop. My mom gushed about how good I looked and how "normal" I seemed and how great it was to have me home. She claimed to have missed me terribly.

"Missed me?" I asked. "You never see me when I'm here. You barely talk to me, so how could you have missed me?"

My mom frowned and blinked at me a few times. "I had hoped that the rude way you were treating me before you went into the hospital wouldn't continue when you got out. I don't understand where it's all coming from and I'd like you to knock it off."

"I'm not being rude, I'm being honest," I said. One thing I was keeping from my mania was my new relationship, if you could call it that, with my mother. No longer was I going to be that daughter who just accepted all her b.s. without calling her on it. Her not visiting me in the hospital had taken its toll. It was proof to me that she really didn't give a damn, and I had a problem with that. A big problem.

"Just stop," Maya said. "Let's try and celebrate that you're home."

"You'll be happy to know that you've been admitted to a new school for your senior year," my mother announced. "West Hills Prep offered to take you back once I told them that your misbehavior was due to your medical conditions—the kidney failure and all. But I requested that they give you a good recommendation to another school instead and they agreed."

"You could have asked me before you made that decision," I said. "I would have preferred to stay at West Hills. And do you really think it's better for everyone to think I have a failed organ than to know I was in a psychiatric unit?"

"There's a stigma associated with mental illness," she said. "And besides, there isn't anything wrong with you mentally. You're not bipolar. You just had an allergic reaction to a medication."

"What's the school?" I asked.

"It's called Evergreen, and it has an excellent reputation. We were very lucky that they happened to have a space," she said. "It's all the way across town so you won't know anybody there. They don't have a crew team, but they have all kinds of other sports. They even have golf. Golf is a great game you can play your whole life. It's much more useful than crew."

What's so "perfect" about not knowing anybody in your senior class? Who wants to start at square one making new friends in their final year of high school? And what about the rowing career I'd been diligently plugging away at for years that was supposed to help me get into college? Now golf was supposed to take its place? I hated swinging at things.

The doorbell graciously interrupted and terminated the conversation. A visitor had arrived. Her name was Valentina, and she looked to be in her early twenties. She was cute and pert with shoulder-length brown hair and dark eyes and an accent that made her sound like an international spy. Actually, she wasn't a visitor—she was a stayer.

"I'm from Ukraine," she said. "I was a nurse there. I'm so excited to be living with you." She reached for my hand and squeezed it so tightly and for so long and pumped my arm up and down so vigorously that my fingers ached and my shoulder felt like it was going to dislocate.

"Valentina will be staying with us and watching over you while you adjust to being home from the hospital," my mom told me as Valentina, whom I realized had something of a greeting disorder, worked over Maya's hand and arm.

"I would take care of you," my mother said. "But, I'm not a nurse." I couldn't imagine why I needed a nurse. It wasn't like I had shots to be administered or I couldn't walk on my own.

After we'd finished dessert, a raspberry tart, I gave Valentina a tour of the house and showed her to the guest room. She gushed over the television in her room and marveled over the walk-in closet, the "flooffy" pillows and down comforter. "I've never been in house so beautiful and big," she said. "Unless you're a rich Russian, you live in an apartment in Ukraine."

Valentina was a total fob—so fresh off the boat you could smell the sea breeze in her hair. "I've only been in America one month," she said. "But now I'm here forever." I hoped she wasn't planning to stay at our house forever.

Valentina was giddy when I showed her my bathroom, which we would be sharing. "Only the two of us?" she squealed, revealing that she had shared one bathroom with three generations since she was a child. "You do realize that you are the luckiest girl in the world," she said.

"Lucky?" I asked. "I may have my own bathroom, but I also was kicked out of high school and just spent two weeks in a mental ward."

"Spit over your shoulder three times," she said.

"Gross," I answered. "Why?"

"I just told you that you were lucky. After someone tells you that you're lucky, you must spit over your shoulder three times or else whatever it is that makes you lucky might be taken away," she explained. "You don't want to start sharing your bathroom with ten people."

I pretended to spit over my shoulder and then left her to unpack.

I spent the rest of the night with Maya, watching TV and talking while she knit me a sweater, the long plastic needles clicking when they touched. Knitting seemed like an old lady hobby, but Maya was a little old lady-ish. She'd probably gotten that way from mothering me from such a young age.

"I don't get why Mom has the Ukrainian chick here," I said. "I must be the only seventeen-year-old in this entire city with a full-time nanny."

"Valentina will drive you to your doctor appointments, since Mom has confiscated your keys. Also, you're on different medications that need to be kept track of, and somebody needs to make sure you get enough sleep and chart your moods, too. You've been really, really sick. According to

Dr. Prateek, your mania was off the charts. He said you're not completely recovered—it's still a bit of a jungle up here," she said as she tapped very lightly on my forehead with her fist. "I was the one who insisted on Valentina. If Mom hadn't hired somebody, I wouldn't be going to summer school. I don't trust Mom to care for you, and I feel guilty enough for not stepping in before your illness got so acute. I'm never letting that happen to you again. I promise."

"Don't feel guilty," I said. "How were you supposed to know what was going on? You weren't here."

"So you forgive me for putting you in the hospital?" she asked. "You were really furious with me when we admitted you."

"The place is hateful," I said. "But now that I've come down from the mania, I get that I probably did need a little medical intervention. I'd gotten myself pretty far out there."

"You don't know how happy I am to hear you say that," Maya said.

An expression of great relief spread across Maya's face. I had told her the truth. I wasn't mad at her anymore. She had done what she thought was right and she had been there for me all along. It felt good not to be angry with her – even though I no longer thought she would always be there to make sure I was okay. She wasn't that powerful. It had been an illusion. I did still feel a distance between us. Maybe it wasn't a distance. Maybe it was just that the new me had gone through an experience she had no way of fully understanding. Being the younger one, it always seemed like whatever I was going through, Maya had experienced three years ahead of me – so she could guide me through it. But, I had veered off the path she was forging. I had diverged and set out on my own path. A path she'd never go down. It made me miss Ebony and Leopoldo.

After two days back at home I realized that having Valentina around wasn't all bad because, for some reason, I was so ADHD that I couldn't even organize a coin purse. I would take a shower and then, in the middle of getting dressed, remember that I hadn't brushed my teeth. I'd smear toothpaste on my toothbrush and hear the dogs barking and remember that I hadn't fed them. I'd go downstairs to feed the dogs and realize I was hungry and put a piece of bread in the toaster. Then I'd return upstairs to finish getting dressed and realize that I had forgotten to feed the dogs. So I'd go back downstairs to feed the dogs, and I'd smell the toast burning and take it out of the toaster and put in a new slice of bread. Then

I'd return upstairs to get dressed and hear the dogs barking and return downstairs to feed them. Then the doorbell might ding and next thing I knew it was noon and cause for celebration if I was dressed.

The other thing Valentina provided was a Yasmine buffer. Somebody had given Yasmine too many quarters, and she was calling me several times a day, asking for help suing the police department. I didn't really like Yasmine and had no means of helping her, so I was glad that Valentina wouldn't allow me to answer the phone. Valentina took Yasmine's calls and told her, repeatedly, that my phone had been confiscated because I needed to pour my energies into recuperating. But that didn't put the brakes on Yasmine's dialing finger. Eventually, to get rid of Yasmine, Valentina found the number for a civil rights attorney with the slogan "Sue Anybody but Yourself—and Win." She gave Yasmine the number and told her the lawyer was a "real whale." (I think she meant a shark.) Yasmine's calls dwindled to once or twice a day and then, hallelujah, ceased altogether. It was much easier to forget about the hospital when I wasn't hearing from her, knowing that she was calling me from inside there. I really didn't want any reminders of the dreaded place.

Valentina having strict control of my phone and computer, however, had a big downside, which was that I couldn't contact my friends or Ebony and Leopoldo. I whined so much about wanting to at least see Ben's face, if I couldn't contact him, that Valentina caved and finally let me check out his picture online. I stared and stared, drinking him in, wishing I could step into cyberspace and wrap my arms around him.

Valentina looked at Ben over my shoulder. "He is cute, but his eyes don't smile with his face, which means he could be a liar—or at least be hiding something. I had a boyfriend with eyes that didn't smile with his face. He cheated on me with a stripper from Belarus."

One thing Valentina wasn't caving on was my request to visit the West Hills website. I told her about the revolution of sorts that I had started at my high school and that I was very curious to see if classmates were talking about it. I wanted to at least see what had become of it—if the revolution had amounted to anything or if it was just a big, misguided, mania-induced fantasy in my head.

"Revolution is good," Valentina said. "Revolution for equality is bad. The Soviets killed fifty million people trying to make everybody equal. What do you want? The People's Republic of High School?"

"I wasn't trying to make everybody the same," I said. "I was just trying to get everybody equal treatment."

"Now that sounds smart," she said. "Maybe if you had been at my high school I wouldn't have had to eat lunch alone everyday because I was twenty pounds overweight and had eczema. I guess high school is cruel everywhere."

I still had a burning desire to visit Brookside Assisted Living and get to the bottom of what was going on with my mother's donations and visits there. I hoped they'd let me volunteer even though I hadn't shown up for my scheduled appointment. I pretended to Valentina that I wanted to go there and volunteer because I thought it would be therapeutic, since I didn't think she'd go for me starting in on some sort of detective case. But, she was having none of it. I needed to get myself in shape before I was in condition to help others was her reasoning.

After a few weeks, when I was sleeping eight hours, talking slowly, and able to sit still for more than ten minutes, Valentina judged me "adjusted enough" to leave the house, and my mom scheduled a visit to Evergreen. My mom arrived in my room at seven a.m. holding a grey skirt and matching short jacket that looked like a flight attendant's uniform. "A pair of low pumps and a blouse and you're ready to go," she said as she handed me the suit. "I'd flatiron your hair. It looks a little wild. You want to look put together."

Valentina hated my outfit and insisted I wear a red necklace and earrings to balance it out. "All the apartments in Kiev are that same ugly, grey color. You don't want to look like a Soviet apartment."

It was a good thing Valentina and I left the house promptly at eight because we needed plenty of time to get to Evergreen. The drive from the Westside all the way across town to Pasadena in morning traffic took over an hour, which meant that I was going to be spending close to three hours a day on the road once school started. I'd leave a Saskatchewan-sized carbon footprint by graduation day. West Hills had been so convenient. This new school was already unappealing.

Evergreen, which certainly didn't look very green, was on a busy street filled with chain stores and fast food restaurants and painted a drab brown color. We drove into the parking lot and I got out of the car. After searching through a labyrinth of hallways, I reached the office of the headmaster, Dr. Mane, and took a seat. Dr. Mane was tall and rangy, with an undertaker's pale complexion. He pulled out my file and told me how delighted he was to have me at his school. "You have good grades and good recommendations from all your teachers. You're an athlete, too," he said. "I bet you're sorry to be leaving West Hills Prep and your crew team, but now that you're living so far east, it makes sense. You don't want to be commuting from here all the way to West Hills everyday."

Hold on. We moved over here?

Dr. Mane told me how sorry he was to hear about my kidney problems and launched into a lengthy story about his uncle, who had recently received a kidney transplant and was now "good as new." Both of his uncle's original kidneys had shriveled up from a staph infection. After he asked me a few questions about my condition, it dawned on me that I was going to need to buy a *Kidney Disease for Dummies* book and bone up on what was allegedly wrong with me, since the only kidney-related word I knew was "dialysis."

Dr. Mane gave me a tour of the campus, which was impressive. The classrooms were filled with all the latest technologies, and it would have taken a baseball stadium of PhDs to read all the books in the library. The science lab looked like it belonged at NASA. Even though I didn't want to go to Evergreen, I had to admit it seemed like a pretty good place to land if I wasn't going to be able to return to West Hills, though I was going to miss my friends. I hoped the place wasn't too cliquey and that I'd be able to meet people and not spend my last year of high school eating lunch alone.

Once we'd completed the tour and small talk, Dr. Mane walked me to the parking lot (where Valentina was waiting—reading a map while rocking out to the radio) and shook my hand. He told me that he'd spoken to the administration at West Hills and that I would be able to make up the homework and exams I'd missed—which would keep me on track for applying to college. That was good. The thought of having to delay college and spend more time living with my mother was not appealing.

"Don't worry about being accepted into college. Your GPA is good; you'll do fine," he said. "And believe it or not, the story of your illness will look good on your applications. Colleges tend to have a soft spot for handicaps—and serious illness is considered diversity." I hoped the colleges wouldn't request my medical files because my certification papers probably weren't the kind of diversity they were seeking.

When I got into the car, Valentina pointed to her map excitedly. "Look how close we are to Hollywood," she squealed. "I can't believe I'm this close to movie stars." Valentina had been yakking about celebrities since her first night at my house.

"I've got a deal for you," I told her, laying a trap. "I'll show you around Hollywood if you will drive me past Ben's house."

As I'd suspected would be the case, Valentina's obsession with things show biz won out over her sensible nurse side. "Okay," she said. "But you will not get out of the car—even if you see him on the street. You haven't adjusted enough (God I was sick of the word "adjust"!) and are too fragile to spend time with a lover who you're not sure is actually your lover. It's too risky for the emotions. We need the emotions calm."

I was antsy the whole stuck-in-quicksand two hours Valentina and I spent touring Hollywood Boulevard—where I snapped photo after photo of her posing next to likenesses of celebrities in the wax museum and standing over stars on the Walk of Fame.

The drive to Ben's house seemed to go on forever. Finally, we were cruising down his street. My heart was pounding. As we approached his house, I saw his car in the street. Valentina slowed as we got close to his house. I quickly scanned the front yard and the windows on the first floor—nothing. I looked upstairs—no dice. Then, just as we were directly in front of the house, I saw a shadow in Ben's window – Ben's shadow. I gasped. Then another silhouette appeared—a girl-shaped silhouette. Then it all disappeared as Valentina sped on. "You saw his house," she said. "Now we go home."

"I saw him," I said. "And a girl. They were in his bedroom." I felt the air being sucked out of my lungs. Did Ben have a girlfriend? Valentina was right. This felt way too hard on the emotions.

"Maybe it was his mother—or his sister," Valentina said.

"You're right," I said. "It had to be."

I turned around and glanced back at Ben's house and the big oak tree with branches that extended up to his window. An image of me climbing the tree passed through my mind. Then there were words in peanut butter scrawled across his window.

"I think I might have written 'I like you' on Ben's window—in peanut butter," I told Valentina. "Is that weird in a way that would make somebody not like you?"

"It's strange, but it's not bad," she said. "It's nice words—not curse words. And they're in peanut butter. Who doesn't love peanut butter?"

I crossed my fingers that Valentina was right, but I wasn't sure. Writing on somebody's window in peanut butter was a very strange thing to do. I couldn't imagine why I'd done it and I wished I hadn't. All I could do was be hopeful that it hadn't sent Ben running in the opposite direction.

The next morning, Tiffany and Nell arrived to take me to the beach. Valentina had deemed me well enough to spend some limited time with them. They had to wait forty-five minutes while I struggled to get ready. As we climbed into Tiffany's car, Valentina sped out of the house and hopped into the backseat. "Which beach are we going to?" she asked.

"You don't need to come, Valentina," I said. "I have my friends with me. Take the day off and chill."

"Oh, no," Valentina said as she shut the car door. I noticed that she was carrying a straw bag. "Your mother wants me with you at all times. And I love the beach. I hope there are big waves."

As the car pulled out of the driveway, Tiffany and Nell commenced with the "It's so good to have you back" and the "We missed you so much" and the "You seem so much better than when we saw you at the hospital."

Once they were done, I brought up topic number one. Actually, it was topic number two. Number one would be saved for the beach. "So, were there any positive changes I made at school or was my whole crusade just in my head?" I asked, nervous for the answer. I still badly wanted to think of myself as a sort of revolutionary, but it was starting to seem like a kindergarten fantasy, where you pretend you're a famous rock star or movie goddess.

"It's hard to say exactly, because there wasn't all that much left of the school year when you left," Nell answered. "The parking lot arrangement was a little different. Stella complained that people were parking in her space."

"I ate a couple cafeteria grilled cheese sandwiches," Tiffany reported. "And Dickens was still hanging out in the Atrium by the time school ended."

"Did kids ask about me or get angry that I wasn't on the ballot for school president?" I asked. "I haven't been allowed to text or call or e-mail anybody or check the school website yet."

"Both of us were so freaked out that you'd been carted away—so, between that and finals, we barely noticed what was going on around us," Tiffany said. "There were jokes about you and different rumors about where you'd gone. Zeke and Fiona wanted to send you flowers, but I told them I didn't know where they should send them. We didn't say a peep about the psych ward."

Jokes? Rumors? None of this conversation was at all reassuring. And, again, why did the psych ward have to be such a closely guarded secret? It's not like I was in prison.

We arrived at the beach and Valentina peeled off her sarong and T-shirt to reveal a bikini the size of a handkerchief. She tugged on a pair of flippers and asked if we wanted to join her in the water.

"It's a little cold," Nell said.

"Don't you want some sunscreen?" I asked as she skipped across the sand.

"I want a tan," she said.

"Isn't a tan a little eighties?" Nell asked me.

"I guess they don't have skin cancer in Ukraine," I said.

"They have a high cancer rate because of Chernobyl," Nell (the expert on disaster and tragedy) said. "Would you rather have lived through Chernobyl or Hurricane Katrina?"

"Some of those Red Cross guys I saw on TV were cute, so I'd go with the hurricane," Tiffany said. She turned to me. "So, tell me some of the wild stuff that happened in the hospital. Did the dude who thought he was a vampire try to bite you?"

The word "hospital" immediately made me feel like I was suffocating.

"For God's sake, Tiffany," Nell said. "Give Jane a break. Do you really think she wants to talk about that pit of hell?"

"She's not uptight like you, Nell," Tiffany said. "Not everything is O.L. with Jane."

"It's off limits today," Nell said. "I want Jane to have a peaceful morning."

It was finally time for topic number one. "What I really want to talk about is Ben," I said. I felt my pulse quicken with a mixture of excitement and dread, depending on what the news would be. "What's going on with him? Did you give him the necklace I made for him?"

Tiffany and Nell shared a nervous glance. "Uhm . . . not really," Tiffany answered. "No."

"I think we should talk about Ben later," Nell said.

"What happened? Out with it, now," I demanded.

"It can wait," Nell said. "I don't want you to get . . . emotional. Let's talk about something else."

"Tell me!" I demanded. "I need to know."

"Let's just say . . . that ship has sailed," Tiffany said. "He's back together with his old girlfriend, Gabriella."

So that's who I'd seen in Ben's window. "Maybe he's just waiting until I'm back in the mix and then they'll break it off and we'll start seeing each other. I honestly think he likes me," I said.

"He might have," Tiffany said, looking uncomfortable.

"Why are you so sure he doesn't like me?" I asked.

"Okay, I'm going to give it to you straight up for real since you're so insistent," Tiffany said. "When I walked up to him with the necklace you made and told him that you wanted him to have it, he told me to give it to somebody else it and walked off. A couple crew guys told me you burned him bad, but they didn't know what you did."

Burned him? How could I have burned him? We'd never even gone out. I hadn't expected news this horrible. "I was going to text Ben as soon as I got my phone back," I said. "I could ask him what he's upset about and iron things out."

"I'd hold off on that," Tiffany said. "You didn't see the look on his face."

"At least give it some time," Nell said.

"Like maybe a few years," Tiffany said. "Forget about him for now and think of all the new, cute guys you'll meet at Evergreen."

Tiffany turned on the radio, and I lay down on my towel, pulled my hat over my face, and shut my eyes. What had happened to make Ben so sour on the subject of me? The answer was hidden somewhere in my messed-up memory – if only I could unearth it... I meditated on Ben's smile and homed in hard on the image until it dissolved into his house in the dark. I focused on the front door. Ben opened the front door, shirtless and scratching his head. I saw the stairs. I climbed them one by one. I saw his dimly lit room. Our clothes were in a pile on the floor and we were kissing and giggling. So far so good. Then we were laying on the bed and he was on top of me and I was giddy and my head was swirling. Had we gone *that far*? Then I saw a photo of an apple hanging on the wall and a photo of a homeless person hanging next to it. And, try as I might, I couldn't see the two of us anymore. The images on the wall crowded out everything else. There was the apple and the homeless person and nothing else.

I was jolted back to the present by the voice of none other than Stella— just about the last voice I wanted to hear. I opened my eyes and sat up. I could see Ariana and Alexis arranging towels and a big umbrella a few yards behind Stella.

"Hey, Jane," Stella said, standing over me wearing a shiny gold bikini and a self-satisfied smirk. "Haven't seen you in a while. I heard a rumor that you were in the hospital. I hope you're okay."

"She's fine," Nell said. "She was only in the hospital for a little while."

"For what?" Stella pressed. "Was it something serious?"

"Why do you want to know?" I asked.

"You don't have to get huffy," she said. "I'm just trying to make conversation and show some concern. I heard that there was something wrong with your kidneys . . . or your liver . . ."

"Are you really concerned?" I asked. "Because if you are concerned, then I would like you to please not ask me questions about my kidneys and liver because I don't feel like talking about them—or any of my organs."

"Fine. Be that way," Stella said.

Stella was cut off by Valentina, who shoved past her, grabbed her beach bag, and stuck her hand inside. "Time for your afternoon dose," she said, pulling out a pillbox and a bottle of water.

"Who's this?" Stella asked.

"I'm a nurse . . ." Valentina began.

"This is Valentina. She's my cousin from Ukraine," I said as Valentina handed me a couple pills and the water bottle.

"I didn't know you were Ukrainian," Stella said. "You certainly don't look Ukrainian."

"What is a Ukrainian supposed to look like?" Valentina asked as I rolled up my towel and shoved it into my beach bag.

"C'mon, guys. Let's go," I said, motioning for the others to leave.

"But, we only got here an hour-and-a-half ago," Tiffany said.

Nell picked up her beach bag and folded her towel inside it. She winked at Tiffany. "I have to get home. I've got that babysitting job."

"Oh, yah. That's right. You're babysitting," Tiffany said, winking at me.

Valentina, who had a sixth sense for creeps, turned to Stella. "If you don't have any important business here, then why don't you go enjoy the water."

Stella sighed, sneered, and walked off.

During the ride home, I buried my head in one of Valentina's gossip magazines and read about which celebrities were getting divorced and who had gotten liposuction – anything to distract me from the miserable morning I was having. I wished I'd stayed home. "Don't let Stella ruin your day," Tiffany said. "She's nosy about everyone and everything—always trying to dig up dirt."

"She reminds me of a rich Russian," Valentina said. "So obnoxious and proud. Ignore her."

"It's not Stella in the singular that I'm so concerned about," I said. "I'm betting there are a lot of nosy Stellas out there. And I don't feel like rereading the last few chapters of my life and answering a bunch of prying questions every time I go out. And I won't always have you two and Valentina to guard me. Plus, I practically need notes to keep track of all the lies my mom made up about me."

"She's just trying to save you from humiliation," Tiffany said. "'Bipolar' and 'mental institute' are loaded words."

"You don't call the psychiatric unit a mental institute, Tiffany," Nell said. "They don't give lobotomies anymore or lock you up in Bedlam."

"I think I might have slept with Ben," I blurted out.

"Whaaaat? How can you not know if you slept with someone?" Tiffany asked.

"I was manic, remember? It's called dissociative amnesia or something," I answered. "What if it was really bad? What if that's why he acted creepy when you tried to give him the necklace?"

"Stop torturing yourself," Nell said. "Just put the whole thing in the rearview mirror and move on. Tiffany's right. You're going to meet a whole crop of new guys at Evergreen. Maybe guys who live in Pasadena are cuter and cooler than the lame ones over here."

It wasn't going to be so easy to put Ben in the rearview mirror, especially since he had stretched out and taken up residence in my brain. I had to believe there was at least a bit of hope for us. Tiffany and Nell barely knew Ben. Maybe Tiffany misinterpreted what he said—or was trying to say. If they were right, then big heartbreak was around the corner for me.

The rest of the ride, Tiffany asked questions about "Ukrania." Once Tiffany's questioning of Valentina was finished, Valentina began chattering about the Hollywood factoids she'd learned and Tiffany and Nell chimed in with celebrity gossip. The conversation was shallow and, like when Tiffany and Nell visited me in the hospital, I sensed a vast divide between us. It wasn't their fault and I still loved them. It was just that I'd changed and they hadn't, and they hadn't a notion about where my head was at. I felt alone enough that I wanted to actually be alone.

The car hadn't even reached the end of my driveway or come to a complete stop when I hurled myself out of Nell's car and raced for the front door of my house. "Thanks for driving," I yelled to Nell without turning back.

Valentina came down to breakfast the next morning with my daily reminder pillbox and a bright pink sunburn. "Look how tan I am," she said delightedly. "Let's go back to the beach this afternoon."

"I think you got enough sun damage yesterday," I told her.

"Well, is there anywhere you want to go after your appointment with your psychiatrist?"

Psychiatrist? Ugh. A psychiatrist's office was about the last place I wanted to go. I didn't want to talk about feelings or the hospital or medicine. I didn't want to be reminded that something was not right with me. "Instead of the beach, why don't we go to Disneyland or Universal Studios or another fun attraction?" I suggested. "Of course, it would take all day, but surely my doctor's appointment could wait one day. Right?"

Valentina's face lit up like a Christmas tree. I could see her practical, responsible side duking it out with her rabid enthusiasm for sightseeing and entertainment. "I've been talking to your doctor everyday, so she knows what's going on with you . . ." she said.

"Right. So, what would it hurt? Maybe you'd like to check out the boardwalk in Venice or the zoo," I suggested. I didn't actually want to go to any of these places, but tourist attractions were safe places to go if I didn't want to run into people I knew—since no one who lived in Los Angeles ever visited any of them. Hearing about how much embarrassment and shame everybody was trying to save me from was making me feel, well, embarrassed and ashamed and wanting to go undercover in some kind of witness protection program for crazies. What things had I done that nobody was telling me about? Just how much did I need to be embarrassed about—and how embarrassed should I be? Was there something so horribly wrong with who I really was that an entire new persona had been invented for me? Were my insides that completely unacceptable? Was I going to have to hide unalterable and basic parts of my self for the rest of my life?

Valentina's adventurous side finally won out. The first spot Valentina and I hit was Disneyland, where I videoed her with her arm around every character from Mickey Mouse to Pluto. I pulled the same ruse the next day, and we spent six hours at Universal Studios. My scam worked for the rest of the week, during which we went whale watching, bought a map of the stars' homes and scoured Bel Air and Beverly Hills tracking down the alleged addresses, took a boat to Catalina, and explored Malibu and Muscle Beach.

Valentina loved shopping for souvenirs and trinkets to send back to friends in Ukraine, so I took her to gift shops. We made frequent stops at cafes, where Valentina drank cappuccino after latte after espresso shot, claiming, "This is so tasty. The coffee in Ukraine tastes like the juice of boiled socks."

I was supposed to be the one who was partially hypomanic, but I could hardly keep up with Valentina. I became grateful for the break in the action I got during my visits to the clinic, where I was being administered so many blood tests (to check levels of different medications and the functioning of my organs) that my arms looked like they belonged to Keith Richards.

The week wasn't all torture, because Valentina turned out to be a lot of fun. She liked to laugh and she appeared to like me, although she was being paid to like me. "I've always liked people who have the bipolar," she said. "Your minds are so imaginative. The schizophrenics, now they are more work." It was nice to have somebody around who wasn't afraid of the word "bipolar" and didn't dance around the subject. "The bipolar is a very tough one to be dealt, but we all get something. I got ugly eczema, a slow metabolism and an alcoholic father—not as hard as bipolar but not good," Valentina said. "And you never know who's going to get cancer or dementia. So, don't think you've been singled out."

Finally, I got Valentina to agree to let me visit Brookside Assisted Living. I called the director and told her that I was sorry I hadn't shown up at my scheduled time, explaining to her that I'd gotten ill and was in the hospital with kidney problems. She was very sympathetic and we set a date for me to volunteer the next week. I was excited. Even though I was deeply resentful of her, I still wanted to solve the mystery of my mother and whatever was inside Brookside Assisted Living Center that she was hiding.

Once the week had drawn to a close, and we'd exhausted Los Angeles's supply of tourist traps, Valentina was done falling for my scheme and announced that the doctor's office visit could no longer be put off: "No if, ands, or probably." Valentina hadn't quite conquered American slang.

# FOURTEEN

/HE NEXT MORNING, I walked into the sunny office of Dr. Faith Fontaine (or Dr. Faith as she told me to call her.) She smiled at me as I sat on the comfy couch across from her—and it was love at first sight. Her smile was so warm and kind that I felt like I was meeting an angel. She even looked like an angel. She had flawless porcelain skin; big, aquamarine-colored eyes; and blonde, fluffy hair the texture of cotton candy. All she was missing was a pair of gold wings.

Dr. Faith stared into my eyes before she spoke. Her expression was overflowing with empathy and trust and understanding and acceptance and caring and kindness and sugar and spice and everything nice. She told me that she had studied my medical files and had had a meeting with Dr. Prateek. "You've been through so, so much," she said to me. "More than I like to see anyone have to go through, particularly somebody your age. Is there anything you'd like to talk about?"

I shook my head "no."

"I understand," she said. "Trauma is frightening."

"It doesn't feel like trauma, it feels like . . . avoidance," I said.

"That's trauma," she insisted. "Take your time. Tell me something that you can talk about that doesn't upset you."

Somehow, Dr. Faith got me talking—about how the things that made sense during my mania (what I could remember) made less and less sense everyday, how I was starting to feel like my brain had betrayed me.

After everything I said, Dr. Faith would pause and ask if there was more I wanted to express and then either quietly back off or listen some more, her gaze never leaving my eyes. She was like a snake charmer, magically coaxing out the hairball of confusion and distress that I hadn't coughed up yet. She quoted all the latest research on bipolar disorder and knew the pros and cons associated with the different treatments. She even knew the truth about St. Joan's Psychiatric Unit. "It's trapped in the 1940s," she said. "All of them are."

"We don't have to talk about memories just yet," she told me later in the visit. "But they'll continue coming up, and you must process them. You need to visit me regularly so that I can monitor your moods and medications." She also told me that, unfortunately, I wasn't going to be able to forget the cycle I'd just endured and that she wouldn't lie to me—it wasn't going to be all smiley faces from here on out. There was plenty more healing to do. "Your brain is in shock. Think of your brain as though it has stitches. It's still mending."

Although I was beginning to feel somewhat balanced, she said that I was still bipolar and that I (still burning through the mental manual) was caught in the grip of a new code number: "ACUTE STRESS DIS-ORDER DSM 308.3: . . . Occurs after traumatic event (rape, serious accident, severe episode of depression, mania, or psychosis). Symptoms include: numbness, detachment, difficulty concentrating . . . avoidance of stimuli that arouse recollections of the trauma (i.e., thoughts, feelings, activities, places, people) . . . flashbacks of traumatizing event."

Dr. Faith told me that my nonexistent attention span, like my tremor, was a side effect of lithium. "I'll give you a prescription for a blood pressure medication that cuts down on the trembling," she said. "But there's nothing to be done about your attention span. And brace yourself for another side effect that might arise once you've come all the way down from the hypomania. Fatigue and increased appetite. The antipsychotic you're on is sedating and it causes weight gain."

"One of my pills is an antipsychotic? Which color? Am I schizophrenic now, too?" I asked, panicked at being slapped with *that* label. Bipolar was bad enough.

"It's the blue pill. And you're not schizophrenic, but you were psy-chotic when you checked into the hospital. That's why they put you on it," she said. (Phew. I'd dodged another DSM code.) "And don't be frightened by the term 'antipsychotic.' That class of drugs is used for all kinds of mental disorders—not just psychosis and schizophrenia."

Dr. Faith promised me that as long as I followed the treatment she laid out for me, it was unlikely I'd land in a psychiatric unit again and that my quality of life, with fine-tuning here and there, could be just as high as anyone else's—although I'd never have one of those phone-it-in lives. My brain would always be like a Xerox machine. Drop in a paperclip and a team of qualified technicians would have to toil for hours to get it copying again.

"I starred in my own personal campaign to demolish the social hierarchy at my school. I was so proud and so sure I was making this great step for humanity," I said. "I had this huge ego and thought I was really God's gift. Now it's starting to seem like some. . . deranged illusion or... sleight of hand of my brain."

"Don't discard all that you did and felt during your cycle as nonsense," she advised. "Hypomania and mania are very creative states. No doubt some of what you did and thought was delusion, but some of it may have been inventive and keenly observant. And your grandiose perceptions of self aren't all wrong. Often a manic state brings on confidence and ego that should have been present all along. The grandiosity has to be scaled back, but not extinguished."

When the hour with Dr. Faith was up, I didn't want to leave the warm tea cozy that was her office. I felt like I could drop my soul in her hands and she would see to it that it never touched the floor. I wanted to crawl into her pocket and live there.

Maybe it was power of suggestion, but a few days after my appointment with Dr. Faith, I woke up feeling like I had anvils in my shoes. I tried to go for a run and I made it two blocks from my house and had to turn back.

"I've never seen you eat so much," my mother commented at lunch after I'd polished off four brownies, two bowls of carrot soup, two grilled cheese sandwiches, one bag of potato chips, and a partridge and a pear tree. I had already eaten a three-course breakfast and a midmorning snack.

"I can't get enough food," I said, feeling poured into a pair of jeans that used to fit loosely. "I bet I'll be hungry again in two hours."

"I wonder what this is all about," she said as she rapidly gathered the plates and cups and potato chip bag from the table and bussed them to the sink. She grabbed the tray of brownies I was eyeing as I wondered if maybe I should stuff down a couple more.

"It's one of the drugs I'm on," I said. "The side effects . . ."

"Let's get manies and pedies," my mom said, cutting me off. "Your nails look ragged."

"You interrupted me," I said. "Why do you always do that?"

"I don't think it's healthy for you to dwell on your medicines and treatments," she said. "Go get Valentina and tell her we want to get out of here in ten minutes before the salon gets too busy." I stomped out of the room, too tired to even get into it with her.

On the way to the nail salon, I asked my mother to pull over at a liquor store, where I bought two extra-caffeinated, stimulant-enhanced energy drinks. I'd already put away a double espresso and a pot of black tea, but I still felt like I was running on fumes. I drank one energy drink on the drive to the salon and another while I sat in the spa chair. But I still managed to nod off midmanicure.

After reading and cuddling with Storm (who had always been my favorite to snuggle with) most of the afternoon, I cancelled plans with Tiffany to go to dinner and a movie. The food part sounded good, but walking from the car to the restaurant and the movie sounded too energy intensive, and the hours were way past my new bedtime of nine.

During my next visit with Dr. Faith, she stated that she was concerned about my sluggishness. "How is your mood?" she asked, as usual, and I realized that I didn't have a mood. I was numb. I didn't have the energy to feel anything.

"It's like my brain has flatlined," I told her.

Dr. Faith said that the blue pill was pulling me down too far and I probably didn't need as much of it anymore. "We'll start cutting back on the dose." She sent me off with one of her reassuring smiles and written instructions on how much less of the blue pill I would take each few days.

I reached my car and flopped into the backseat and napped while Valentina drove me home.

My energy was back full force when the day I was to visit Brookside arrived. I couldn't wait to get inside. I decided to bring Hollywood, our newest dog, because she was the smallest. I figured I needed a dog I could hoist up onto beds and a dog who wouldn't threaten anyone. Hollywood was sweet and compact.

Valentina pulled into the Brookside parking lot and got out a book. She was going to read while I did my pet therapy. I put Hollywood on a leash and we walked through the front door of Brookside and up to the receptionist's desk.

"I'm here to volunteer," I told the receptionist. She remembered me from my previous visit to the facility and welcomed me back. She set out some very simple guidelines. I could visit all the rooms, but I had to knock first and enter slowly so that I didn't frighten any of the patients. If I got any kind of negative reaction at all I was to leave immediately. She told me not to be put off by any of the patients' behavior. Some of them had "mental problems" and could get rude and aggressive. Then she pointed to the hallway and invited me to get started.

After knocking on a few doors and getting no answer, I reached a room that was open. Inside was an elderly woman in bed hooked up to an IV. Next to her was a young woman who was massaging her hands. I poked my head inside. "Excuse me," I said. "Would you like a pet visit?" The elderly woman smiled and told me she'd love to meet my dog.

Hollywood quickly charmed both women and they giggled as they pet her. They loved Hollywood so much that it seemed like they were never going to let her go. Meanwhile, I was getting antsy. I didn't think these two women had anything to do with my mother and I was on a mission. I finally swooped up Hollywood and told them I needed to see the other patients.

Next, I visited a woman who clearly had dementia. She petted Hollywood and smiled at him, repeating "Bee, bee, bee, bee" over and over. I left when she asked me to please go and get her husband. I found a nurse and told her that the woman in 204 wanted her husband. The nurse thanked me and told me not to worry about it. Apparently, the woman asked for her husband repeatedly, even though he had been dead for years.

I popped into several more rooms and then into the cafeteria, where they were serving lunch. Most of the people in the cafeteria were elderly, but not all of them. There were a few people that looked to be in their forties and fifties. Women outnumbered the men three to one. Hollywood was a hit. Everybody wanted to love her up. I had to continually stop people from feeding her scraps.

I wasn't loving being inside Brookside. It was reminding me of the hospital–institutional and with nurses running around and plenty of people with obvious mental problems who were making no sense. Before lunch was over, I left the cafeteria. I was discouraged. I'd visited almost a dozen rooms and had probably met or at least seen most of the people living at Brookside – and I wasn't any closer to figuring out how my mother was related to the place. I took off to visit the rooms I hadn't yet made it to, hoping I'd find at least some tiny thing related to my mother.

I wandered down the last hallway in the facility and came across an open door. I poked my head inside and said "hi" to a woman who was no older than fifty. She was clearly in poor health. She was gaunt and she had an oxygen tank next to her and a breathing tube in her nose. She waved me in and smiled at Hollywood.

"Oh! What a cutie! I love dogs!" she said, her face all aglow. Hollywood sensed she had a fan and jumped right into the woman's lap. She introduced herself as Colette and told me that she'd always had a dog until she moved into Brookside. She'd begged them to let her have a dog, but they wouldn't. "It's probably for the best. Now that I have the oxygen tank, it would be hard to walk a dog," she said.

I asked her what was wrong with her and she told me that she had emphysema – advanced emphysema. Clearly, she was on her last legs. I wandered around her room while she happily cuddled and cooed over Hollywood. At her bedside table was a grouping of photos. I bent over to look at them. They were photos of her with different people, smiling and looking much healthier. I froze when my eyes landed on a photo at the back of the table. I gasped and reached out my hand, instinctively grabbing the photo. It was a photo of what appeared to be Colette with my mother and grandparents, all of them much younger. Colette and my mother looked to be in their teens. I stared at the photo, speechless. After a couple minutes, I turned to Colette. "Who… who… are these people?"

"My family," Colette answered. "My mother and father passed, but my sister is still alive."

My hand was shaking so badly that I dropped the photo to the floor and the glass frame shattered. I dropped to my knees, quickly collecting the bits of glass. "I'm so sorry!" I said. "I'll buy you a new frame and bring it to you when I come back."

"It's no problem," Colette said. "Don't worry about it. I have other frames."

I felt the circuits in my brain crossing—the fuses crackling and burning out as the news hit me full frontal. My mother had a sister? I had an aunt?

Why had my mother never mentioned her? Why had I never met her? She seemed sweet and presentable, so why hide her? I felt light-headed as I stood and tossed the glass shards into a trash can.

"Are you okay?" Colette asked me. "You look... wobbly."

"I'm... I'm... fine," I stammered, barely able to spit out the words. "I have to go." I scooped up Hollywood and headed for the door, shaking.

"Please come back with her," Colette called after me.

"Sure," I said as I darted away. I sped down the hallway and made a quick stop at the receptionist's desk. She thanked me for coming and I told her I'd return and then disappeared out the front door.

I ran to the car as fast as I could and hopped inside. "Drive," I told Valentina.

"What's wrong? Are you okay?" she asked, concerned. "Did something bad happen?"

"I'm fine," I answered. "Just get me out of here." I didn't say another word the entire ride home.

I stayed alone in my room the rest of the afternoon, staring at the ceiling and trying to digest what I'd learned. My mother was no longer a mystery to me. She was a perfect stranger. A liar with a giant secret. I didn't know who to talk to about Colette. To say I was angry and confused was an understatement. Learning who Colette was had left my mind scrambled and jumbled and searching for answers.

After several hours, Valentina barged into my room and demanded to know what was wrong. I told her I was fine and she wasn't buying it. "I'm taking you straight to your psychiatrist if you won't tell me what is going on with you."

"My mother has a sister that I never knew about," I blurted out. "I met her at Brookside for the first time."

Valentina wasn't interested in why my mother had kept Colette a secret. Instead, she was mad at me. "You're healing from a nervous breakdown and you go out and make it all worse? This is just the sort of thing you don't need," she said. "We're trying to repair your life and you go out and track down news that shakes up your world. This isn't healthy for you."

Valentina told me that until I had fully healed I was to leave the subject of Colette alone. I wasn't allowed to confront my mother about it and get into a dramatic situation with her. She didn't even want me to talk to Maya about it. She wanted me to put it on the back burner until I was well enough to confront it calmly. I didn't know how I would ever be able to confront the subject of Colette calmly. "Forget about her. Don't talk about her. Don't think of her," Valentina demanded. "I'm sure there's a perfectly good reason why you've never met Colette." She said this, but even she couldn't come up with one earthly reason as to why Colette had been kept in the closet.

I agreed to Valentina's demands, but there was no way I'd be able to stop thinking about Colette. Meeting her was one of the most confounding experiences I'd had so far. I was going to get to the bottom of what had happened with Colette. I would just have to wait for the right opportunity. In the meantime, I would never be able to look at my mother the same or believe anything she said.

Valentina clapped the next morning when I told her we were going rowing with Audrey and Ella. They both apologized on behalf of all my crewmates for kicking me off the team and "not understanding what was going on" with me (although I didn't think they fully knew what had gone on with me.) I didn't necessarily want to sit in a shell and dwell on the fact that I'd be missing out on the only sport that mattered to me for the rest of my high school career—and the wasted efforts and lost opportunities rowing might have afforded me. But Audrey and Ella had been texting, and I felt guilty putting them off any longer. Plus, I was missing being on the water, and I knew I needed to give bored Valentina a little action. She seemed to be going stir-crazy sitting around the house with neurasthenic me. And she claimed she'd been rowing since she was a little girl.

When it was time to carry the boat to the water, I was grateful that Valentina was along to pick up the slack. I could barely lift my arms. "I'm a little under the weather," I told the girls.

"We're gonna miss you next season," Audrey said. "But at least we don't have to compete against you."

"You sure don't," I said. "Evergreen is about as landlocked as it gets."

Audrey and Ella were cool enough not to mention any of the lulu stuff I'd done around them, some of which I remembered vividly as soon as I lowered myself into the shell—like plopping myself into the stroke seat and declaiming that mighty me was the answer to the team's prayers and rowing so out of sync that I ejected myself and a few others from the boat.

How could I have been so egotistical and… irrational? I asked Audrey and Ella to apologize to the others for my "bad manners" and that was about all I had in me to say. Valentina filled the lull in conversation (posing again as my cousin), prattling on about the temperature of the water in Ukraine and who owns boats in Ukraine (rich Russians) and camping in Yosemite, which she'd been bugging me to do.

When I got home from the marina, I noticed that the emotional numbness was wearing off and I was starting to feel things. Only I didn't like what I was feeling—or remembering. I had a vision of myself traipsing through a party dripping wet and wearing a bathing suit. Definitely strange. I had an even-stranger memory of me carrying boxes of athletic socks to crew practice. And there was one very distressing image of me in Spanish class, grabbing backpacks while the class watched. More strange. I had been proud of trying to desegregate the parking lot, but now the image of me directing traffic and telling students where to park was cringe worthy. It was a double-edged sword, because I didn't want to remember, but I had to remember if I wanted to know what I'd done—what I needed to rectify, what I needed to be embarrassed about, and what I could (hopefully there was something) be pleased about.

A couple days later, Tiffany hit me with a hard-sell invite. "The party isn't a long drive away," she pleaded. "If we don't like it, we'll leave. But I know we'll have fun. Esther's hired a band and everything. You can't stay home forever."

"I recorded a bunch of TV shows that I want to watch tonight," I said.

"What? Are you a retiree living in Miami? This whole lack of spunk of yours is starting to freak me out. It's reminding me of when you were depressed," she said. "Throw on that black dress of yours that has the pink tie around the waist and a pair of sandals with heels and be at my house in half an hour. And leave your babysitter home. Don't bring Charles Dickens either—like you did when we went to Jason's party."

"Charles Dickens? I brought Charles Dickens to a party?" I asked.

"Oh, good," she said, sighing.

"Oh, good what?" I asked.

"Oh, good that . . . you don't remember," she said, and then she hung up as fast as she could, probably saving me from another upsetting memory.

The party was huge and the band was okay. It was a cover band, but they covered good bands and good songs. There weren't any kids there I knew because Esther, the hostess, didn't go to West Hills. I danced with Tiffany for a few minutes and then hit up the appetizer table, sampling every snack that didn't contain meat. I finally pulled myself away from the spread, with a mouthful of chips and salsa, and went to find Tiffany and coax her into leaving. I'd been on my feet plenty long.

"Hey, aren't you Martin Luther King Jane-ior?" I heard. I flipped around to see a short, stocky guy with braces smiling at me.

"Excuse me?" I said.

"Yah. You're the one who ran for president at West Hills. My brother goes there. He videoed your speech," he said. "You were talking about a revolution you were heading – trying to get rid of the social pyramid at your school. It was hilarious."

I stood paralyzed. An image of me standing at a podium declaring revolution appeared in my mind.

"Hey, Lance. It's Martin Luther King Jane-ior. The girl from the video," the short guy said, motioning for another short, stocky guy to join us. "I hope you don't mind the nickname, but it's what my brother and his friends started calling you after the speech."

The other guy started laughing. "I saw the video too. It was rad!"

I shoved past the two idiots and darted away as fast as I could, desperately searching for Tiffany. I was sweaty and nauseous and wanted to leave the party more than I had ever wanted to do anything.

Figuring Tiffany was probably belly up to the bar, I frantically elbowed my way into the kitchen, where a keg and a row of booze bottles were lined up on the counter. I was half way into the kitchen when my heart plunged into my socks. There was Ben, leaning against the sliding glass door leading to the patio with a beer in his hand. Next to him, so close she practically had her feet in his shoes, was a tall girl with giant hazel eyes, honey-colored skin, perfectly straight, white teeth and ample curves. Her dark hair was short and spiky, which most of us can't get away with, but her face was sufficiently gorgeous that she would have looked good bald and wearing a ketchup-stained McDonald's uniform. This had to be his girlfriend, Gabriella. And it was worse than I thought. Nobody could compete with this goddess. I stood staring at them, unable to look away. It was like gawking at a fatal pile up on the highway—disturbing and yet, somehow, mesmerizing.

Gabriella had her arm around Ben's waist and her head against his chest. He was clearly hers and nobody was getting near him. Gabriella pulled Ben's head down closer to her and whispered into his ear. Then she moved away from him toward the counter with her empty glass, leaving him alone. I hesitated for a second, debating what to do, feeling more sweaty and more nauseous. I had to get out of the party before I was spotted again and had more humiliation flung my way and/or threw up. But if I could pull it together and endure the torture just a few minutes longer, I might be able to solve the Ben riddle. It was now or who knew how long from now when I'd have another chance to explain myself or gauge how he felt about me—if he really despised me like Tiffany and Nell seemed to think he did. And I had to move fast, before his security guard returned to his side.

With king-sized unease and queasiness that had turned into almost gagging, I willed myself to the back of the room and stopped when I was facing him. He glanced at me and frowned.

"Hi, Ben," I said meekly, my stomach churning and my hands sweaty and trembling. The room started spinning.

"Hey," he answered blankly, his eyes fixed on something at the other end of the room, probably Gabriella, appearing so indifferent that he couldn't even get it up enough to dislike me. That ship hadn't sailed. It had sunk—in the Bermuda Triangle.

I could feel my face growing red as a stop sign. Everything in my body was cringing and cowering. I was wishing upon wishing that I had turned on my heels the second I had laid eyes on Ben and not made the horrendous decision to approach him. I spun around and bumped right smack into Gabriella, spilling her drink down the front of her blouse. "Oh, God," I said. "I'm so sorry. I'll get you some napkins."

"Don't worry about it," she said. "It gives me an excuse to leave. This place is way too crowded." She reached for Ben's hand and pulled him toward her. "Come on. Let's go home." Hand-in-hand, they shoved their way through the crowd and off into the sunset. They weren't just leaving. They were going "home," with all that implied.

My knees buckled and the room got blurry and I couldn't catch my breath. Dizzy, I leaned against the wall as the whole appalling scene came rushing at me, flooding my mind: I was back in Ben's dimly lit bedroom. We were lying on his bed, wound around each other with him on top of me—kissing, panting . . . There were photos on the wall—the apple, the homeless person. I couldn't stop looking at them. Apple, homeless person. Apples, homeless people. Then I was shoving him off me. I jumped from the bed and he struggled to stand and get his footing, looking aghast and horror-stricken. Then he hugged me and I shoved him again, nearly knocking him over. His jaw dropped and his eyes widened and he whimpered. Then I was running—out the door, down the stairs, out of the house, to my car . . .

I regained my balance and plowed my way through the kitchen and into the living room, choking back tears. I pulled Tiffany from the chair she was sitting in. "We have to go. Now!" I dragged her to the front door.

"Slow down," she said. "What's wrong? What's wrong?"

"Everything," I said, bursting into tears.

# FIFTEEN

HE MEMORIES WOULDN'T STOP COMING. They were like war flash-backs: being shackled to a table with restraints; pounding on the walls of the pitch-black seclusion room in the hospital; running through the psych ward and being tackled by laughing security guards; being shackled to a table in the psych ward while security guards laughed some more; shoving Ben off me; Ben's stricken face; an angry policeman shouting at me while I unpacked crates of apples on skid row; Ben's stricken face; Ben's stricken face. The memories rained down on me, drenching and drowning me.

It was official. My worst nightmare had come true. I was the laughing stock of West Hills and maybe the whole county. I would never be able to go back to being an anonymous B person. My cover was blown. The true weirdo that I was—the weirdo I'd carefully kept concealed for so long—had been outed. I'd flown my freak flag. Yes, I was going to a new school, but due to gossip and rumors and a little thing called the Internet, I wasn't going to be able to completely shake my new reputation no matter where I went, unless, maybe, I moved out of the country. I wasn't even a C or a D person. I was at the very bottom of the lower-archy, a certified F person—freakish, finished, f***ed. . . . I detested that girl who had paraded around school like the star of a bad reality show, deliv-ering Marxist rants and performing saucy stunts and thumbing her nose at everybody who was anybody. She had ruined normal for me and might have ruined my whole life.

"So, there are some dumb people who made fun of you and think you're nuts?" Valentina said, dabbing my eyes with a tissue. "All my friends think I'm selfish for leaving my country. Their thoughts have no power. They don't trip me or steal my purse or crash my car. Now, if these thoughts could get out of their heads and punch us or spend our money, then you could worry about what other people think of you. So, there. Who cares what other people think?" I cared. I had always cared, with the exception of several regretful weeks.

The weightiest decision of every day became couch or bed, with bed victorious four times out of five. Tooth brushing was reduced to once a day, and showering was an every-other-day affair. Nothing was on the schedule but sleeping and watching television snuggled up with Storm and whatever other dog felt like hanging out. I wasn't discriminating about what I viewed, either—infomercials, reality shows, sitcoms, movies, cartoons, news—everything but fitness shows. I didn't get absorbed or distracted by any of the moving pictures. TV was just something for my eyes to do.

Leaving my bedroom began to require more gumption than I had. I fantasized about living in a studio apartment where all my belongings would be within arm's reach. I even considered buying one of those metal sticks with a grabber on the end that senior citizens use to reach canned goods on the top shelf, so that I wouldn't need to exert much effort when I had to retrieve the remote control or a pillow that had fallen off the bed. When I didn't feel like walking all the way to the kitchen, Valentina would bring me room service, but the raising of the fork and glass and sawing of the knife required more stamina than I had. I answered the phone only for Maya, and she could barely lure more than a few paragraphs out of me. I didn't want to admit it, but I was on the elevator riding down to the bargain basement or, better yet, the boiler room. The burly black beast of depression had awakened from hibernation and left the cave and was scratching at my door.

Valentina's liveliness was like a dog barking at me to keep tossing a ball, long after I'd lost interest in the game of fetch. She wanted to go to the movies. She wanted to go for a hike. She suggested we go to a waterpark. "When can we deliver the two weeks notice?" I asked Maya.

"We promised her a job through the summer," she said. "I thought you liked Valentina."

"I like her a lot, but she won't stop bugging me to do things I don't have the energy to do," I answered.

"Valentina says she's trying to distract you from negative thoughts you're dwelling on."

Thankfully, my mom got Valentina busy organizing closets and drawers, running errands, grocery shopping, and stuffing envelopes for the Furry Friends quarterly newsletter. But Valentina still hovered over me and pestered me to "get active" every chance she got. "Sitting in your room alone is the worst thing you can do for your mood," she said. "Let's get you out on the water and row, or at least take a stroll. Even reading a book would be better than what you're doing. And stop looking at that boy on the Internet."

Valentina had caught me more than once staring at Ben's picture on the West Hills site, picking at the scab until it bled. "If he is the right boy, he understands," she said. "If not, there are plenty others. Boys are like buses. If you miss one, another one will come along in five minutes—or fifteen minutes, if you are in Kiev."

Slowly, and all at once, the Beast began talking. Stronger, louder, and more cruel than before, the Beast screamed at me without pausing to breathe during the steady stream of: "You'reajoke. You'realoser. You'recrazy. Everyoneatschoolislaughingatyou. Everyonewillalwayslaughatyou. Everyoneatschoolthinksyou'reafreak. Everyoneonthecrewteamthinksyou'reafreak. Everyonewillalwaysthinkyou'reafreak. There'snowheretogowherekidswon'tthinkyou'reafreak. Benhatesyou. Your chanceswithBenaredone. You'llneverfeelbetter. You'llneverfeelbetter. Giveup. Giveup." Over and over and over, like a scratched CD, the voice played on in a never-ending, deafening loop.

The blistering dialogue metastasized. As it grew louder, I grew weaker —I had no immune system to fight back. My body and mind were caught in a Herculean undertow that was pulling me down, down, down into something monstrous and bottomless and starving for me. I was trapped in a house of horrors that had no doors or windows. Everything ached. Even my freckles.

All day long, I was reminded of every shortcoming of mine; every bad grade I'd received; every race I'd lost; every fight with a friend; every time I'd gotten into trouble or been punished; every opportunity I'd screwed up; every stupid thing I'd said; every mean name I'd ever been called; every embarrassment; every criticism; every worry I'd ever had; every disapproving look I'd ever been given; every dream I'd given up on; and, especially every *stupid, crazy, whacked out, shameful* thing I'd said and done while I was manic—particularly what I did to Ben. It was as if I'd never

ever done one right or worthwhile thing. I longed for the good old days of my previous depression. It had been a common cold compared to this stage four cancer.

"The force that through the green fuse drives the flower" had, following the progression of the poem, become the force "that blasts the roots of trees" and was my "destroyer." I had imploded. I was rotting inside my head. And all the kings' horses and all the kings' men couldn't put Jane together again.

I went to sleep (if I slept at all) crying and woke up crying, wondering if I'd cried all night. My eyes burned. The tears were wearing divots on the inside of my eyelids—like rocks that had been worn down by centuries of current rushing over them. I was a corpse with a beating heart. Life was the saddest curse I'd ever been dealt. How lucky are the dead, I thought.

When I caught a flu that grew into bronchitis, I asked the doctor not to prescribe an antibiotic. "The infection is more alive than I am," I told him. "It's survival of the fittest and the virus is more fit."

Oddly, the only words that provided anything in the way of comfort were the stanzas of my new code that I made Dr. Faith read to me. If there was a number for the horribleness I was experiencing then that meant I had somebody in the snake pit with me. "Major Depressive Disorder 296.2X: Condition characterized by severe low, empty, hopeless mood. Symptoms include: decreased pleasure in activities previously enjoyed, sleeping too much or insomnia, greatly reduced or increased appetite, intense sadness, crying, irritability, feelings of worthlessness . . . lethargy and exhaustion . . . preoccupation with death and suicide . . ."

Tiffany showed up on the doorstep one afternoon, even though I'd told her to steer clear. I didn't want her or anyone else competing for my nonexistent attention and treating me like a cripple. And I couldn't tape a smile onto my face for anybody. I'd scared off Nell a few days back when she texted me: "Would you rather run through a large vacant field filled with 500 angry King Cobras or three landmines?" I texted back: "I'd like to be bitten and poisoned by the snakes and then blown up by the landmines." Tiffany's perkiness was unnerving, and I would have killed for her problems. "Can you believe I have to get braces?" she asked. "Who starts senior year in braces? What if I have to get headgear? Tal will never want to hook up with a girl with braces. Who would?"

"Why don't you knock out your teeth and get dentures instead?" I asked.

"Thanks for caring," she said. "At least I'm not bedridden over a guy who wasn't even my boyfriend."

"You think this is about Ben?" I asked. "I could never get this upset about a guy. I'm not happy about what went down between us, but I'm way too much of a 'chicks rule' girl to go completely catatonic over a guy not liking me—no matter who he is. You know that."

"Well then, what is it?" she asked. "You've got it all. You're cute. You wear size twenty-six jeans. You have a nice house. Your mom lets you do whatever you want. You're a good athlete. You get good grades."

"You don't get how little I care about that stuff," I said.

"You say that now."

"I would gladly be an uneducated, two-hundred-pound tub of goo living in a tent if it meant I didn't have to feel like this anymore."

Tiffany paused, her face growing more serious. "I'm sorry," she said. "It's just . . . I don't know what to say. I love you... I miss you... Nell, too. We're scared. You won't do anything drastic, will you? Like, you know. . ."

"Suicide would be redundant," I said. "I'm already dead."

Tiffany left sufficiently freaked out that I doubted she'd return, and I didn't want her to. She hadn't a sliver of an idea about what I was going through and I didn't have the words to describe it. There was nothing about her that I could relate to and that made me feel even more alone.

"That girl is sweet and cute," Valentina said, after Tiffany had driven away. "But her brain is the size of a walnut."

The only thing that held my interest anymore was returning to Brookside. The mystery of Colette still captivated me when absolutely nothing else did. I begged Valentina to take me back, but she wouldn't. I kept working and working on her, hoping that she would get sick of me asking her and finally relent. It was so hard to be around my mother and not bring up Colette. Luckily, I didn't have to much. She was avoiding me more than usual. I suspected that the reason was that she didn't want to confront my deep unhappiness. It was too much ugly reality for her. She preferred to live in her dream world where Pumpkin was doing fine and required nothing in the way of emotional support from her.

"Why are you even bothering with me?" I asked Dr. Faith during one of our visits. I was sprawled across her couch wishing I could move in with her and crash on her living room floor. The depression didn't lessen when I saw her, but I felt safer when she was near. My mother may have birthed me, but Dr. Faith was my real mother—my fairy godmother.

"To save one person is to save the world," she said.

"But I don't deserve to be saved. I have money and a home and an education," I said. "There are people living in plastic trash bags who aren't complaining as much as I am."

"I've met plenty of poor folks who are happier than you are," she said. "Do you really believe the American idea that privilege equals happiness? You're carrying some of the worst pain there is, in my opinion. The most basic instinct and drive in life is to stay alive, and depression snatches that from you. People who lose their homes in hurricanes—even starving people—don't necessarily feel as bad as you do mentally. It doesn't matter how fortunate or unfortunate your circumstances are. Pain is pain."

On route to my next session with Dr. Faith, I found a loophole in her "pain is pain" theory in the form of homeless, mentally ill people. Their pain had to be worse than mine.

When Valentina got stuck in traffic next to a bus stop, I hopped out of the car and took the arm of a filthy, bedraggled bag lady who was yelling loudly and angrily at nothing.

"What are you doing?" Valentina screeched. The traffic had started moving again. She pulled over to the curb and stopped as I tried to drag the woman toward the car door.

"I'm bringing her to see Dr. Faith," I said. "She's going to have my appointment." The woman smelled like rotting garbage and wasn't budging. "I'm getting you help," I told her.

"Get your hands off me! Stop!" she wailed. "Let go! Help!"

Valentina raced to me, pulled the homeless woman from my grip, and planted her back on the bus bench. Then she shoved me back in my seat and slammed the car door and turned on the childproof-lock button.

"Dumb, dumb, dumb," she kept repeating. "I'm telling your doctor." I'd never seen Valentina so angry before.

"You can't just abduct people. You could be arrested," Dr. Faith said, after Valentina marched into her office and recounted what had happened. "That wasn't smart."

"But aren't I right? Doesn't that woman need help more than I do?" I asked.

"So, I don't get you up and running because the homeless woman is in the dumper?" she asked. "It's not like two dysfunctional people equal one functional person."

"It's just that I see people out there who could be me if I was disadvantaged," I said. "It gives me guilt. I should be helping them."

"Look, it's a crime that so many mentally ill people live on the streets," she said. "But, it's a crime that you didn't commit. You didn't put them there and you can't save them all. All you can do is clean up your side of the street. Put on your oxygen mask."

"What do you mean?" I asked.

"You know how flight attendants ask parents to put their oxygen masks on before they put their kids' masks on when there's a drop in cabin pressure?"

"What's that got to do with anything?" I asked.

"It's so the parents don't pass out before they can help their kids," she said. "How will you ever be able to help anyone if you're a puddle? Let's get you balanced and send you back out there to be a productive member of society. Our world doesn't need another depressed person lolling in bed or killing themselves and carving indelible scars in the people who love them."

Miracle of all miracles finally happened. I had hounded Valentina so doggedly about visiting Brookside that she caved. I think she realized that I was in bad enough shape that I couldn't get worse, no matter what happened at Brookside, so why keep me away from doing something I wanted to do so badly? I also think she understood that it was the only thing in life that I had any enthusiasm for. She was desperate to find *something* I was interested in and this was it.

I made an appointment for a pet therapy visit with the receptionist and she seemed happy that I wanted to return to the center. "I was afraid the patients scared you off," she said. I arrived in the afternoon with Hollywood and proceeded to visit a few patients. I wasn't interested in seeing any of them. All I wanted to do was get to Colette's room, but I didn't want my visit to seem suspicious.

After I'd visited several rooms, I headed for Colette. My heart was pounding. I didn't know what I was going to say to her or ask her. I was considering telling her I was her niece. I was considering asking a bunch of questions about her family, my mother in particular. Or maybe I would just ask her all about herself and try and get to know her better. Maybe we could strike up a friendship and I could visit her regularly.

My knees were shaking as I reached her room. The door was shut and I knocked. I could hear shouting coming from inside. It was Colette. "Get your hands off me! No! Stop it!" The door opened and a nurse peeked out. I glanced inside and saw Colette being restrained by two orderlies. The nurse looked at me and Hollywood and frowned. "Now isn't a good time for Colette to have pet therapy. She's not in the right condition for it," she said.

I couldn't stop staring at Colette. A nurse was injecting her with a needle. "Colette, you need to breathe and try and calm down," the nurse said. "Nobody is trying to hurt you. We're trying to help you."

"Did you hear what I said, Miss?" the nurse asked me as I stood there, still gaping at Colette, not moving. She stepped into the hallway and shut the door behind her. I could hear Colette continuing to scream at the staff. "Thank you for bringing your dog by. I know Colette loves dogs," the nurse said. "I hope this scene won't frighten you away."

"What's wrong with her?" I asked.

"I'm afraid I can't discuss patients' medical conditions with anyone but family," she said.

"I'm her niece," I said.

"Heather is your mother?" she asked.

I nodded. "I didn't realize she had a daughter," the nurse said. "Colette is having a psychotic episode. Now and then she'll refuse to take her medication and this is what happens. I'm sorry you had to witness it."

The nurse opened the door and stepped back inside the room. "You take care," she said as she shut the door. I picked up Hollywood and sprinted away from Colette's room faster than I had during my previous visit. I raced past the receptionist's desk without even saying good-bye. I wished I'd listened to Valentina and stayed away from Brookside. Now I knew the ugly truth. Colette was like me. Her fate was my fate – middle aged and locked up in a home, raising holy hell while being stuck with needles. If my world as I knew it had shattered when I met her, now it had been ground down and swept away.

Valentina was waiting outside. I jumped into the car and burst into tears. She chastised herself for letting me visit Brookside. "I never should have taken the chance," she said. "What bad judgement. I'm supposed to be keeping things like this from happening to you." It took Valentina hours of her listening to sentences punctuated with choking sobs to shake out of me what I had witnessed. "Just because Colette has psychotic episodes at her age doesn't mean you will," she said, as convincingly as she could. "The nurse told you she doesn't take her medicine. You take your medicine, so you won't wind up like her." But, no amount of convincing was going to make me believe that a place like Brookside wasn't what I had to look forward to.

Learning the truth about Colette made me feel worse. Now that I knew my depressing fate, I had nothing to look forward to. What was the point of even trying to get well? And I hated my mother. I couldn't stand living under the same roof as her. She repulsed me. It was clear to me now what had happened. She was ashamed that she had a sister who was mentally ill, so she hid that she had a sister at all. It was probably what she wished she could do with me. She was obviously visiting Colette out of guilt. Colette's emphysema seemed serious enough that she would most likely die soon. Even a heartless person like my mother would probably have a hard time forgiving herself if her own sister died without some final show of concern.

I told both Maya and Dr. Faith about Colette. Maya was intrigued, but not enough to want to meet Colette. She didn't see the point. "If Mom wants to keep her a secret then let her," she said. (She added that she'd often wondered why some of my mother's childhood photos were cropped. I'd never noticed.) Since I'd come out of the hospital, I'd noticed a change in Maya's attitude towards my mother. Whereas before she had been curious about my mother and also felt resentment towards her, she was now completely indifferent. How my mother had dealt and was dealing with my illness angered her to the point that she'd washed her hands of her.

Dr. Faith wasn't surprised that I had an aunt with bipolar disorder, which is what she determined Colette's problem was, since it was genetic. But, she didn't see Colette's fate as my fate. "She went off her medication,"

Dr. Faith said. "That's why she's psychotic." She told me that people who won't take their meds are hard to help and can have tragic lives. "That doesn't need to be your life. You'll stay on a regime and have a happy and successful life." I wished I could believe her, she sounded so convincing, but the image of Colette being restrained and poked with a needle was so vivid and horrifying that it cancelled out Dr. Faith's theory.

One night, while I was in the bedroom gulping down handfuls of water from the sink faucet (I had chronic medication-induced dry mouth), I glanced in the mirror. There were dark circles under my eyes and my skin was a sallow green and broken out and my cheeks were hollow. My upper body looked like an X-ray or an anatomy lesson. It was a pitiful looking face and body. The longer I stared in the mirror, the more I didn't like what I saw, and the more that I didn't like what I saw, the more agonized I felt. I started banging my head against the mirror.

"You're pathetic, you're pathetic," I repeated over and over with the Beast. "Loser, loser, loser, loser. Give up. Give up. Give up. Die, die, die, die."

As I pounded my forehead harder and faster against the glass, I noticed that my throbbing head was having an unexpected and welcome effect. Focusing on the physical ache was shifting my attention from the psychological ache, and it was a relief of sorts. It reminded me of rowing a 2K, where the exhaustion made it impossible to feel anything but exhausted.

I continued banging my head until I hit it so hard against the glass that the mirror cracked. I didn't stop. Blood was trickling down my face and dripping into the sink. Shattered pieces of the mirror began falling noisily to the counter and floor. I shut my eyes so that I wouldn't get glass in them and continued banging my head on the mirror. As the pain grew more and more intense, my mental burden crept further away. The nonstop hatred-of-myself dialogue was growing quieter. The pain on the outside was snuffing out the pain on the inside.

Valentina, whose room was next to mine, heard the broken glass hitting the counter and rushed into the bathroom, where she pulled my head away from the mirror. "What are you doing?" she wailed. "Stop! You're ruining your pretty face."

She carefully plucked the shards of glass from my forehead and then used a wet towel to wipe the blood from my face and neck. She took my hand and plastered it against the towel over my forehead. "Keep the pressure on it," she ordered. "It will stop the bleeding."

I arrived at the emergency room still holding the towel against my forehead. "I was carrying a glass of water upstairs to my room and I tripped and fell on it. I guess I should have turned on the light," I told the doctor who was stitching me up. It turned out the bleeding was more dramatic than the actual cuts were. Six stitches in all and the doctor said that they probably wouldn't leave scars.

"Swear you won't tell my mom about this," I begged Valentina as she drove me home from the hospital. I had explained to her that I wasn't necessarily trying to do myself in, but that the pain felt good in a weird, masochistic way.

"Your mother will know you've been hurt when she sees the bandages, but I guess we could tell her you fell," she said. "But I have to tell the psychiatrist. You can't be hurting yourself."

# SIXTEEN

THE EXPERIENCE OF CRASHING against the glass gave me a newfangled obsession. I daydreamed more and more about making the big, final transition into oblivion. Actually, it wasn't a new idea. It was an idea I was considering more earnestly. It was comforting to know that suicide was always there for me if the pain inside got any more excruciating. As the writer and philosopher Friedrich Nietzsche said, "The thought of suicide is a powerful solace; by means of it gets one through many a bad night." The problem was how to go about getting the job done, especially with Valentina keeping vigilant watch over me like I was a newborn.

Soon enough, an opportunity presented itself. My mother went to the hair stylist and Valentina left the house to pick up some prescription refills of mine. She ordered me not to "try anything funny" and said she'd be back in less than half an hour. As soon as she was out the door, I pulled myself from bed and began a tour of the house—looking for a method of ending it all.

First, I headed to the kitchen and checked the drawers for knives. As I suspected, the big chef's knives had been locked up somewhere, but the serrated bread knife was still available. I pulled it from the drawer and delicately grazed it across my wrists and neck, getting a feel of how a fatal slice might be carried out. Apparently, it takes a while to die once you've slit your wrists. I decided that I didn't want the gruesome experience of slowly drowning in a puddle of blood.

I wandered into the garage, thinking maybe I could turn on the car engine and wait inside until I was asphyxiated. Then I remembered that the car keys were locked up when the cars weren't in use.

Back in my room, I pulled a selection of belts from my closet and stood on top of a chair under a light fixture and glanced up, trying to figure out how one might tie a belt to the light fixture. But, the belts were too stiff to tie around the light fixture and the light fixture probably wasn't strong enough to hold me up. I couldn't find anything else in the house to hang myself from or with.

I climbed into the attic and opened the window and stared down at the concrete patio in the backyard. The attic probably wasn't far enough from the patio to ensure death by defenestration. With my luck, I'd become a paraplegic—forever unable to kill myself because I couldn't move any of my muscles.

I left the attic discouraged. I didn't have the know-how or guts for a do-it-yourself disposal of myself. Or did I? As I passed Valentina's room, I noticed that the cabinet next to her bed was ajar. The cabinet where all the medications in the house—even the cold medicine and homeopathic remedies—were normally locked up tight.

Overdosing on pills was the primo choice—no pain, no bravery required—but I never imagined I'd have the chance to get my hands on even a bottle of baby aspirin, since Valentina guarded all of the pills so closely. She must have checked on what needed refilling before she left for the pharmacy and then forgotten to shut the cabinet.

My heart was pounding as I walked to the cabinet. Suddenly I felt giddy, happy even. Relief was on the way. It could all be over in minutes. I could cease to feel. I was going to die someday anyway, I reasoned. I was just speeding up the process by sixty years or so. Sixty miserable years.

I reached the cabinet and pulled out bottle after bottle of pills, hunting for my sleeping medication. Luckily it wasn't a prescription that needed to be refilled. The bottle was full. I took the bottle and headed to my bathroom, where I poured a nice, big glass of water. I wasn't going to think about this and weigh my options. I wasn't going to second guess myself. I wasn't going to debate why or why not. I wasn't going to wonder about what was next—if anything. I wasn't going to write a note. I wasn't going to worry about Maya's feelings or my friends' feelings. I had little time left before Valentina returned home—and this opportunity might never present itself again. It was going to be like jumping into a cold pool. I didn't want to be alive, and if I didn't want to be alive, then I had to die. There was no other way to not be alive. I was going to just do it. Die. Done. The end.

My hands were trembling as I stuffed the pills into my mouth, four at a time so I didn't choke, and washed them down with gulps of water. When the bottle was empty I dropped it in the trash and left the bathroom to find the spot where I wanted to fade out and leave. I had some time before the pills kicked in.

After touring the house, I returned to my bedroom and crawled in bed, deciding that I wanted death to be as comfortable as possible. I lay on my back with my hand over my heart, waiting to feel its last beat. Then I started feeling fuzzy and dreamy and dizzy and nauseous. I was gagging and I wanted to throw up, but I wasn't going to. Throwing up would ruin everything. I had to keep the drugs inside me. I was feeling sicker and sicker to my stomach, but I was also feeling lighter and fluffier. I felt like I was hovering over the bed. I felt warm. Peaceful. The best I'd felt in weeks. I wasn't having that last gasp of "Oh, no! I don't want to die! This was a mistake!" Death was going to be easy, painless. Tons of people had already died. If they'd done it, so could I. Death was as natural as birth.

Soon… I was really sleepy and dreamy and then… I started feeling too nauseous to hold it in. I leapt up from the bed to run to the toilet, but after about three steps I fell, way too dizzy to walk. The room was bobbing and my legs and arms felt limp. I rolled on my side and started puking and puking and puking. My stomach was cramping and the vomiting wouldn't stop. I was retching and heaving and still struggling to stand and walk to the toilet, but now I couldn't even move my head.

I don't know how long I vomited—the seconds and minutes ran together. I kept hoping that I'd stop vomiting long enough to slip away. Why was I still hanging on? Was there still enough medicine inside me to get the job done?

Then I could hear Valentina shouting. It felt like she was shaking me. I didn't want to be shaken. I wanted to tell her to stop shaking me and shove her away, but I couldn't get words out of my mouth.

Then there were bright lights and loud noises and I was on a bed that was moving. I felt myself being carried inside a car or a truck, and the door slammed shut and I was moving again, with Valentina still shouting at me. I was feeling more and more tired, but she was yelling too loudly for me to slide into peaceful slumber.

Soon I felt myself being lifted and moved somewhere else, with more bright lights and people talking. I heard the whir of a machine as something was stuck down my throat. It felt like a hose, and I gagged and gagged and tried to pull it out, but somebody had pinned down my arms. I felt air whooshing through my throat and my stomach cramping. It was like I'd swallowed a vacuum. Then... nothing...

I stayed in the hospital for a day and a half, hooked up to IVs of fluid and being asked, over and over, why I did it and was I going to attempt it again. I answered, in different words, the same thing over and over: I did it because I hurt too much not to do it and I promise I won't do it again. The promise felt hollow, but I'd tried to end it all and it didn't work. Now I didn't have faith I *could* make it work. But the suicide option wasn't going anywhere. I could put it on the back burner for now and try again later if I wanted to and, hopefully, do a better job of it next time.

It seemed like whenever I opened my eyes, Valentina was there—she and the doctors and nurses whispering and rifling through papers. I saw Maya once, and all she did was cry. Then my mother visited. She tried to hold my hand and I pulled it away. I was feeling short on inhibitions and impulse control, which was not a good combination for my mother. "Stay away from me," I told her. "Go home."

"Calm down, Pumpkin. I'm just here to check on you and make sure you're better," she said.

"I know what you did. I know all about Colette and how you hid her from us because you're embarrassed she's bipolar," I said. "I met her. You're a worse person than I ever even imagined."

My mother's jaw dropped. She stared at me, dumfounded. "Colette? How did you meet Colette?"

"I went to Brookside. That's how. I know you visit and send checks to make yourself feel less guilty now that she's dying," I said. "I bet you'd disown me if you could now that I'm bipolar, too. But, it's too late. Everybody already knows I'm yours. You can't just crop me out of photos."

"Pumpkin, you don't understand," she said. "I'm not ashamed of you or Colette. You don't know the story of Colette. You don't know what happened."

"I know all I need to know," I said. "Please leave. I can't be around you right now." My mother grabbed her purse and shuffled off. I hadn't intended to confront her about Colette. I was just going to freeze her out. But, I was glad I'd told her off. She deserved it. Whatever semblance of a relationship we'd had before was officially over and at least now she'd understand why.

Minutes later, Dr. Faith visited. When she walked in the door, I started bawling and begged her not to put me back in St. Joan's. She told me that she wasn't going to put me back in the psych ward, but that I would not be left alone for even a minute until she was convinced I wouldn't hurt myself again. Valentina would be with me at all times.

"I'm sorry I did it," I told her between sobs. "But it's like I'm in a meat grinder all day, everyday. There's no break. I needed a break and there was no other way to get a break."

"It's part of the cycle," she said. "What goes up must come down. But you will get a break. I think you've bottomed out and can only go uphill from here."

"When? I've been waiting and waiting. How long will this last?" I asked.

"I don't know," she finally admitted.

"What if it never ends?" I asked.

"All you can do is be patient," she answered. "The depression will subside. I've never had a patient who I couldn't help. Remember—'suicide is a permanent solution to a temporary problem.'"

Dr. Faith decided to wage a blitzkrieg on all the neurotransmitters in my brain—dopamine, norepinephrine, serotonin. She upped the doses of all my medications and added a purple pill that would take the place of the old blue pill but, hopefully, wouldn't have so many side effects—the sedation and enormous appetite. The purple pill would act as a glue to help fuse the mucked-up pieces of brain back together.

"I'm also putting you on a hormone replacement," she said. "Your last blood test (I was still having so many blood tests that I was a pin cushion) indicated that your thyroid levels are down. Lithium can do that. It is also impairing your kidney function." Ironically, my mother's make-believe stories about my kidney condition had become reality.

"I want you to start eating more and try and get outside everyday. Have your mother or Valentina or Maya, when she's home, take you somewhere," she said. "Sunlight is good for you, and an outing might provide a bit of distraction. Try to get your heart pumping, too. Exercise helps."

"But, how do I get out of bed and face the day when I haven't slept all night?" I asked.

"I'll give you a prescription for a stimulant to take in the morning," she said. "It's one that airline pilots and truck drivers use for energy during long shifts."

I wished I hadn't OD'd, because the last thing I wanted to do was to add more meds to my cocktail. I was already ingesting so many pills that if you shook me I would have rattled. I had a pill for every color of the rainbow. And even though I took different medications at different hours of the day (the hours were programmed into Valentina's phone), each set required not one but two glasses of water to wash them down. My most important possession was my pill cutter. Dr. Faith did say, however, that once (if ever) I was stable, we could cut down on the meds.

The new purple pill turned out to be a gift from the heavens. Within a half hour of taking it, before bed, I was out cold. And it wasn't a sleeping pill or a downer, so it wasn't addictive and I wouldn't build up a tolerance. If only I could have taken a second dose in the morning and spent the day unconscious, but Valentina made sure I was awake and doing things all day, and she wouldn't let me out of her sight. She slept in my double bed with me and even sat outside the bathroom when I used the toilet.

People say that after an attempted suicide, the victim often has a new appreciation for life and is happy that he or she didn't succeed. I wasn't happy to be alive and had no appreciation for a life that was nothing but pain. But trying suicide did change something for the better. Now that I knew I wasn't afraid of dying, I felt like less of a wimp. I was choosing to be alive. I wasn't just staying alive because I was scared of death. I had stood up to the Beast and let him know that I actually had more power than he did, because I had the power to kill us both. I'd stood up to God too, and told him, "You can't fire me. I quit." Also, Dr. Faith had convinced me that I'd hit rock bottom, so I didn't need to worry that I would ever feel any worse unless, of course, I was trapped in the hospital again. Strange how the threat of sticking me in the hospital if I tried to off myself again was actually keeping me from making another attempt. I couldn't go back to that place.

Suicide also gave me an interesting insight into life: how terrified everyone is of death—theirs and yours. Dr. Faith was the only person who talked to me about my attempt. Maya couldn't discuss the subject without bursting into tears. My mother took different routes around the house so she wouldn't have to bump into me, though that could have been the result of our unpleasant conversation in the hospital. Even practical Valentina danced around the issue. None of them wanted anywhere near the subject of my pill overdose, which was a blessing, because that meant that I didn't have to answer any questions or defend the choice I'd made.

Valentina eventually made a stab at a suicide conversation, but I could tell it was hard for her. "I didn't look after you carefully enough," she said, squirming uncomfortably. "It's my fault what happened. I'm not taking my eyes off you until you're out of your depression. I don't care if I have to stay awake all night every night. You're the only person I feel close to that doesn't live six thousand miles away from me. I'd be devastated if something happened to you."

I told Valentina to give herself a break. She was doing an amazing job. But, Valentina was a perfectionist and what I'd done was proof to her that she wasn't doing her job perfectly. I had to admit it was a secure feeling knowing that somebody as fastidious and loving as Valentina was in my corner.

As per Dr. Faith's instructions, I started each day with a fruit juice, soymilk, and protein powder smoothie (all I could choke down) and began my dreaded daily outings. I practically needed a wheelchair to cart my brain out the door. During the drives to various "uplifting" locales, I could think of nothing but the innocent bugs being squished to death under the car tires and the pollution spewing out of the tailpipe.

Valentina brought me across town to the lovely Descanso Gardens. "Isn't the nature so pretty?" she chirped as we twisted through a path in the park, passing a forest of multicolored camellias. I lowered myself onto each bench we passed. But, Valentina wouldn't let me sit. "No, no," she said. "You need the exercising." We snaked through the rose garden. There were roses in every color. "Mmm," Valentina said, with her nose stuck in a giant, fragrant, yellow rose growing from a bush that was leaning far left, all its branches tipping sideways. I sniffed the rose and smelled nothing but decay. The rose was brown at the edges. It would soon wilt and lose its petals and they would drop to the dirt and decompose into mulch. *"And I am dumb to tell the crooked rose my youth is bent by the same wintry fever."*

The lilac and iris gardens were a sea of purple. Bees hovered above the flowers buzzing, collecting nectar. No doubt there was a hive nearby where they worked tirelessly for a greedy queen bee. "Can't we go now?" I asked.

"Not until we see the Japanese Garden and the California Garden and the edible plants," Valentina said, her head buried in a map of the garden. "It's such a perfect sunny day. We can't leave yet." But I was ready to split. I'd had enough of the soon-to-be-dead flowers, and the sun wasn't doing it for me either. The sun looked bright now, but it would burn out in a few billion years and leave the planet as barren as an empty shoebox.

The next day, Valentina drove down to the boathouse and tried to stick me in a boat, but I refused, so she shuttled me downtown to the historic Biltmore Hotel for tea. I sat slumped at a table across from her, picking at dry scones and dainty sandwiches that I didn't want to eat and drinking tea that tasted bitter, while Valentina read from a tour book. "The hotel was built in 1923. Can you believe that?" she asked. "And it's still in such good shape. It's an example of Renaissance-style architecture."

I studied the plaster columns and ceiling with elaborate woodcarvings and pure gold gilding. I wished the epic architecture dazzled me. But I saw cracks in the ceiling and pits in the stone columns. Slowly the cracks would lengthen and branch out and termites would gnaw away at the building's innards and the stone and plaster would disintegrate into fine dust until there was nothing left but a pile of dusty rubble.

Maya came home for a weekend. Ever since the incident with the pills, she'd been calling multiple times a day and visiting more than her schedule could permit. She took me to the beach and we walked the shoreline in bare feet. "Try to breathe deeply," Maya said. "The clean air is good for your health. It smells good, too."

The air did smell clean, and I was sorry to have to dirty it with my lungs, which were probably fairly filthy after the bout of bronchitis I'd just kicked. Maya and I rolled up our pants legs and waded in the cold water. "I've always loved the sound of the tide," Maya said. "It's the only sound that's both loud and peaceful at the same time."

As we ambled down the beach, we reached the storm drain. "We should turn back," Maya said. "The water gets dirty here."

My mind fastened itself to the word "dirty," and the rest of the walk I obsessed on the storm drain runoff that contaminated the water when it rained and poisoned fish.

I looked behind us as Maya and I continued back down the beach. I choked up when I saw that the foamy tide had washed away our footprints in the sand—like we'd never even been there.

That night, Maya and I lay in lounge chairs in the backyard and admired the stars. "Doesn't it feel good to be a part of something so giant and majestic?" she asked. "It makes me feel safe. Like there's a plan for all of us and we don't even have to work that hard to be part of it. The stars and planets are lifted and spun in circles without trying—and we're taken care of, too."

"Sorry to be such a pessimist, but I don't feel cared for or held up like the planets," I answered. What the vast expanse of the sky inspired in me was a feeling of insignificance. I was but a tiny speck of lint in the universe. How could I be so small when my sadness was so big?

It was hopeless. I was darkening every lovely locale I visited with the black cloud that followed me around. Before Maya headed back to school, she insisted we visit one last spot for lightening the spirits—the Natural History Museum. It was a quick trip. We meandered through the lobby and into the North American room, where there was a woman offering up various relics for visitors to touch. She handed me a trilobite encased in amber. I held it in my hand, studying it. Then I burst into tears, and Maya rushed me off to the restroom.

"It's just nature and history," Maya said. "What's the problem?"

"We all struggle and suffer and then all that's left are bones—or fossils if you're lucky," I explained. "In a hundred years everybody we know will be gone. We'll all be forgotten."

Poor loving and devoted Maya drove me home and spent the afternoon and night with me. I begged her to focus on her summer school classes and stop calling and visiting so often. I hated all the worry I was causing her. But she wouldn't give up on me. She was going to keep me on life support as long as she could. There was no way she was signing the "Do Not Resuscitate" order I wished she would sign. "You're not alone," she told me at least once every day. "We're in this together."

One night, Valentina walked into my room with a colorful calendar featuring the streets of Kiev. "Not now," I growled when she opened the calendar and waved it at me. I had just taken my evening dose of downers and I was antsy to lose consciousness.

"This will only take one minute," Valentina said. She flipped through the calendar until she reached July, and then she used a thumbtack to hang the calendar on the bulletin board above my desk. "I did this for my grandfather after my grandmother died," she said. "He was so down, and it helped him. I wish I'd thought of this before." She uncapped a black marker and began X-ing out each day on the calendar until she reached the thirtieth. "This is today," she said. "Come and X it out. This day is over."

I moved to the calendar and she handed me the pen. I drew a big black X through the day. "There," she said. "The day is done. You never have to live it again. You see all these Xs? These are all the days you've made it through. Each X'd out day is a day you never have to live again. Think of this as a crew race and keep paddling. The finish line gets closer every day."

It was satisfying to see the collection of Xs. I was like an alcoholic chalking up days of sobriety or a general gathering my troops to finish off the battle. I had to admit, I felt a subtle lift—a pride of accomplishment. I had come so far, maybe I could soldier on a few more miles.

Each evening, after the sun left to go and wake up the east, I pulled out the black marker and drew an X through the day and another soldier popped up. My battalion was growing. There was a long wake behind me and I was just a few boat lengths from the finish line. Catch, drive, finish, recover . . . A resolve to finish the race was surging inside me. I wasn't giving up just yet. "Is that all you've got?" I yelled at the Beast. "Bring it. I can take it. I've still got a stockpile of ammo."

# SEVENTEEN

$\mathcal{D}$R. FAITH WAS THE FIRST TO NOTICE. "I've got to get it together before I start my new school," I told her.

"Did you hear what you just said?" she asked.

"Yah. So," I answered.

"You're talking about the future. About going to school," she said. "You're planning on sticking around and getting well enough to tackle something as big as school."

"I don't know if I'll be *able* to go to school, or to survive school," I said. "I'm just hoping I *can* attend school."

"Hope suggests that you're seeing at least a little light at the end of the tunnel," she said.

She was right. It was only a birthday-candle-sized flicker, but it was a flicker.

"Let's cling to that," she said. "Try to focus on the flashlight that's guiding you out."

Pulling myself from the chin-deep cement I was stuck in didn't happen all at once. I'd feel a minute or half an hour of something akin to peace and I'd cherish it. "Come on, don't leave me," I'd plead. I was like a baby learning to walk. I'd use a piece of furniture to pull myself to standing and then take a few wobbly steps on my own before I fell to my tush. Each time I stood I walked a little farther until I was making it all the way across the room.

I didn't trust the sense of well-being to stick around. When I felt good, I was waiting to tumble back into the darkness or hotfoot up into mania.

And when I felt not good, I was pretty sure I was stuck there for good. But soon the anxiety had toned down enough that I didn't need a sedative during the day. I didn't need the sleeping pill at night anymore either. Everyday I left my bed for a little bit longer. I started showering more often and drying my hair after I washed it and putting on makeup before I left the house.

Valentina was overjoyed when I agreed to go for a three-mile hike with her. "You have color in your cheeks," she said, beaming. "You're picking up your feet when you walk." After the hike, I suggested we go to the bookstore. I hadn't had the concentration to read anything for weeks. I was ready to lose myself in a novel, and Valentina loved to read and had been tearing through the books in the den. We spent a couple hours in the bookstore and then went out for coffee. Valentina, as usual, consumed massive amounts of espresso. "I'm still making up for all the years of bad coffee I lived through in Kiev," she said.

"You might not believe this," Valentina told me on the way home. "But, you're the best patient I've had. You never did the 'why me?' whining. You should be proud of yourself."

I thanked Valentina for the compliment and then noticed that she looked sad. She'd been really quiet all day. "Is something wrong?" I asked her.

"I'm supposed to be asking you about your feelings, not vice versa," she answered.

"No, seriously. You've barely spoken a word all day," I said.

It took me a while to shake it out of Valentina, but she finally admitted the problem. "I'm so glad you're better," she said. "But, that means I won't have a job much longer. I'm going to miss you. You've become like a sister."

It hadn't passed through my mind that Valentina would leave, but she was right. I wouldn't need her much longer. Still, I didn't want to her to go. "I'll work something out," I promised her. "Maybe you can get a new job and pay my mom rent and live with us. She wouldn't charge you much. She's generous. It's one of her few good qualities." Valentina smiled at my idea. I smiled, too. Valentina knew me inside and out. She'd seen me at my absolute worst – seen it all hang out – and now she was telling me that she was still going to like me even when she was no longer receiving a paycheck for liking me. It doesn't happen often, but now and then life drops something totally unexpected and amazingly awesome in your lap. Valentina was one of those things.

One afternoon, I returned home from a visit with Dr. Faith and stepped into the kitchen for a glass of ice water. I hadn't reached the faucet when I heard wailing. I followed the cries into the backyard, where I found my mother sobbing while Valentina rubbed her back. I quickly counted the dogs. All were present, so a dead dog wasn't the problem. What was all the caterwauling about? I rushed to her side. "What is it? What happened?" I asked, now starting to get frantic that maybe the problem had to do with Maya.

"It's Colette. She died. Last night. The emphysema got her," Valentina said.

"It's so unfair," my mother said through her blubbering and sniffling. "Colette was too young to die. Why did she have to be taken away? She was a good person. No, no. It can't be. Not my dear sister."

"There, there," Valentina said. "She's with God now."

"You don't know what it's like. You have Maya," my mom said. "You'll always have Maya. I have nobody." Nobody? Maya and I equaled nobody? Even in her mourning she was insensitive.

I called Maya to break the news, but Valentina had already told her. "The funeral is tomorrow," she said. "I'm coming down."

"You're going to her funeral?" I asked. "You've never even met her. You wouldn't even know about her if it hadn't been for me."

"She was my aunt," Maya said matter of factly. "She's family. I have to go."

"Just to let you know, I'm going to the funeral for Colette, not Mom," I said. "I couldn't care less how she feels. The only reason she's so upset is that she feels guilty."

"Try and put aside all your problems with her, at least through the funeral," Maya said. "See you at ten."

Valentina pulled me aside later in the day. "You need to show more sympathy," she said. "Your mother is devastated. She's lost her sister. How would you feel if something happened to Maya?"

"I'd be devastated," I said. "But, I would never hide Maya and be ashamed of her if she was mentally ill. I'm not buying any of this mourning routine my mom is going through. It's all about her. She wants sympathy."

"We don't know that for certain," Valentina said. "I think your mom is truly upset over Colette. You have to be there for her. She doesn't know how she's going to make it through."

I didn't bother arguing with Valentina, but I wasn't going to "be there" for my mother. She had never been there for me. And it was my guess that she'd never been there for Colette until she was dying. She didn't deserve my support. The thought of even handing her a tissue to dry her tears made me wince.

A hearse pulled up in our driveway the morning of Colette's funeral and we climbed into the backseat. We arrived at a Catholic church and followed the casket inside. The church was largely empty, save about three pews of people. I recognized a couple of them as nurses from Brookside, but I'd never seen any of the others before. My mom's cousin, Francesca, was the sole mourner I knew. She was actually the only member of my mom's family I'd ever met, aside from my grandparents. I wondered if she approved of Maya and me being in the dark all these years about Colette.

The priest began the service, and my mother pulled out rosary beads and began fingering them. I'd never seen my mother with rosary beads before. I didn't even know she owned them. In fact, I only knew of her going to church for funerals. She didn't visit on her own. She shut her eyes through the mass and bowed her head in prayer. So things got rough for my mom and suddenly she was big buddies with God? I hoped that if there was a God, that he could see through her phony baloney.

The funeral was blessedly, no pun intended, brief, and afterwards we rode to the cemetery in the hearse and watched as Colette was lowered into a hole in the ground—my mother a faucet the entire duration of the ritual. I bent down over the grave and hung my head. "Dear Colette," I said quietly. "I only met you once, but I feel like I know you—or at least know what you went through. I'm so sorry you suffered so much and that none of us could help you. I hope you're at peace now." I hesitated, wondering if this was a situation that called for God. I'd never given much thought to God. I'd actually been hiding from him, hoping that if he was real I wasn't doing something that offended him. Dr. Faith had been scooching me toward the notion of God as a loving spirit that offered comfort and strength and guidance. "God bless you and stay with you, Colette," I said. "I'll visit again soon."

There was no reception after the funeral, just tea and crumpets at an overpriced teahouse (where they charged five dollars for an extra dollop of clotted cream) with Francesca.

When we got home, I offered to drive Francesca back to the church where she had left her car. I wanted more information about Colette, but I didn't want to endure talking to my mother to get the information. And there was no guarantee she'd even give me the truth. "You're aware that I never knew Colette existed until recently when I tracked her down at Brookside Assisted Living," I said. "Why is that? She seemed sweet. Why did my mom keep her a secret? What happened?"

"It's a long story," she said.

"It's a long drive back to the church," I said.

"I don't know that your mother would want me to tell you the story. She's always been very private about what happened," she said.

"I already think my mother is a heartless twit, so anything unflattering that you might tell me about her won't make me think any less of her than I already do," I said.

"It's not unflattering information about your mother," she said. "It's unflattering information about Colette."

"Out with it or I'm going to force my mother to tell me about Colette," I said. "And I won't wait until she's done mourning or trying to get attention or whatever it is she's doing. I've been kept in the dark about my aunt for long enough."

"Okay, okay. You should probably know. Here it goes," Francesca said. "Your mom and Colette were close growing up. Kind of like you and Maya. Colette was a delight. She was funny and sweet. She was the golden child—smart, talented at everything she tried. She was two years older than your mother, and your mother worshipped her."

"Good so far," I said.

"They went to college together, and when your mom graduated, they got an apartment in West Hollywood," she said. "Everything was okey dokey for a few years and then Colette got really weird."

"Weird how?" I asked.

"She became reclusive and morose. She would shut the curtains and stay in bed for days sometimes," she said.

"So she was depressed," I said.

"She wasn't just depressed. She was angry and irritable and would go into rages. She whacked your mother over the head with the handle of a tennis racket once when she used a face towel as a hand towel. Colette was paranoid. She wouldn't eat any of the food your mom bought or cooked because she thought your mom was trying to poison her. She was so convinced that people were following her that she left the apartment dressed in disguises. It was a nightmare," she said. "Your mom moved out and went to stay with your grandma and grandpa."

"Why didn't somebody try to help her? Obviously she was mentally ill," I said. "I'm pretty sure she had bipolar disorder."

"They tried to help Collete. They dragged her to a psychiatrist, but she wouldn't take the medicine he prescribed. She thought he was trying to poison her too." I felt my eyes getting misty. "They got her committed once, but my lord, you can't imagine what institutions were like then. Despicable places not fit for man or beast. Patients locked in tiny rooms and being injected with big needles – wailing and staring at blank walls. Horrible." She shivered in disgust.

"Hasn't changed much," I said.

"Medications weren't what they are today, either," Francesca said. "They put poor Colette on all kinds of really strong tranquilizers and antipsychotics. I think they even put her on Thorazine. She was sane but she was a vegetable, and when she was aware of what was going on, she wasn't having any of it. We kept trying to help her, but the situation grew more and more hopeless. Then . . . later . . ."

"What? Did she try to kill herself?" I asked.

"She attempted that a few times . . ." Francesca stopped. "You can't let your mom know I told you this part... Colette turned on a space heater and placed it on a stack of magazines and matchbooks and lit your grandparents' house on fire in the middle of the night."

The car went silent while Francesca caught her breath. "Was anyone injured?" I finally asked.

"No," Francesca said. "But almost, and she burned the house to the ground. Your grandparents didn't press charges, but they got a restraining order against Colette and cut off all ties. It was too dangerous to have her in their lives."

"So what happened to Colette after that?" I asked.

"Your grandparents eventually got rid of the restraining order, but by then Colette would have nothing to do with them or your mother. She hated your mother and grandparents for cutting her off. She wouldn't see them or talk to them. I kept tabs on her through a social worker and tried to visit her every six months or so and give her a wad of cash. She kicked around from one crummy job to another. Had a husband for a while who was a drug dealer. Got arrested once—committed here and there. She lived in halfway houses—and in her car sometimes. Your mom and your grandparents never saw Colette. I was the only family member Colette would talk to—probably because she needed the money I gave her. And the money was actually your mother's. She would give the money to me to give to Colette."

"But, why did she have to be kept secret?" I asked. "My mother was ashamed of her, wasn't she?" The gears in my brain were grinding as I struggled to process what Francesca was telling me.

"Not ashamed," Francesca said. "She was traumatized by Colette. She was protective of her, too. She didn't want people knowing about her problems and judging her. She thought that telling you about Colette would be upsetting to you somehow and that you might want to meet her, and that wasn't possible."

"Did she ever get better?" I asked.

"For the past five years or so, she was doing pretty darn good, except for her lungs," Francesca said. "She stayed on her meds most of the time, and when she was on them she was as sweet and fun as she was when she was a girl. I convinced her to let your mother back into her life two years ago when her emphysema got severe—and your mother started seeing her regularly. Your mother moved her into Brookside when she started deteriorating and couldn't take care of herself anymore. Her life was a tragic one – and very painful for your mother."

"Why didn't my mom let us meet Colette when she started seeing her again?" I asked.

"I tried to persuade her into it, but your mother thought it was too late," Francesca said. "She felt that all it would do was confuse you two and make you feel that you'd been deceived. And she still didn't trust Francesca. She went off her meds from time to time and would get completely wacky and very aggressive. It was disturbing."

After I dropped Francesca off at her car I drove to the beach and sat on the shore for three hours, trying to digest what I'd learned. My view of my mother had done a one-eighty. She wasn't the two-dimensional, insensitive person I'd known all these years. I had thought I'd never understand my mom. I'd gone my whole childhood knowing nothing about her and developing no bonds. Finally, I had insight into her insides. But, it was too late. I wasn't going to get over all the resentments I had, and I doubted she would change. But, at least I didn't hate her anymore. I pitied her. She was a broken down, damaged person. I started feeling guilty about how I'd been treating her, even though I wasn't going to let her off the hook for being a bad mother. She could have tried harder. But, I wasn't going to punish her anymore.

Dr. Faith was all over my mother's history. "I knew there had to have been something in her past that numbed her emotionally," she said. "It all makes sense. She lost the two people she loved most—her sister and then her husband—and won't get close to anyone again so that she'll never again have to deal with emotional devastation if somebody else near and dear is stolen away."

"So that's why she isn't close to me and Maya?" I asked. "Because she doesn't want to lose one of us and have her world fall apart again?"

"Exactly," she said. "She pours her love all over the animals because they're a safe place to stow it. I don't doubt your mother genuinely loves her pets, but generally it's easier to grieve a dead cat than it is to get over the death of a child. Your early memories of her being more motherly suggest that she could handle intimacy then—and probably your dad's death pushed her over the edge."

"I see what you're getting at," I said. "I've actually started to feel sorry for her instead of feeling so . . . discarded by her."

Dr. Faith said that my mother's reflexive change of topic whenever my illness came up, her neurotic habit of minimizing my disorder and her creative rewriting of my recent episode to put an upbeat spin on it were proof that she couldn't bear to imagine that the same condition that had flattened her sister was living inside me and left me susceptible to Colette's wretched fate.

Before we wrapped up our session, I slapped Dr. Faith with my newest worry, which was, in my humble opinion, exceedingly creative. "I'm worried about the future," I told her.

"Everybody's worried about the future. It's unknown," she said. "We fear what we don't know—what might be lurking up ahead. But it honestly shouldn't get harder for you, Jane, not with all you've been through psychically. You're one of those rare seventeen-year-olds to whom I can say that. Of course, there will always be challenges because that's life. If it gets too easy, then you're not doing it right."

"No," I said. "I don't mean the future. I mean *the future*. The next life."

"Huh?" Dr. Faith said. I'd outdone myself.

"I think I've got the rest of this life covered," I said. "I know there's lots more to go and tons of stuff I don't know and haven't experienced and plenty of pain in store and the Beast is still living inside me, but I'm pretty sure I can get through this life."

"I'm glad you feel that way, and I agree," Dr. Faith said. "I have faith that you'll be able to handle whatever comes your way." (I loved it when Dr. Faith used the word "faith.")

"But, the next life," I said. "Now there's an unknown. What do I do if the next life is harder than this one? What if there's no you in the next life to help me and no Maya and not even a Valentina somebody can buy me to be my friend? And what if my depression is so much worse that it makes the recent unpleasantness look like a skinned knee? And what if they don't have suicide in the next life, so if you feel hideous you just have to go around feeling hideous until you die? Or maybe you don't die. Maybe it's just anguish and agony forever and ever. I don't want to come back bipolar. I'll come back with one eye, club feet, phenylketonuria, you name it. But I didn't get a say in this life, so I probably won't get a say in the next, either. I could come back bipolar with boils and spinal stenosis and so dumb I don't even know I'm dumb and a mother worse than the one I have now and . . ."

"I want you to stop and take a deep breath," Dr. Faith interrupted. She capped her pen and shifted in her seat. I squirmed, my horrific next life flashing in front of my eyes. I took in a sharp, labored breath. "Another one," she said. I continued breathing in and out.

"How about we just take it one life at a time," she said. "Can you do that?"

"Okay," I said.

"Jane," Dr. Faith called out as I left her office. I turned around.

"I'll find you the next time around. I promise," she said.

When I returned home from Dr. Faith's office, I found my mother in her bedroom crying, holding a picture of Colette. I sat on the bed next to her. "Mom, I know all about you and Colette," I said. "Francesca told me. I'm so sorry."

My mom turned to me and looked me right in the eyes. They were such sad eyes – red and puffy and glassy. She stared at me silently and then wrapped her arms around me and held me tighter than she had ever done before. We hadn't hugged many times in my life, so it was an alien feeling to be in her arms. "I'm sorry, too," she said. "For everything I didn't do for you when you were sick. You're such a strong, brave girl. I hope you know how much I love you."

My mother had never told me that she loved me. Her words seemed genuine and left me speechless. Was it possible that my mother really did love me? I felt myself leaping over the giant canyon that had separated us my whole life. For a moment, I wondered if this was the beginning of a whole new relationship for us. Were we going to become a genuine mother and daughter? Were we going to have heart to hearts and laugh and have fun together? But, in an instant it was over. My mother pulled away and grabbed a tissue. She patted me on the back and then got up. "I need to get to the grocery store," she said. "We're out of everything." And with that she was out of the room with an XOX. For sixty seconds I had known what it felt like to have a mother – and that wasn't nothing. I would cherish those moments because they'd probably never happen again.

As I clawed my way out of my depression, I started getting fired up about starting a new school. I found out there was a bus to transport me across town, which meant I wouldn't be making a hellish daily drive to the farthest edge of the east. Also, Evergreen had a Mandarin Chinese program. I'd always wanted to learn Mandarin, if only because the alphabet looked so exotic. I didn't want to learn to play golf, but they did have an archery team, and I had loved playing with bows and arrows since I was young.

Dr. Faith continued cheering me on, promising me that though there might be some setbacks and relapses in my mood and state of being, I was on the path to full recovery. And, thank God, there was no code number for "recovering." Dr. Faith said I was probably done with collecting DSM codes.

Another reason for optimism was that, according to Tiffany and Nell's texts and e-mails, nobody was talking or asking questions about me at West Hills. I was last year's news, which meant my "crazy as a box of birds" label might not follow me across town, or at least not in a big way, and that I might be able to carry on as a normal teenager at Evergreen. Then, in a year or so, I'd leave for college, where a freshman class of five hundred or a thousand strangers confronting a brand-new environment wouldn't know, or be all that interested in, how I behaved during the second semester of my junior year.

And as for the kids who still might be judging me harshly for what I did during my mania or digging up dirt on what was "wrong" with me: "Who cares what they think?" as Valentina said. (I was still working on that one.)

And Ben? "Stop driving yourself batty about what happened between you two and put on your big-girl pants and e-mail the boy with the eyes that don't smile with his face and apologize. If he accepts the apology, you might get a second chance. If he doesn't, he's not worth it."

I thought about Valentina's suggestion for a day and then spent the next day agonizing over what to write Ben. I wasn't sure I was going to actually send a note, but I wrote one nonetheless. After drafts one through fifteen, I wound up writing: "I'm so sorry for what I did during the time we spent together at your house. It had nothing to do with you and everything to do with the illness I was struggling with. I hope that you can forgive me and that we can be friends."

"Very good," Valentina said, looking over my shoulder. "Short and sweet. Boys hate long notes full of feelings words and questions about feelings." Then, without even asking me, she hit the send button.

I jumped up from my chair. "How could you? I wasn't ready! I wasn't even sure I was going to send that!"

"You were never going to be ready and it needed to be done," Valentina said. "It's the only way you can move on—or maybe even have a future with Ben."

I checked my e-mail several times a day, jittery and amped-up each time I logged onto my account. But each time I checked my inbox, there was a big, glaring nothing where I'd hoped his address might be.

Soon after I was allowed to e-mail Ben, Dr. Faith and Valentina allowed me to text Ebony. I wanted to text Leopoldo, too, but I couldn't find his address. Valentina and Dr. Faith had wanted me stable before I got in touch with anyone from the hospital. They knew how traumatic the hospital had been for me and they didn't want me having any reminders until they thought I was ready. Ebony had already e-mailed and texted me, and Valentina had gotten back to her and explained the situation. I sent Ebony a lengthy text with a précis of my post hospital crash and apologized I hadn't gotten in touch sooner. I suggested that once I'd settled into Evergreen, we get together.

Ebony texted me back almost immediately and told me she was sorry I'd bottomed out. She thanked me for helping her to believe more in herself and said that it had made her brave enough to ask Anton to marry her—and he said, "Yes!"

I had been working with Dr. Faith on beefing up my self-esteem and remembering that the ego I had when I wasn't manic wasn't all wrong – it was just overblown. Here was something I'd done that I could be proud of—and I probably wouldn't have had the guts to dig into Ebony and lecture her without the confidence that my manic, inflated sense of self gave me. Looking back, it was easy to see how much I had limited myself for so many years and how mania had opened the box I'd stuck myself in and set me free. There was no point in crawling back inside the box and pretending to be small again now that I knew what it felt like to live large.

# EIGHTEEN

THE NIGHT BEFORE school started, I got a text from Nell: "Would you rather meet us at the Verona or not know any of the juicy West Hills gossip?"

I reached the Verona about half an hour later and found Tiffany and Nell waiting for me at a table against the back wall of the coffee shop, buzzing with anticipation. "Are you sitting down?" Tiffany asked.

"Not yet," I answered. "I'm going to get a hot chocolate first."

"No time. Big news," Tiffany said.

I pulled over a chair. "Tal is gay. Apparently he and Ariana's boyfriend, Kyle, had been having a secret affair. Kyle left Ariana to be with Tal. Now Ariana and Alexis hate Kyle. Both guys are hanging out at the Benches now."

"Interesting," I said. "Is there anything else?"

"Probably," Tiffany said. "But there's only been three days of school, so that's all for now. Subject change. I need to get into reality. How clueless was I to think that a gay guy liked me? Maybe if I spent less time obsessing about dumb stuff and more time studying, I'd actually know something useful."

"Amen," Nell said. "Now for my news."

"Are you sitting down?" Tiffany asked.

I pointed to my chair.

"Owen asked me out and I said 'yes' and we're going to a party at Jason's this Friday!" Nell said.

"The Owen who hangs out in the CEA and wears the porkpie hats and holiday-themed sweaters?" I asked. "The one you said is 'fashion challenged?'"

"I know, but it turns out he's kinda cool. His family joined our beach club and we hung out over the summer. He hates all the same things I hate," she said. "I figured, if you could embarrass yourself the way you did, then I can embarrass myself a little by going out with a guy who wears plaid with houndstooth."

"Thanks... I guess," I said.

"Way to go, Nell. Totally rude thing to say," Tiffany said. "Subject change. You. What's going on? Are you excited about Evergreen?"

We spent the next half hour talking mostly about Evergreen and was I excited or nervous to start and what classes I was taking, etc. "Okay, my turn for a subject change," I said. "I sent Ben an e-mail apologizing for my wacked-out behavior that night at his house. He hasn't e-mailed me back."

"I told you not to do that," Tiffany said. "I told you he'd moved on."

"I had to be absolutely certain he'd moved on before I could move on," I said. "I got my answer and I'm done." Truthfully, I was still checking my e-mail constantly, but I'd gotten used to the idea that I wasn't going to see Ben's name in my inbox, and I'd thanked Valentina for making me put on my "big-girl pants" and face the sad truth where he was concerned. She was right. It was the only way to get closure, even though closure meant accepting a giant, heartbreaking disappointment.

"What a relief," Tiffany said. "I thought you were going to obsess on him forever. That's what I would have done. Anyway, with Ben totally out of the picture, now you can focus on all the new guys you'll meet at Evergreen."

"Speaking of Evergreen," I said, glancing at my watch. "I should probably get some sleep. I have to catch the bus at six forty-five."

"Okay, but there's one more thing we need to talk about," Nell said. "We wish you were still at West Hills. I totally get why you're not coming back, but we miss you."

"So much. It's not the same without you," Tiffany said.

"Lots of people have come to me and asked why you're not there," Nell said. "It's not so bad as you think. Nobody's even talking about your episode last spring. Teenagers have short attention spans. Plus, we're all so focused on ourselves and our dramas that we don't have lots of time to think and talk about somebody else." That was almost exactly what Dr. Faith had told me, but I hadn't believed her—that teens are the ultimate narcissists, and narcissists don't think all that much about others (unless it's a love interest.)

Tiffany and Nell collected their belongings and wished me well and left while I waited in line to get the hot chocolate they hadn't allowed me to get because they were too busy yakking. I finally got my drink, with lots of whipped cream on top, and started toward the exit. As I was opening the door to leave, a guy with a little too much energy burst into the cafe, bumping into me, and spilling half the hot chocolate down the front of my new sweater. "I'm so sorry," he said, pulling off his sweatshirt and using it to clean up my sweater. I'd been so consumed with the mess that I hadn't even looked at the guy. As I moved aside from the dark doorway, I did a double take.

"Tal?" I said.

"Jane?" he said. "I'm so glad to see you. Let me get you another drink."

"It's alright. I need to get home," I said, but he insisted.

"Come, sit," he said once he had the drinks. "I've been wanting to talk to you. Please. Just for a few minutes."

I took my new hot chocolate and sat. "I'm not sure if you heard that Kyle and I came out," he said. I nodded. "I want to thank you, because I'm not sure if I would have if it weren't for you."

"I'm not gay," I said.

"No, but you were so open last spring," he said. "I've heard rumors that maybe you weren't totally well, but what you did made me want to be honest and open, too, and just let the truth flow. I didn't feel so scared to be who I really was. You changed things for me. And Kyle."

"I'm so happy for you both," I said.

I drove home slowly, letting it all sink in. Valentina and I had a long talk while we waited up for my mother to get home. Then my mom and I had a long, serious talk, inasmuch as such was possible with her. The next morning, the three of us talked some more, and my mom made a few phone calls and had a few uncomfortable conversations and I made a phone call and had an awkward conversation. Then, my mother went off to the gym and I texted Nell and Tiffany and told them the news.

# NINETEEN

$\mathcal{I}$ DELIBERATED OVER where to park as I drove to school the next morning. I was returning to West Hills with my head held high, but I didn't need to make a huge splash—I'd done plenty of that in the spring. The B lot seemed like the obvious choice, but I changed my mind when I pulled into the parking lane and saw Nine's motorcycle and Dickens' "coach" parked on either side of Stella's car in the A lot. In solidarity, I drove my car into a modest space on the outskirts of the A lot and took a deep breath. Nobody had seen me yet. There was still time to turn back and say it was all a big mistake and leave the scene of the crime and make it to Evergreen in time for second period.

I felt dizzy and breathless as I walked through the Atrium. "You can do this," I repeated to myself. There were several faces I didn't recognize, but the standbys were there—Stella, the A sisters . . . Charles Dickens was swinging in the hammock, wearing a smoking jacket and puffing on a pipe.

"Jane, my lady!" Charles said, waving his pipe at me. "How simply divine to see you!"

Stella looked up from her phone and choked on the Diet Coke she was drinking. "Jane? WTF?" The others looked mostly confused. And that was it. My knees were shaking, but I was fine. What was there to be afraid of? What could Stella, or any of the other students, do or say to me that would be worse than what had already happened to me?

I took more deep breaths as I left the Atrium and started on toward the CEA. I saw Fiona and Zeke sitting together, eating breakfast burritos. "Jane!" Zeke shouted. He jumped up from the table and bolted for me

207

and gave me a big hug that smelled like eggs. "Please tell me you're back for good and not just visiting."

"I'm enrolled here again," I said. "You were right, Zeke. It's liberating to hit rock bottom. There's so much freedom in not having to protect your reputation."

"Yes, yes," he said. "I always say it's like an inmate on death row getting the flu. Who cares? But, you're not socially rock bottom. Look."

I turned to see that a small crowd had formed around me, waving and smiling. Fiona reached me and squeezed my hand. "J-j-jane, guess what? I joined c-choir like I always wanted to. And I'm good! I don't s-s-stutter when I s-sing."

"It has to do with the prolongation of syllables," Zeke said. "If only life were a musical, then Fiona wouldn't have any problems."

I glanced at the kids—some faces I didn't know, a few Bs, but mostly Cs. "Why are you back hanging out at the CEA after all the fun you had in the Atrium?"

"Because this is where the food is," Zeke answered. "By the time I bring my breakfast or lunch to the Atrium, my food is cold. The Atrium isn't really where it's at anymore. The trees in the Atrium grew over the summer, so it's dark and cold there. The Benches, on the other hand, have no shade, and I have fair skin that burns easily. But, the A parking lot rules. I try to get here early so I can park there."

Just then somebody clamped their hands over my eyes from behind. "Guess who?" The accent was a dead giveaway.

"Tal!" He removed his hands and we had a quick hug. Then he and Kyle moved into the CEA to grab some breakfast.

My phone chimed and I pulled it from my pocket. It was a text from Nell: "Would you rather have all guys be gay and look like Tal or all guys be straight and look like Zeke?" I saw her waving to me from across the lawn before she disappeared into the school building. I texted back: "I hate to be mean about Zeke, but I'll take my chances with the former. Hopefully there'd be one Tal who would be able to stomach girls occasionally."

As I made my way through the campus there were, of course, a few kids who pointed at me and giggled and whispered (and I heard a muffled "Martin Luther King Jane-ior"), but most of the students seemed fine with having me back.

Tiffany tackled me. "Yay! You made it! I told you it would be okay. Blodgett said we're getting another student in our class starting today— that means you! Now we can cut p.e. together!"

"I thought you were going to start working harder in school," I said.

"Except for p.e. You don't learn things in p.e. that will help you get into college," she said.

The bell rang and we swarmed to the school building in a mass exodus. Claire pounced on me in the hallway and made me promise I'd go back on the team. She said that seat four was in flux and that Coach Beverly would probably let me try out for it now that she knew what my "disturbances" during spring practices were due to. She also told me that the day I hopped into the stroke seat, we clocked one of our fastest sprint times. Something else to feel good about. The mania may have made me do some embarrassing stuff in the boat, but it also allowed me to reveal how good I really was at my sport. I promised I'd visit the boathouse by the end of the week.

My first period was history. I entered and noticed Nine sitting in the back row. We were having yet another semester of history together. She grinned and gave me a thumbs up as I took the seat next to her.

Vegas entered and greeted us. He gave the class a quiz, motioned me to his desk, and handed me a syllabus. "Principal Hodge told me that you apologized for your unruly conduct last spring and that you promised you wouldn't be upending classes with rowdy behavior. I hope you're planning on sticking to that agreement."

"I am," I said. "I was unfair to you teachers. I've actually learned a lot here. I know this is a prep school, and you're just trying hard to prepare us for college."

He leaned in close to me, whispering. "Between you and me and for nobody else's ears, the focus of this school shouldn't all be on the destination. It should also be about the journey. But change takes time. And criticizing and attacking the staff will only make things worse."

"Point taken," I said.

I was spent by the end of the day, but I was satisfied. I'd done it. I'd faced the paper tiger. I'd returned to school—no masks, no apologies (except to some of the teachers.) I gave myself a pat on the back and headed for the parking lot.

As I reached my car, I saw Ben walking towards the B lot. He saw me and stopped. I felt my pulse soar as the old feelings came rushing back. He looked hotter than ever. His hair had grown out and he was tan, which made his eyes glow greener, and he'd grown at least an inch. He stared and stared. I stared and stared. I took a step toward him. He took two steps toward me. Then he took three steps backwards, turned, and walked to his car.

It looked like Ben was one problem I wasn't going to be able to fix. He was a casualty of my "experience." I still felt plenty embarrassed about how I'd acted with him. I'd liked him so much, but it seemed I'd done irreparable damage to the sweet, warm connection that had been between us. Our crush was star-crossed. Sadly, very sadly, some loves just aren't meant to be.

# TWENTY

*I* WAS TUCKED INTO MY BED and sleeping soundly on freshly washed and ironed sheets that I had spritzed with lavender and then expertly fit over the mattress. I was sleeping that comatose kind of sleep that only a concussion or, in my case, the exhaustion of the first week back at school, brings on. I was dreaming about a support group for bipolar people—probably because Dr. Faith had been encouraging me to join a support group. The mentally ill have no way of identifying and supporting each other because we hide our disorders, fearing prejudice, and we can't pick out one another in a crowd—unless, of course, you're really off your rocker and standing at a freeway onramp, using an umbrella to battle an imaginary extraterrestrial enemy. So we miss out on supporting one another. I had fought off joining a group so far, mostly because I feared that suggestible me would take on everyone else's troubles.

In my dream, I was standing in a circle surrounded by about a dozen teens drinking hot chocolate. "Hi," I said. "I'm Jane and I'm crazy."

"Hi, Jane," the group replied in unison. I stood frozen as a noise started up. It was a "ping, ping, ping" sound that didn't fit into the scene. I guess my brain didn't want to wake up and was trying to blend the sound into the dream. So the kids in the group started pulling minimarshmallows from the hot chocolate mugs they were drinking from and chucking them at me. But the marshmallows hit me as softly and soundlessly as snowflakes; the loud pinging continued.

"It's been about a month since my last episode . . ." I stopped as the group pulled pens and pencils from their bags and began tossing them at me.

"Boo," the crowd hissed. The pens and pencils weren't explaining the pinging either, because I couldn't feel them hitting me as the kids continued tossing them at me. Finally, the pinging noise drew me out of slumber. I sat up and glanced around the room. The sound was coming from the window near my bed. I pushed aside the curtains as something tiny hit the glass. I pushed open the window and looked outside. I made out a dark figure on the front lawn. The figure was waving. "Jane!"

"I'll be right there," I shouted. I grabbed my bathrobe and threw it on as I charged out of my room and down the stairs.

I flung open the front door and there stood Ben, the porch light ringing a faint halo around his head. He was smiling one of his irresistible smiles. "Hi, Jane," he said. "Did I wake you up?"

"Uh, no," I lied. "I was reading."

Ben held out a handful of tiny pebbles. "I didn't have any peanuts," he said with a chuckle.

Speeder and Storm raced up to see if they could be of assistance, barking loudly. "Shhh," I said, grabbing their collars. Speeder threw himself at Ben, panting and slobbering. Luckily, Ben didn't seem to mind. He crouched down and pet Speeder and then shooed him inside for me. Then he quietly shut the door and leaned back against it and jammed his hands into his pockets.

"So, how are you?" he asked.

"Pretty good," I answered.

"Did you have an okay summer?"

"I'd give it a D+. Yours?"

"Mine was mostly rowing. And I went to Greece . . . with my family. It was pretty okay, except for the family part," he said, studying the porch steps. "It was kinda more humid than hot this summer, didn't you think? Sort of weird weather for L.A."

I shrugged, curious about just what he was getting at. Had he really come over here in the middle of the night to talk about the weather? I'd seen him five times during my first week at school and he hadn't so much as grinned at me. Why was he suddenly being so . . . nice?

"So… I was at the party over at Jason's house tonight," he said.

"Tiffany wanted me to go with her, but it's was a big week for me. I'm sorta wiped out."

"I thought you weren't coming back to West Hills," he said. "So I was surprised to see you at school."

"I was feeling really weird and embarrassed about all the kooky stuff I did last spring. I worried I'd be treated like some kind of . . . leper at West Hills," I said. "But, then I decided... what the hell. I can't hide out the rest of my life. So far, most of the kids have been cool about it all."

"I'm glad you came back," he said. "And by the way, you provided some much-needed comic relief last spring."

"I also made a spectacle of myself, but that's something I'm dealing with."

Seeing Ben was bumming me out. He was so cool and thoughtful and fine (Ebony's word.) Why couldn't I have stayed away from him during my meltdown? Why, of all people on earth, did I choose him to make a complete freak show of myself in front of? Why did my disorder have to drive him away and not a guy I didn't give a rip about—which was pretty much every other guy I knew.

"Anyway, I was at the party," Ben continued. "And Tiffany was drunk and . . . she sorta... well... spilled it."

"Spilled what?"

"Everything. About you. What happened. About you being bipolar and the mania and the depression. Everything. She told me where you lived, too, and which bedroom was yours."

"She never has been able to keep her mouth shut," I said. Judging from the smug "I know you want me" look Ben was wearing, her loose lips had also let tumble out that I still had a thing for him.

"She told me that when you were in the hospital it wasn't for your kidney."

"The kidney ruse was for my mom. She was hyper about nobody knowing I was in the psych ward. She thought it would taint me. A lot of people found out the truth anyway. I'm surprised you didn't hear about it."

"I didn't want to think about you, so every time I heard your name I zoned out," he said, sitting down on the front step. "And I deleted your e-mail without even reading it. I'm sorry."

"Don't be. What I did to you was appalling."

"But it wasn't you. It was your illness," he said. "I thought you were winding me up and dissing me to torture me or screw with my head—to make me look like an idiot. I worried that maybe when we got personal, it turned you off and gave you the heebie-jeebies. I was so wrapped up in how burned I felt that I wasn't able to notice that you were maybe having troubles."

"Hey. I pissed off and confused a lot of people. Thank you for coming over to make amends, but it wasn't necessary. I have only the nicest thoughts of you and I wish you the best." I turned for the door. "It's late. You're probably tired."

"Why didn't you tell me?" He took my hand and swiveled me around and pulled me down so that I was sitting next to him.

"I didn't really think the details of my nervous breakdown would turn you on," I answered.

"It doesn't bother me at all," he said. "I like that you're not so . . . ordinary."

What was Ben Sanders doing sitting on my porch, holding my hand, and smiling coyly at me? Was it possible that this guy was still interested in me? I glanced around the yard. Was this a joke? It was too early for April Fools. I kept waiting for somebody to jump out of the bushes with a video camera and yell, "Gotcha!" But instead, Ben cradled my face in his hands and kissed my forehead and then my lips. I swooned. This kiss felt even better than the last, maybe because I had come to think that it would never ever happen. That ship had sailed and then sunk. Then I remembered *her* and pulled away.

"We probably shouldn't be doing this," I said. "I don't want Gabriella coming after me with a pistol."

"That's history," he said. Yay! "Gabriella's too clingy and jealous. I can't talk to another girl without her squawking—even if it's a ticket taker or a barista. She's a good person, but I think I liked how she looked more than I liked her. Shallow, huh?"

"There are worse reasons to go out with somebody," I said. "And she is stunning."

"You're sexier . . . to me," Ben said. Then he leaned over and started kissing me again. I was floating. There was every indication that I was going to get a second chance with him.

"Do you want to come in?" I asked. "We can go up to my room. You could spend the night. My mom never has a clue what I'm doing or where I am."

He pulled away. "I'd love to spend the night here, but no. I want to do it right this time. I want to know you first." He kissed me again and then pulled me up to standing. "We've never even left the house together. I don't know your idea of a perfect day or what you want to be when you grow up. I don't know your middle name. I haven't met anyone in your family. I've never even bought you lemonade or a sandwich. I'm not going to mess up again."

"You didn't mess up. And the middle name is Rose," I said. "You were great. I loved being with you. And you didn't make me do anything I didn't want to do."

"We'll get to all that again, and I can't wait. But, now I have to go because I'll never be able to stick to my plan if I keep touching you and looking at you." He hugged me and squeezed my hand and took a few steps away from me.

"Wait," I said. "I've been wanting to talk to you about that Dylan Thomas poem you like."

"Sure," he said.

"Well, I read the whole poem and it blew me away. The words were so lush and beautiful. But then I read a description of what it was about, in a poetry textbook, and, as usual, I was disappointed. The poem was all about death. I thought the 'green fuse' was the energy and creativity of mania and the force that 'blasts the roots of trees' was the destruction and devastation of depression. And I was sure the 'wintry fever' was bipolar disorder and 'the crooked rose' was a bipolar flower. In fact, I related to that crooked rose."

"Maybe that's what the poem is about," Ben said. "Nobody was in Dylan Thomas's head when he wrote it. A poem can be whatever it means to you. I used to think the poem was about growing up, but now I think it might be about a guy who likes a bipolar rose."

We both laughed and Ben continued down the steps. "I'll come over tomorrow at seven if that works for you. We'll go out—anywhere you want."

"Sounds good, and I promise I won't do anything weird," I said.

"Weird is okay, just not running-away-for-no-reason weird," he said.

"Got it," I said.

He turned and walked to his car. A few steps later, he turned and waved again. I waved back and continued waving as he drove away. I watched Ben's car until the taillights disappeared around the corner, then I thought about how far and how long it had taken to get to this point. I wasn't just starting a new relationship; I was starting a new life as me.

# ACKNOWLEDGMENTS

HANKS TO the most amazing agent a writer could ask for—the brilliant Fonda Snyder; editors Deirdre Greene and Kate Eagan for their help and advice in shaping this story; writer Rachel Brown for sharing her vast knowledge of the world of book publishing; dear friends and earliest readers and cheerleaders Alex Byrne and Kristine McKenna; my sort-of brother-in-law Luke Kreinberg for his keen insights into bipolar disorder; and, of course, my steadfast, encouraging and loving family, who was alongside me during the exciting and challenging project of writing this book. And a shout-out to my goofed-up brain, which understands Jane a little too well.

Thanks for reading my book! I love hearing from my readers and getting your honest reviews on Amazon and Goodreads. Like me on Facebook at Kati Rocky Author. Follow me on Twitter: @Kati Rocky. Contact me: KatiRockyAuthor@gmail.com